Dirty Tricks

Dreda Say Mitchell

Big Mo Crime Series Book 1

First published in 2020 by Mitchell and Joseph Ltd

www.dredasaymitchell.com

Paperback format ISBN: 978-1-9164202-4-3
e-book format ISBN: 978-1-9164202-3-6

Book cover Stuart Bache at Books Covered
https://www.bookscovered.co.uk
Formatting Polgarus Studio https://www.polgarusstudio.com

Huge huge thanks to Christine Dunlop for her expert editorial eyes during the second phase of edits.

Dreda Say Mitchell

International Bestselling Author Of:

SPARE ROOM

'The scariest, creepiest and best
psychological suspense you'll read this year.'

Lee Child

Praise for Award-Winning Author Dreda Say Mitchell

'As good as it gets.' ***Lee Child***

'Great book written by a great girl.' ***Martina Cole***

'A truly original voice.' ***Peter James***

'An exciting new voice in urban fiction.' ***Guardian***

'Zippy, twisty plot… and a bevy of memorable supporting goodies and baddies.' ***The Sunday Times***

'Thrilling.' ***Sunday Express Books of the Year***

'Awesome tale from a talented writer.' ***The Sun***

'Fast paced and full of twists and turns.' ***Crime Scene Magazine***

Amazon Readers Love The Big Mo Crime Series

'Top class.'

'Little Mo captures your heart.'

'Absolutely fantastic read.'

'You must read this book.'

Prologue

1992

'Knock her friggin' teeth down her throat.'

'Scratch her eyes out.'

'Rip all that curly-wurly hair out of her head.'

The schoolgirls, baying for blood like a pack of dogs frothing at the mouth, savagely screamed and spewed hate and poison at ten-year-old Maureen Watson. Curly-haired with polished light-brown skin, no one called her Maureen. She was known by one and all as Little Mo because she was a tiny, wee thing, still inches off five feet. And that's why the other girls ganged up on her, classic bullies who used their bulk and bluster to intimidate a much smaller girl. Cowards, every last one of them is what Little Mo's grandfather would have told her. Not that he had told her that, because Mo hadn't breathed a word to him about this spot of bother that was being dished out to her at school.

'Titch.'

'Short-arse.'

'Pint-sized dwarfy.'

The other girls tightened their menacing ring around Little Mo around the corner from the school gates, snarling and abusing her all the way. The other kids, milling out of the school, scented blood in the water. In a flash they encircled Mo and her tormentors, clapping and chanting, 'Fight! Fight! Fight!'

The children loved nothing better than witnessing a proper bashing after being cooped up in school all day.

The boss girl of the bullies was Lulu Lawson, who took pride in her nickname, Loopy Loo. You better believe she was crazy! She was big for her age, broad-shouldered with long arms that ended in hammer-like fists that had been knocking other kids around since the age of four in the nursery. There was nothing she liked better than performing to an audience. It was a reminder to the other children that she was the undisputed Queen Bollocks-Bee of their School. Anyone who thought different ended up with two shiners and a bloody lip.

Loopy's eyes lit up with malicious glee as she went to work with a solid shove that slammed Little Mo into the wall. With all the force she could muster, Mo shoved her attacker right back. The crowd gasped and sucked in their breath with horrified disbelief. Mo Watson must have a death wish.

'You're dead,' the bully barked, a splatter of spit flying from her mouth.

With one of her deadly hands, she yanked a fistful of Mo's blouse, sending a button flying in the process. She lifted Mo to the tips of her toes but before Loopy could deliver a killer blow

Mo kneed her in her soft tummy. The other girl staggered slightly back, an audible grunt of stunned air whooshing past her lips. Mo pressed her advantage, swinging and kicking for all she was worth. She was no contest against the much bigger girl who slammed a fist to the side of Little Mo's head. Dazed, Mo wound up face down on the ground. If she'd stayed down, Loopy and her mean-girl crew would've left her alone, no doubt high-fiving each other, congratulating themselves on a job well executed.

But Little Mo didn't stay down. She never did. 'Stay down' wasn't in her vocabulary. Little Mo climbed to her feet, moving her head to shake off the foggy dizziness. Then she tilted her chin with determined defiance, swinging punches left, right and centre. But they missed their mark. The other girls were too big and there were too many of them. The girls steamed in, knocking seven bells out of Mo. So over the pavement she went again.

It was so much easier to stay down. But she got up again. Mo might be small, but she wasn't letting anyone push her around. Never-Ever. Sneak over the fence at the back of the school to avoid the bullies was what her friends begged her to do. But Mo's answer was always the same. 'Why should I? I ain't scared of them.'

Mo stood strong and proud despite the wicked pain that pierced through her like the heated blade of a knife. Her school blazer was torn, shoes scuffed, the strap hanging loose from her new bag and her socks marked with the dirt from the kicks she'd taken. Her face was bruised and scraped. She boldly stared Loopy and the other girls in the eye, clenched her fists and gritted her teeth.

As she did so, an angry man's voice in the distance roared, 'Oi!'

The crowd collectively spun round to see who had the brass nuts to interrupt their after-school entertainment. Loopy nastily twisted her lips ready to give the guy a proper, ripe mouthful but when she clocked his face the blood drained from her face leaving her shaken. Her gobsmacked expression was mirrored on the faces of a few of the other kids. The bullies and the other kids scarpered as if a wand had been waved by Mo's fairy godfather.

Surprised, Mo watched them go. When they'd disappeared, she tried to mend the broken strap on her bag. She loved this bag. Her beloved grandad had got it for her down the Leather Market in Petticoat Lane Market or The Lane as everyone locally called the East End institution. And now look at the state of it? It resembled something a dog had mistaken for its dinner.

Mo forgot all about her busted bag when she felt the shade of a dark shadow cast over her. Her head snapped up to find the man who had scattered the crowd standing over her.

'You alright there?' His voice was deep and typically East End. 'What was that row about?'

He was suited and booted, tall, very tall indeed. Muscular and wiry, wearing a baseball cap that shadowed most of his face and shades that hid his eyes. Mo squinted up at him. The guy looked familiar. Then she remembered why. He'd strolled into the chicken-n-chip shop on the High Street, noticed the lengthy line of schoolgirls queuing up, including

Mo, and told the guy behind the counter to let them have their lunch on the house. The bloke on the counter didn't argue. The big guy collected his takeaway on the house too.

Mo's Mum had warned her, finger stabbing in her face to emphasise her words, not to speak to any strangers, especially men.

Mo didn't heed her Mum's advice as she finally gave him an answer. 'They duffed me up because I'm little. They wait for me, regular like a dose of castor oil, at least once a week at the school gates.'

His lips twitched at the corner like he was holding back a laugh. 'What's a young 'un like you know about castor oil?'

Mo's little nose wrinkled. 'Enough to know I'll bite the fingers clean off the next fool who tries to get a spoonful in my mouth.'

He let out a bark of loud laughter. Then quickly composed himself, his expression turning serious again. 'That's not very nice of those girls to be ganging up on you. Why don't you tell your teachers and get them to do something about it?'

'Tell the teachers? You having a laugh?' Mo snorted in disgust. 'I'm not no grass.'

The man nodded. 'Fair enough. Maybe you could just climb over the back fence instead and avoid them that way?'

Mo snapped back with the same explanation she'd given her mates on that account. 'Why should I? I'm not scared of them. I'm not scared of a living soul.'

'You could get some back-up?'

Mo wasn't having that either. 'I don't need back-up. I fight my own battles.'

The man looming over her smiled. 'Hmm, I can see you're going to go far in life, young lady. What's your name?'

'Little Mo. Coz I'm little and my name is Maureen.'

He folded his arms over his immense chest and sighed. 'Well, Little Mo, why don't you let me help you out? The next time them girls start up on you, tell them I'm a relative of yours. That'll soon put a stop to their little game of soldiers. You'll see.'

Mo folded her arms just like he had. In fact, she shifted her whole body so that she mimicked the way he stood, feet slightly apart. Mo liked the feel of that. It made her feel steadier. Powerful.

'Why should I? Who are you?' Her tone was belligerent.

He seemed to loom even larger over Mo. 'Don't you know who I am then?'

Mo's face screwed up slightly. 'No. Why should I?'

His big hand patted her on the head where her curls were now a tangled mess. 'Don't worry about who I am. Them girls won't be bothering you no more, that's all that matters.'

Grinning, the big guy set off down the street. Little Mo went back to trying to put her bag to rights.

Her new guardian angel was well down the road when he stopped and shouted over his shoulder, 'and another thing, girly. You'll need to change your name if you want to get on in life. Tell them kids and anyone else who crosses your path that your name isn't Little Mo. It's Big Mo. And if they forget to use your new handle, give them a slap to jog their memory.'

'Change my name?' But Mo was talking to the wind. Her saviour was already gone.

That was the day Little Maureen Watson started thinking big.

Chapter One

2000
Eight years later

'Come on, everyone! You all know this one!'

Robert Steele was in his element, at the piano in his local pub, surrounded by his mates and with the rest of the crowd all joining in the sing-song. He'd always been handy on the old Johanna. It was a gift he'd inherited from his grandfather, who'd once played the organ in his local cinema back in the 1920s when silent films needed accompaniment. The poor old bollocks enjoyed his work but was put out of business when the talkies arrived. As a teenager Robbie had played piano for various local bands, but his Dad had put the kybosh on that.

'You don't want to end up like your grandad with sweet FA but old movie posters to put in the fireplace in the winter. Pack it in and that's an order.'

So Robbie packed it in. His Father, known by everyone as Jimmy Southpaw from his boxing days, wasn't a man who took kindly to having his orders disobeyed even by his oldest son and heir.

A cheer went up when Robbie played the opening bars to, 'Yes! We Have No Bananas!' but rather than launch straight into the song, Robbie played a brief solo. He turned to look at his audience as he played. But then his fingers froze in surprise on the keys. Two familiar figures lurked at the back of the crowd. The newcomers were neither expected nor wanted.

'I'll tell you what,' Robbie told the crowd, keeping his tone jaunty, 'why don't we have a brief intermission while you get some refreshments.'

This was met with disappointed groans from the crowd.

Robbie turned to the barman. 'Davey, sort out some drinks on the house for these good people?'

Groans forgotten, there was a stampede for the bar.

The two fellas at the rear didn't join in though, instead came to join Robbie by the piano. Robbie's friends drew closer while he eyed the men carefully.

'Good evening,' he said lightly. 'And what can I do for you two gentlemen?'

The older of the two who looked in be in charge gestured at the piano. 'Still practising are you, Robbie?'

Robbie closed the lid. 'Yeah, I am. I'm just like the Old Bill in that respect. I can never quite get it right. So you two boys in blue have given up arresting innocent people and become music critics? Is that right?'

'No, we were just wondering if we could have a little chat?'

Robbie was uncomfortable. What was going on? His Dad had an arrangement with the local plod. 'Peace for peace' his Dad called it. If the cops didn't poke their nose into his business, he wouldn't poke his beak into theirs. But now these two detectives had turned up at Robbie's local, in front of his friends, with a view to running him in without warning or explanation. That was bad enough. That was strange enough. But he also knew these two detectives, Carlson and Philips, and something was badly wrong if they were behaving like this.

'A chat, you say?' Robbie probed. 'Sure, why not? Get yourself a drink and pull up a chair.'

Philips was hanging back. Carlson, the oldest of the pair, kept doing the talking. 'We'd prefer to talk in private, Robbie, down the station.'

'There's no need to be embarrassed, officer, I've got no secrets from my friends here.'

'I'm sure,' the cop bit out. 'But when you hear what we want to discuss, I think you'll understand why we don't want any prying ears.'

Robbie was silent while he tried to work out what they were playing at. His mates, who served as his security detail when necessary, took that as a sign he wasn't going. One of his boys stepped in while others armed themselves with chairs and glasses. 'Listen, mate,' his guy murmured menacingly. 'We're trying to have a quiet evening here and we don't need two Rozzers popping by and spoiling the atmos.' He shifted his muscled bulk closer. 'You heard the man. He ain't going. Now why don't you boys do one.'

Carlson was gently pushed and jostled, so he got the message. Robbie noticed that the cop was unruffled. He was obviously confident that Robbie was going to call his dogs off. And because he was so confident, Robbie did.

He stood up. 'Leave it out, boys. No need for any fisticuffs here. If these gents want a chat down the nick, that's fine with me. Always glad to help Her Majesty's finest keep law and order on the streets.'

Carlson looked very pleased with himself. 'Wise decision, mate. You always had a wise head on your shoulders.'

Robbie was down the station for half an hour before he finally managed to get Carlson in private. Left alone in an interview room for half an hour, Robbie had mentally gone through every possible explanation for this bizarre turn of events, but none of them made any sense. Carlson and his sidekick Philips had remained schtum on the drive here, despite Robbie's repeated questions, nor was there any hint of what this chat was going to be about when they arrived.

When Carlson appeared in the interview room, casual and expressionless, Robbie went off on one. 'What the fuck? I mean, what the actual fuck? You can't drag me down here on false pretences. When my old man hears you've run me in, he'll go mental. You know what he's like. He'll come down here mob handed. You can't do this to Jimmy Southpaw's kid. You know that.'

Carlson drew close and whispered, 'There's things going on at the moment that I can't talk about. All will become clear in due course, but for now you're just going to have to trust me.'

Robbie's eyes glinted so fiercely that it could have been

his old man talking. 'Of course, I don't trust you, you're a fucking copper.'

Carlson straightened, obviously taking offence at the younger man's tone. 'I'm going to have put you in a cell for now. But please, stop worrying. I promise you we'll be laughing about this in the morning.'

The detective went to the door and shouted, 'Officer! Could you escort this gentleman to a cell, please?'

The detective disappeared to get on with whatever it was he couldn't talk about. Robbie was led by the uniformed cop past a string of cells to his new home for the evening. He noticed they all seemed to be empty. 'You're quiet tonight. Is there a strike on?'

'It's early. The drunks will be here soon.'

The cell door slammed shut in his face.

It wasn't the cell that bothered Robbie, he'd been in those before but never for very long, his Father had always seen to that. It was Carlson and Philips. What were they up to? And why together? He'd never seen them acting as a pair before, but they were both in on it whatever it was.

But what was 'it'? Robbie considered whether to demand the right to make a phone call. The old man would have his briefs down here straight away, no doubt dressed up in their gowns and wigs. But the fact that Carlson knew he could do that meant he was confident he wouldn't. Robbie wasn't even sure if he was entitled to a phone call. He wasn't actually under arrest nor had he had actually been booked in on arrival. Neither was he cautioned. As far as the law and the outside world were concerned, he wasn't even there.

It made no sense at all.

There were footsteps and the sound of slurred singing outside in the corridor. The cell door opened, and a man was thrown in. The guy was tanked out of his nut and fell flat on his face, all the while keeping up with his tune. His accent was distinctive, but the poor bloke was so pissed it was difficult to make out.

Robbie got off his bunk and gestured at his new cellmate. 'What's this?'

The cop on the door was impassive. 'It's a drunk, sir.'

'I can see that. But what's he doing in here? You've got an entire suite of empty cells down there.'

The officer mocked, 'If you wanted a single room, sir, you should have paid the single room supplement.'

Robbie ignored the sarky jibe and asked, 'Any sign of Carlson?'

His answer was the cell door clanging shut.

Robbie looked on with rank disgust as the drunk, still singing away, pissed up against the wall in a corner of the cell. Usually Robbie wouldn't stand for that kind of shit in his presence. But he let it stand this time. He had too much on his mind. Occasionally, when the old soak forgot the words to the song, he'd pause for a moment and Mumble to himself while he retraced the lyrics. It was during one of those moments that Robbie was sure he could hear something from inside the building, coming from upstairs. It echoed down the corridor. A high-pitched ringing noise that wouldn't stop. It sounded just like a fire alarm.

Twenty minutes later the police station was a raging, red inferno as fire fighters struggled to contain the blaze. A group of senior officers from the police and fire service stood in a group well back from the station building being consumed by smoke and fire. The discussion was clipped and serious.

'Is everyone out?'

Someone nodded. 'The place was nearly empty. Most of our guys were in town today policing a demo, not many arrests locally so we think we're OK. Everyone's accounted for.'

'Neighbouring buildings?'

'All secure.'

A senior cop stepped forward, a quizzical expression on his face. 'That's a hell of a fire and it spread so fast. Any idea how it started?'

'We're going to have trouble finding out. There'll be nothing left but soot when it's finished.'

'It's an old building. It was one of the stations designated for closure. Apparently, it's being converted into flats later this year. Lucky break for the construction company, they'll have a vacant site. Alright, we're done here. We'll let these boys hose the place down and then we'll see where we are tomorrow.'

Only then did the group notice a sweating and anxious uniformed cop trying to catch their attention.

'Is there a problem?' The most senior officer asked.

'Yes, sir.' The uniform was flustered and breathless. 'We think there might have been someone in the cells who got left behind in the chaos. He was booked in on the computer for being drunk and disorderly, but we couldn't get a name out of him so we don't know who he was.' His chest rose and fell as he took in all the faces before him. 'He might've got out though. We're just not sure.'

Pensive looks and angry muttering followed his announcement. Finally they agreed that a search should be organised for the missing man who might still be inside the inferno.

But the hunt for the drunk wasn't the only search going on.

A frantic and sweating Detective Carlson searched ambulances, police cars and control vehicles. He hurried through the crowds that had gathered behind the security tape to watch the blaze. He consulted colleagues, but without being too specific about who he was looking for. In the end he was reduced to asking passers-by whether they'd seen a certain man who matched a certain description. After his thankless and increasingly desperate hunt drew a blank, he returned to watch the flames consuming what was left of the building. The roof caved in with a roar followed by the chimney stacks which showered the spectators in burning embers and smuts.

Finally, like a man possessed, he rushed desperately towards the burning building and had to be manhandled back by two fire fighters. He struggled and threatened them with arrest before he realised that the senior officers nearby were staring at him.

Desperate and disconsolate, he left the scene, shoulders slumped and walked aimlessly down a neighbouring street. Finally, he stopped and screamed at the top of his voice to the empty street. 'Robbie! Where the fuck are you?'

Chapter Two

'Rest in Peace?'

Jimmy Southpaw's roar inside the church as he read aloud the RIP message on the wreath was terrifying as he stood next to his son's coffin near the altar.

'He knackers my boy and then sends a wreath to the funeral?' he continued in furious disbelief.

The packed rows of mourners at the funeral of Robbie Steele gasped in jaw-dropping horror as they watched one of the East End's most feared gangsters take swift revenge on this outrage. He grabbed the floral tribute and tore it to shreds with savage violence. His hands shook with trembling rage as he destroyed it like a fox caught by a pack of hounds. Crushed petals and stems fluttered to the floor. But that wasn't enough for Jimmy. He ground and viciously stomped his heels into them. What was left of the flowers he kicked down the aisle.

Jimmy was a big man, an easy six-two. Head clean-shaven, he moved with a quiet and deadly grace learnt in the second home of his youth, the boxing ring. The expression in his eyes was both blunt and sharp. The type of gaze you did not want drilling your way.

Seething through gritted teeth, Jimmy vowed, 'I'm going to get you, Barker. You murdering piece of filth. I'm going to bury you deep enough to reach the gates of hell.'

Barker wasn't present at the funeral of Robbie Steele. And for good reason. He was the one Jimmy squarely pointed the finger of blame at for Robbie's death. Barker was another legendary London Face. Jimmy and Barker had been close associates, blood-brother tight for years and then, just like that, a couple of months back, they'd fallen out. Become the deadliest of enemies.

When news came through that his eldest son, his heir, Robbie, had died in the fire at the police station, Jimmy had let out a gut-wrenching animal scream that could be heard on the neighbouring streets. Convinced Barker had been the one to light the match, he'd grabbed a sawn-off with the intention of hunting Barker down to blow him away. It took at least five men, including his surviving son Harry, to restrain and hold him down. Who knew what had caused the rift between the men, but there was one thing you could bet your life on: no way could Jimmy Southpaw let it stand if Barker had killed his son.

And Jimmy wasn't interested in listening to reports that the fire was caused by the electrics in the police station being older than the ark. As far as he was concerned something strange had gone down in that fire because Robbie wasn't even booked in on the computer. And that strange thing was Barker setting a trap for Jimmy's son and heir to die.

And now Barker had had the front to send an RIP wreath

to Jimmy's boy's send-off, adding salt to Jimmy's grieving, weeping wounds.

No doubt about it. A gangland war was brewing.

Jimmy was a legend in the East End. The kingpin of the feared Steele family empire. Known as Jimmy Southpaw rather than Jimmy Steele on account of the lethal left hook he'd wielded as a boxer in his youth. That same fist he'd used to devastating effect to cement his reputation as one of London's leading gangland Faces. Or businessman was how he liked to put it.

The mourners' hearts went out to him. Admittedly there were a few in the back pew wishing they had popcorn as they settled in to watch the theatrics on display. Mind you, that was the way of funerals in this part of town. If someone wasn't kicking off, it wasn't a proper East End send off, now was it? Nothing was left of Robbie Steele except pure ash, hence the closed coffin. Having to bury your child went against the laws of nature. No parent should have to go through that. Even worse when you couldn't see your loved ones face to kiss him on his way to the world of the angels.

Jimmy's fingers resembled claws as he fought for breath. He wanted to pour out the grief that was ripping him raw inside. It hurt so bad. He would never see his Robbie's face again. Never see Robbie throw his head back, belting with laughter.

Jimmy held back the storm of tears that threatened to overwhelm him. He couldn't cry though. Not here. Every last watchful eye in the church was taking in his every move, his every word. They'd be on the gossip-vine, *Radio East*

Enders FM, as soon as, broadcasting what went down at Robbie Steele's burial. And Jimmy wasn't having his private grief become public property. So he sucked it up and set his features to stone.

And that's when he clocked the congregation gawking at him. 'What are you lot staring at? This ain't no free show. Get your hankies out and start crying. Move it!'

Some of the women did as told, sniffling loudly with grief in to their tissues while others used theirs to mask their relish at the story they'd be dining on for ages about the goings on at the funeral of Jimmy Southpaw's prince. The very nervous looking vicar avoided his eyes. In fact, the man of God looked like he wanted to hike up his cassock and run for it.

Jimmy took his seat among his family in the front pew, wedging between his eldest child, Violet, and his last remaining son, Harry. Violet gently patted his thigh to calm him down. What a good girl she was. Bless her! The only one of his brood still living under his roof.

Jimmy turned to Harry. His son took after his Mother's side of the family with his hazel eyes and fine bone structure, not a bruiser like Jimmy. Mind you, like all of Jimmy's kids, he had his Father's height.

Jimmy hissed, 'What the hell do you look like, you ponce?'

Harry looked down with surprise at his clothing. The young man was hurt. He thought he was kitted out very tastefully in a black suit, albeit the jacket was leather. Harry was a creature of the new millennium, from his clobber to his carefully manicured chin fluff. He had enough bling hanging off him to stock a shop in Hatton Garden.

'This is my best whistle, Dad. It's designer.'

The noise Jimmy Southpaw made at the back of his throat was nasty. Very nasty indeed. 'This is your brother's funeral and you turn up looking like a kid on the pull in Romford on a Saturday night. Where's your respect?'

Harry looked down at his threads again. 'It's cool, Dad.'

Jimmy cast a disdainful gaze along the front row to where Robbie's widow sat, the heat of his rising temper bringing the blood to his face. 'Then again, you're in good company.'

Kristal Steele was what was known in the trade as a busty bottle-blonde. Face contoured to perfection and curves that most women would be trying to shed through the latest dieting craze. Not Kristal. She understood that most blokes appreciated a handful of flesh to hang onto. Not that she was fat, mind. More a generous hourglass figure that made guys grow incredibly tight in the crotch region.

She was almost the picture of the grieving widow, in her tailored black skirt suit, fascinator with veil and delicately dabbing her eyes with her Valentino hankie. Almost. What spoiled the image was the eyeful of cleavage on display. With every move she made her breasts squeezed, bunched and wobbled, threatening to spill out, no doubt giving the Vicar the shock of his life. Well, that's as long as you didn't believe the story doing the rounds that the vicar's housekeeper was serving him more than side salads with his dinner.

Jimmy Southpaw was outraged that she of all people, his Robbie's wife, could be so thoughtless. 'I don't know what she thinks she's turned up for?' he whispered in a clipped tone to Violet. 'Looks like a tart touting for business down some dirty back alley in Kings Cross.'

As if his flash git of a son and daughter-in-law weren't enough to get him frothing at the mouth, he also had to contend with his grandson who sat next to his Mother. He shook his head in stupefied wonder. How that boy had come from Robbie's seed, he would never know. Seventeen-year-old Damien Steele was a weird sod. His habitual way of tilting his head to the right and his soft-bellied figure stuffed into a suit that didn't fit left his grandad's belly churning in disgust. Damien's biggest problem was he was a Mummy's boy. Kristal wouldn't hear a word against him. She got the proper nark when Jimmy referred to his grandson as, 'Damien off *The Omen*.'

Jimmy wasn't a praying man, but he closed his eyes and silently communed with the Lord: *'I mean, what a family. They can't even get a funeral right. They want me to retire and hand my business over. I'd rather give it to the Vicar.'*

Suddenly, Jimmy Southpaw felt old. Bone creaking old. Sixty, for fuck's sake, that's all he was. It was the shenanigans this family got up to every which way that was pushing him ever closer in the direction of an early grave. Jimmy was also troubled because he was going to have to make the decision of a lifetime soon. Now Robbie was gone, who would he choose to be his next in line? His heir.

Jimmy checked his watch. 'I hope that bloke in the dress isn't going to drag this out,' he muttered to Harry. Fire lit up his eyes. 'The sooner we get this over with, the sooner we can arrange for a funeral in Barker's family. That bastard's going to pay for murdering my son.'

Harry hesitantly and cautiously reasoned, 'It might not have been him, Dad. The electrics in the cop shop were—'

Jimmy Southpaw wasn't having it. 'Shut it! Who else would've been able to do a set up like that?'

The bloke in the dress speeded up the service, chivvied along by the dirty looks Jimmy chucked his way. When it was over, the man who'd presided over his family and its various rackets for nearly thirty years waited outside while the coffin was carried out. The workman who'd made Jimmy's dead wife's coffin had also constructed Robbie's. The old fella had come out of retirement as a favour to Jimmy Southpaw. He'd knocked Robbie up a beautiful resting place. Polished walnut and cherry wood gleaming like a new day.

No expense had been spent on the hearse either. A transparent carriage drawn by white horses with long, white plumes standing tall on their heads.

Nothing but the best for his Robbie. Nothing but the best.

The rest of the family and the other mourners stood at a respectful distance while Jimmy prepared to say his goodbyes in private. As the hearse began its slow departure, Jimmy tapped on the carriage window bringing the procession to a halt.

He climbed inside the carriage and embraced the wooden box that contained his son. His voice was clearly heard. 'So long, boy. It was all too short, all too short. Robbie, you were the best son a geezer could ever have. There won't be another one like ya.'

The hushed crowd waited. Waited for him to break down and cry. Instead, he clenched his famous southpaw fist and hammered it on the coffin so hard it shook.

'And don't you worry, I'll sort Barker out. They'll have to collect his body parts together with a shovel and drop them in black bin liners when his time comes. And his time won't be long.'

Five minutes later Jimmy scowled when he noticed a man in a smart uniform and a peak cap.

Furiously, he strode over. 'What are you doing here? Why aren't you waiting with my Bentley?'

'No room in the car park, boss,' his driver smartly replied. 'I had to leave the motor out on the street. When you're ready, I'll go and bring it round.'

Jimmy couldn't believe his ears and fought hard not to lose it. 'You left my Bentley out on the street? Unattended? In an area like this? Them rat kids round here will have had the wheels off by now.'

The driver looked like he was about to lose his lunch. 'I never—'

Jimmy's left fist knocked his cap off. 'You tart.' He pointed at Harry and two of the family's heavies. 'Let's go.'

The four men hurried down the gravel path. When they were past the hearse and out onto the street, it turned out that Jimmy's worst fears were realised. Inside his beloved car was a hooded teen rummaging around like they were on a treasure hunt. Nearby, another group of ragamuffins, faces carefully concealed, posed as lookouts. Clocking the men rapidly steaming their way one pierced the air with a high-pitched whistle of warning.

The gang of teenage thieves scattered and scarpered down the street, shouting and yelling. All accept the one in the Bentley. This one appeared younger than the others although that might have been the impression because the thief was smaller. The hooded teen slammed the door and sent an insolent smirk at the men who were closing in. Then the thief set off after the others as if out for a jog without a care in the world.

Sweating and panting, Harry got ready to rush off in pursuit, but his Dad called him back. 'Leave it! Don't worry about chasing them, I'll find out who they are. I know everyone round here.'

Harry gasped for breath, his shirt sticky with sweat. 'Shall I call the cops?'

Jimmy rounded on him in despair. 'Oh yeah! That's a cracking idea! Let's call the plod.' He mimed holding a phone. 'Hello? Is that Her Majesty's boys in blue? It's Mister Southpaw here. You know, the geezer who bosses this part of London. The number one hard man in the area. The guy who terminates his enemies with extreme prejudice. Well, I'm afraid my wheels have been broken into. Could you send a couple of officers down to investigate? I'd be ever so grateful, don't you know?'

Harry avoided his eyes, pinking over in embarrassment.

Jimmy inspected the damage. On the rear leather seat

was a length of pipe that had been used to smash in one of the windows. He opened the passenger door and looked inside. Nothing seemed to be missing at first. Then Jimmy noticed something. The lock on the glove compartment was forced. That wasn't an easy thing to do because he'd had the lock specially installed by a geezer who knew his way around safes. Using his fingertips, he prised the lid open again and ferreted around inside.

Something was missing. Something close to his heart.

He slammed shut the glove compartment. Looked up the street in the direction the kids had fled. He stared for a long time; a knowing smile played on his lips. Then he remembered he still had to bury his son.

Chapter Three

The hoodie flicked back to reveal eighteen-year-old Mo Watson. East End Teen Tearaway Number One. She was with her crew of juvie delinquents celebrating in a burger bar on Westferry Road, on the Isle of Dogs. Or The Island, the name most people called the Isle of Dogs.

Mo was ecstatic at outwitting whoever was the owner of the flash Bentley and wanted the whole world to know about it. So, she made a big song and dance of strutting and prowling around like the original mutt's nuts. As high as a junkie on a speedball of H and C she was after pulling off the audacious raid on the car. Not that she'd touch heroin or cocaine with a barge pole. Deffo not her scene.

She hadn't grown much more than when those schoolgirl bitches had duffed her over at school. The difference now though was not many dared take the rise out of her height these days. Have the brass to call her short-arse and you'd better be ready to kiss sweet bye-bye to your teeth. Mo had a reputation as a proper firecracker who took nonsense from no one.

Her brown skin and gleaming black curls were the perfect

blend of her Mum's Jamaican heritage and the white Father she'd never known. Mo had also inherited the startling shade of her eyes from her unknown Dad. Steel-grey that seemed to pierce straight through a person's soul.

Now she rested that unsettling gaze on her gang. They were creasing up with riotous glee and high-fiving to the max on the success of their latest criminal caper.

John-John, the baby of the gang at sixteen, sniggered, eyes sparkling mischievously. 'Did you see the cob on that old duffer?' He did an imitation of the guy's intimidating voice. 'Oi! What do you lot fink youse is doing? I'm gonna get ya.'

He topped off his mocking act with a bow-legged walk around the table, hunched-backed as if he were trying to run with a walking stick. The others cracked up big time, hooting and howling for all they were worth. John-John was the joker of the pack, always on hand to add a touch of funny to proceedings.

'We killed it, Big Mo, killed it!' another member of her crew crowed.

Big Mo. That's what her friends and those in the know called her now. Since the day the Big Man had come to her rescue against those bullies, she'd fully embraced her new status as Big Mo.

She'd kept an eagle eye out for the Big Man, desperate to shake his hand for what he'd done for her. Sadly, it wasn't to be. She'd never clapped eyes on him again. A crying shame that. Her nose told her she would've learnt a lot from him about The Life. The criminal life. Working nine-to-five wasn't her bag. The very thought made Mo shudder. She had her eyes and heart well and truly set on making a name for herself in London's criminal world. She yearned to be SOMEBODY. A Face. People would nod with respect when they saw her. Ask her to be Godmother to their baby. Roll out the red carpet. Despite her height she hungered for the day people would look up to her.

And that highlighted Mo's present dilemma. How the living heck was she going to get a foothold in the underworld? Breaking into motors and pinching stuff was strictly small fry. Kids' stuff.

And that's why she didn't join in the rolls of laughter with her friends. If truth be told, John-John's dicking around and the antics of the others were getting royally on her wick. Her crew were playing at gangsters. Strictly Bugsy Malone. Kids trying to walk in grown-ups' shoes. She'd had a bellyful of it. In fact, she'd become well miffed with the commitment most of the others were displaying for quite some time now.

Big Mo made her displeasure known. 'Knock off the Tommy Cooper routine, will you? I've had it to the back teeth with this larking about.'

The laughter was gone in an instant. The others stared slack-jawed at her, taken off guard by her cutting remarks.

Mo strode to the head of the table and widened her stance, a dead ringer for the Big Man's style from all those years ago. 'If we're going to make a name for ourselves as a crew to be feared we need to start using our loaf.' She tapped her temple. 'Plenty of other up-and-coming crews round here playing the Big I Am. The only way we're going to be steps ahead of them is to up our game.'

'Whatcha mean, Big Mo?' Twinkle, Mo's best friend, spoke for the first time.

They'd been besties since primary school. Priscilla Brodie had been given the nickname, Twinkle, when she was six-years-old after performing an excruciatingly, ear-numbing rendition of 'Twinkle, Twinkle, Little Star' during a parents' assembly.

Twinkle was tall, reed-thin, red-haired and freckled with large grass-green eyes. Mo worried to death about her because she was too pale these days. So fragile looking. She shouldn't even really be in the gang. The girl didn't have a bad bone in her body. She was as soft as rice pudding and as gentle as a newborn lamb. Being in Mo's posse was Mo's way of keeping Twinkle close and away from that home of horrors her best friend lived in with her Mother.

'What I mean is we need to start putting our mince pies on bigger prizes. Jobs that will fill up our pockets,' tone softening, Mo slowly explained.

And get us noticed with the right people Mo mentally added.

Someone yelled, 'You mean get our fingernails *really dirty*?' He shook his head in horror. 'My ol' gran will stab me to death with her knitting needles if she gets wind of it.'

Another: 'Once the summer's over I've wangled a place to be a carpenter's apprentice.'

And, to top it off, someone had the audacity to ask, 'Who the friggin' hell's Tommy Cooper, when he's at home? He weren't the guy who owned the Bentley we just jacked?'

Mo held back a shriek of pure frustration. She threw her hands in the air in utter despair. What was the point, eh? She could talk herself silly until Ermintrude and all the other cows came home, but she'd be wasting her breath.

Giving up she let them get back to noshing their chips and burgers and bobbing their heads to Destiny's Child's, 'Say My Name' on John-John's CD player.

Mo pulled Twinkle aside. 'What's up?'

The other girl avoided her eyes. 'Nothing. I feel as fit as a butcher's dog.'

Big Mo leant in closer so the others wouldn't hear. 'I'll tell you straight, I'm worried about you. And don't test me by claiming you've got the painters in.'

Being on her monthlies was Twinkle's usual go-to excuse for looking so mizz, but she didn't do that now. Tentatively, she admitted, 'Just been feeling tired, is all.' Twinkle mustered a tiny smile although her shoulders sagged. 'Ain't been sleeping right.'

Mo compressed her lips in anger. Twinkle was holding out on her and Mo was determined to discover what it was. But one look at her bestie's exhausted, dejected expression made Mo bite her tongue. Twinkle looked awful. The last thing she needed was Mo on her case giving her more grief.

Mo pulled her into a deep embrace. She forced back the gut-wrenching cry when she felt Twinkle's bones poking through her body. Something bad was going on with her bestie. Mo just knew it.

'East End Girls Forever,' Mo whispered in Twinkle's ear.

Her best friend breathed back, 'East End Girls Forever.'

This was their special catch phrase. Their pick-me-up when things looked down.

Mo became aware of the outline of the item she'd stolen from the Bentley's glove compartment in her pocket. The others were none the wiser about what she'd nabbed. And Mo wasn't about to enlighten them.

Her gang had made their decision about what types of lives they wanted to life. And good luck to them. But Mo was following a different road. She'd had a bang-up time knocking about with them, but she was eighteen now. A big girl. It was time to look towards her future.

It was time they parted company. Permanently. Their outlook on the future was very different from hers. Mo only had one ambition.

To be crowned Queen of Crime.

Mo grasped the black railings at the back of the allotment and flipped herself over the top. She deliberately avoided using the main entrance because she didn't want anyone to notice her. Mo was headed to her grandad's plot knowing he wouldn't be tending it today.

She almost tripped over when a couple of sizeable rats scurried out of nowhere, crossing her path. She was startled more from their unexpected appearance than the fact they were rats. Mo loved animals. They didn't tell porkies to your face like humans. All they wanted was a bit of love and to give love in return. Chuck in some food and you've got yourself a friend for life. One of these days, Mo vowed with conviction, she was going to have the biggest, baddest dog there ever was and waltz around town with him. No, it wouldn't be a *him*. Mo fancied a lady dog. What a combo they'd be.

Mo stared down at one of her grandad's pumpkins. What a whopper! It would go down a treat as Cinderella's carriage. With the gentlest of care, Mo took out what she'd thieved from the Bentley's glove compartment.

A gun.

Her heart raced as she looked on it with wonder. She'd never seen a real-life shooter before much less held one. What type it was Mo didn't know, but it was black with a gold handle. A gold handle? Wasn't that unusual, Mo mused? A thread of fear shivered in her gut as it dawned on her that the man who owned the Bentley might be a well-known face in the underworld.

Mo dropped to her knees and used her hands to carefully dig up the pumpkin. She did one last furtive look around. Then laid the gun with the gold handle in the ground.

Chapter Four

What a bunch of freeloaders! That was Jimmy Southpaw's withering opinion as he watched the mourners stuff their faces and liquor up their livers with anything they could get their grasping hands on. These days a funeral was a day trip out, free buffet with drink included. Wild, uncontrollable laughter erupted from a group who stood propping up the bar. Jimmy had to restrain himself. He was tempted, soooo tempted to stomp over there and crack a couple of heads together. Where did they think they were? Eh? An evening out down Walthamstow Dogs? Bile rose bitter and thick in his throat. This was his goodbye bash to his beloved boy, and they thought it was a hahaha moment.

Turf the lot of them out that's what he wanted to do. But that wasn't the East End way. Tradition was folk expected to be fed and watered after an hour or two in a drafty church and wind-swept graveside. The grieving family pulled out all the stops for the farewell send off for a loved one. If the food and drink were light-touch, there would be more grief afterwards with the family being rundown for days, even weeks as being a bunch of cheapskates.

Jimmy glanced about the room attempting to locate members of his family. Ah, there was his Violet. She was doing a bang-up job of circulating among the mourners making sure they didn't want for anything. Violet and Robbie had been close. Truth was his only daughter wasn't the brightest bulb in the ceiling and a bit slow on the uptake sometimes, but Robbie had never turned his nose up at her, not like some. He'd always found time to visit her, spoiled her with gifts and taken her out-n-about in that flash motor of his. His girl was the caring one in the family and that's what she was doing now, ensuring that those gathered were taken care of.

Harry, on the other hand, was predictably chatting up some gormless girl in a dress that seemed to have lost its bottom half. That lad needed a swift cuff around the nut for chasing skirt at his bruv's funeral. Despite Robbie being the one with the heartthrob good looks, it was Harry who was always a hit with the ladies. He had the right chat up lines on speed dial, knew how to make them feel good and how to stare into their dopey eyes as if they were the only person who mattered in the world. Robbie had been more hands-on, whereas Harry was a silver-tongued Lothario.

When he reached his son, Jimmy pulled him aside. 'The bookies. Tomorrow. Midday.'

Jimmy Southpaw was wasting no time organising a management meeting for the family at his HQ, on the Commercial Road.

Harry frowned, his brows slashing together. 'Tomorrow? That's a bit urgent, ain't it?' He touched his Dad's arm lightly with sympathy. 'Let Robbie settle in down the cemetery first before we take care of Barker. Plus, the law will twig it's us if we go for him straight away.'

Jimmy bared his teeth. 'Leave the thinking to me, sonny. Just make sure you're there.'

The sight of his daughter-in-law, Kristal, holding court at the top table like Her Majesty of The East End put his temper back on the rise. He still remembered the day Robbie had bought the girl home. He hadn't liked the look of her from the get-go. Clinging to his boy like poison ivy, those titties pointed like weapons of mass destruction and that chin of hers tilted in the air like her poo didn't pong like the rest of us. Kristal Newbury had her hooks well and truly in his lad and she wasn't letting go for no one. He'd put a discreet someone on the case to dig up everything on her. All the geezer could find out was that the girl worked in a hairdressers and her ol' Dad had recently gone to meet his maker.

End of story.

And that was really Jimmy's problem with her. No one growing from a weed to a woman in the East End could have that boring or saintly a life. Jimmy had given it his best shot over the years ... He couldn't find a speck of dirt on her.

When Jimmy gave her the heads-up about tomorrow's family sit-down, Kristal dipped her eyes at him behind the veil she refused to remove at the wake. No doubt she thought it added an air of mystery to her. 'Out for revenge already, are you, pops?'

He ground his teeth. She knew full well he hated her

calling him 'pops' but she did it, anyway.

His retaliation was swift. 'I'm surprised you're not, sweetheart. He was your old man, after all.'

Kristal lost a touch of her colour under that face full of paint and potions. There had been trouble in his son's marriage. Robbie had kept his obligations to his family but his commitment to his marriage vows ... Well, that had been a bit touch-n-go.

'Just make sure you're there, darling. Alright?' A mocking bite entered his words as he forcefully added, 'And another thing. Don't bring the kid off *The Omen* with you.'

A lightening flash of anger sparked in her eyes. 'I'd be grateful if you'd refrain from referring to my son – your grandson – as *that* Damien. Fed up with it, is what I'm getting.' She shifted her shoulders, wriggling her neck. 'And may I remind you that my boy will be taking over your business one day? He's your only grandkid. I can't see Harry ever having kids. I don't think that guy's got any lead in his pencil.'

You what? Jimmy bristled with righteous rage at the liberties she was taking. First off, making presumptions about his grandson's place in his organisation. And then, calling his son a Jaffa. Casting aspersions on Harry's ability and virility to add to the next generations of Steeles? She should feel dead lucky she was his daughter-by-law because if any other person said that shit to his face, it would be lights out at the end of his legendary southpaw fist.

Jimmy leant down and cupped a palm on Kristal's shoulder with fake family concern. To an onlooker the gesture was the picture of family solidarity. The pressure of his fingers told a very different story.

He harshly whispered, 'You'd know all about pencils, sweetheart. You've sharpened enough of them.'

Kristal kept up the family sympathy-fest with a deceptively grateful smile super glued to her mournful expression. 'I'm not having that. Call me what you like, but I was as faithful to Robbie as the Virgin bloody Mary.'

Her eyes whelmed up with unshed tears as she stood with as much dignity as she could muster. 'I was a good wife to him. I tried my best. I paid my dues in my marriage. Why are you always taking potshots at me, eh? And on the day I had to put my prince among men, Robbie, six feet under?'

When she twisted on her ice-pick thin heels and was gone, Jimmy could've kicked himself. He'd gone too far. True, he couldn't hack the bitch, but you couldn't fault her in doing her duty in providing his son with an heir. And, to give the girl her due she'd never publically shouted the odds when Robbie couldn't keep that wayward willy of his in his pants.

Feeling guilty he went in search of her intending to apologise. Something caught his attention outside. A face. Shock froze him. No way. Can't be. Despite his mental protests Jimmy raced out of the door.

'Sin,' Jimmy yelled at the woman walking briskly down the street, away from the wake.

The impact of his voice was like a whiplash across her back that stopped her in her tracks. Jimmy wasted no time in reaching her. She inhaled as if gathering courage. Then she turned to face him.

His sister.

'Cynthia.' He used her full name in a soft feather-like tone.

His gaze roamed hungrily over his older sister. Her face was hidden beneath a black veil, her body drowning in a coat way too big for her thin body. Jimmy feasted on her. Couldn't get enough of looking at her. His mind rewound back to when they were younger. What a double act they'd been back in the day. Southpaw and Sin. They'd taken the East End by storm. She'd always been the one cheering him on at ringside, not giving a toss if she made a right cake of herself spurring him on.

'Knock his block off, Jimmy.'

'Whatcha doing, you plonker? Keep your right up.'

'Southpaw the Swinger and don't you forget it.'

That was until the day it all fell hideously apart. The day she blamed him for it all. He hadn't spoken to her in twenty-five long, long years. That wasn't the same as not seeing her because he had. They had an agreement. He left her alone if he ever saw her. The agreed distance between them still felt like a knife twisting in his gut.

Sin tilted her chin proudly, the same way she'd done as a young woman. Jimmy was glad to see that hadn't changed. 'The years are treating you well, brother.'

'Why don't you come back with me?' He gently coaxed, laughing nervously to cover the anxiety coursing through him. 'My Harry would be proper chuffed to meet his Aunty Sin. Last time you put eyes on him he was about this high.' His hand dropped to a shade above his knee. 'And you haven't met my grand boy—'

She slammed her palm in the air between them. 'I came to pay my respects. That's all. Now, it's time for me to be on my way.'

She turned, but he grabbed her arm. Sin flinched. Jimmy's grip vibrated with anger. 'You gonna keep punishing me? Eh? After all this time?'

His sister calmly drew out of his hold. Her action left Jimmy feeling agonisingly empty. He wanted to snatch her back. But he didn't. It was as clear as the day she'd packed her belongings and left the Steele family fold that their painful past remained a mountain between them.

Sin took a mini step back as if to underscore his thoughts. 'There's no room for you in the world I've created. I'm sorry about what happened to Robbie—'

'Do you forgive me?' he asked her the one question that had haunted him for years. Jimmy wasn't a man who went seeking forgiveness. Not in his trade. But his beloved Sin…

She didn't miss a beat, her chin dipping slightly so she could hold his gaze. 'I've forgiven many things in my life. Turned the other cheek many a time. I can forgive you too. The trouble is I can't forget. I can never forget.'

She took a meaningful step away from her brother. 'As a brother you're dead to me, Jimmy.'

Jimmy's heart filled with ice and dread at her pronouncement. *She doesn't mean it. She doesn't mean it. She doesn't mean it.* He was lying to himself.

The invisible knife twisted inside him again.

A shrill scream split the air behind Jimmy who pivoted around to see a swarm of older women, some screaming, hightailing it out of the wake as quickly as their legs could carry them. For crying out loud! He'd been gone for less than five minutes.

He turned back to his sister to tell he would have to cut their unexpected reunion short. Jimmy's face fell. His sister was already gone.

The trouble kicked off as soon as Jimmy took off after his long-lost sister. Kristal noted the absence of her Father-in-law and swung into action working the room. At a time like this, speed was of the essence to make sure her version of the line of succession and future of the Steele empire was firmly planted in the minds of everyone gathered. If there was one thing Kristal knew how to do it was work a room.

A gentle tap on the shoulder here, a smile there, a whispered, 'Jimmy doesn't want to make an announcement, y'know, he's keeping it a bit hush-hush for now but he's going to be training his only grandson, Damien, to take over from Robbie – rest his soul – as his successor.'

Not everyone she spoke to was convinced.

'Damien? He's only a kid.'

'Surely Harry will be Jimmy's new guy? He's the other son and the obvious choice.'

Kristal wasn't deterred. She had an answer all prepared for the naysayers. 'You got a problem cowboy, take it up with Jimmy.' With an added, 'Harry's not a fighter, not like my Damien and everyone knows it.'

Noticing the vicar tucking into the nosh obviously in no hurry to get away, Kristal decided that it wouldn't do any harm to have the church's blessing for Damien's new role.

The man of the cloth nearly choked on a prawn cocktail vol-au-vent when he realised that Kristal was sitting beside him. He hadn't even heard her approach.

'Lovely service, Rev,' she purred with a double blink of her false eyelashes. 'I think you hit exactly the right note. Incidentally, my son Damien will be taking over when his grandfather retires and you can be sure if we ever need the services of a man with a dog collar, you'll be number one on our list.'

The vicar was confused. 'Really? My understanding is that Mister Southpaw is hoping his second son Harry will be stepping into his shoes.'

Kristal bared her teeth, outraged. Quite a terrifying sight in the vicar's opinion. 'You're taking the piss, aren't you, reverend? Where did you hear that load of old pony?'

Red-faced now, he told her. 'From Harry himself. He confided in me not five minutes ago.'

He did what? Kristal's pissed gaze searched the room like overactive lasers. In the distance she found her fecking brother-in-law. Look at the twat, cosying up to a couple of Jimmy's key enforcers. And she didn't like the fast-flowing whispering and nodding going on. Were they plotting how to ensure Harry got his lazy bum in Robbie's vacant chair?

Thinks he can screw my Damien over? Nah! Bollocks to that!

Kristal pulled off her earrings meaning business. 'Look after these for me,' she told the wide-eyed vicar, thrusting them into his hands.

She vacated her chair so fast it tumbled backwards,

crashing to the floor. That caught the attention of mourners. They fell silent, some secretly rubbing their hands with relish at the promise of more drama. Kristal stormed, terminator style, across the room, grabbed an unsuspecting Harry by the arm and yanked him backwards.

She could barely contain her fury. ''Ere, what's your game, you grotty little nonce? Going around at my ol' man's funeral canvassing for my beloved's job when he isn't even cold in his grave? What kind of a vampire are you?'

Harry was relaxed. 'Calm down, sister dearest. You're making a total tit and show of yourself.'

He wasn't wrong. The room was deathly silent, people gawking like they had a front seat at the theatre.

He went on, 'I've already spoken to Dad and it's a done deal. Now why don't you go and sob at the graveside like a good widow-woman should?'

Crack! Kristal walloped him a good one with the flat of her hand across his cheek. Harry gingerly touched his cheek with his fingertips. 'It's a good job for you I don't strike women, or you'd be in the ground with our Robbie.'

Crack! Kristal slapped his other cheek this time with the back of her hand. Harry rocked back on his heels, wearing a stunned expression of having a bucket of frozen water flung in his face.

'Really?' His sister-in-law exploded, bouncing on the tips of her toes like she was preparing to do the Ali Shuffle. 'I've heard it's geezers you don't like to strike while women are fair game. Let's see, shall we?'

Harry should've seen what was coming … A right-hander knocked him backwards into the cold buffet. The food flew in all directions. The crowd parted like the Red Sea when a gobsmacked Damien appeared. 'Mum! Mum! What you doing? Leave it, Mum, I'll take care of Uncle Harry.'

He was on his uncle in an instant, dragging them both to the floor. Smeared with coleslaw, egg sandwiches, sausage rolls and other savouries, they rolled backwards and forwards. They grappled like two wrestlers in a mud ring. One of the old dears in the astonished audience, known by all as Odds On Betty, started a book, taking bets on who would come out on top.

The attempts by Jimmy's people to break it up soon turned in to a whole series of other punch-ups depending on who had heard what about Robbie's successor from Kristal or Harry. Bottles flew, chairs crashed, tables overturned. Shouts for some respect to be shown were met with kicks and punches while older mourners either fled or pitched in.

'What's the meaning of this? At my son's funeral?'

The fighting instantly stopped. Every eye turned to the main door. Wearing a face like pure thunder, fists clenched by his side, Jimmy's commanding frame filled the doorway.

All eyes turned from Jimmy towards the Unholy Steele Trinity – Harry, Damien and Kristal.

Jimmy shook with uncontrollable fury at the spectacle his adored son's funeral had turned into.

He yelled, spittle shooting in the air, 'Out! Out! The lot of ya.' He stabbed an accusing finger at his family. 'Get out of my sight!'

No one argued with him, especially his family.

Alone, Jimmy couldn't control himself any longer. A crushing weight pressed tight against his chest. He sank to his knees and put his head in his hands and allowed his private agony to seize him. He sobbed his guts out.

Robbie's gone. My beloved boy's gone.

A part of him had been ripped out forever.

Chapter Five

'Where the bloody hell were you yesterday?' Mo's Mum screeched the following morning like a dodgy boiler about to explode.

Precious Watson stood livid at the bottom of the stairs, fists furiously planted on her hips, glaring up at her daughter. If looks could kill Mo would've surely dropped dead on the spot.

They lived in a maisonette on a housing estate on The Island. They were one of only two families in the block lucky enough to have a French door leading to a balcony that commanded a stunning view over the river. Despite such an enviable position, back in the day, not many people had wanted to live in this part of the East End. Folk claimed that the wind went right through your bones on the Isle of Dogs. Plus, there had been only one bus route that took you on and off it. No Tube, no overland railway. People fought tooth and nail for the council not to house them there. A place by the river on the Isle of Dogs? No thank you very much!

But, in recent times, The Island's fortunes had gone up

in the world. It had a spanking new overland train service, The Docklands Light Railway, which hooked The Island up with other bits of East London and the posh city part up Tower Hill way. And the City folk were willing to pay top dollar for a chance to own the type of picture-perfect view Mo and her family had of the Thames.

As far as Mo was concerned, hand-on-heart, she couldn't wait to up-sticks from The Island. And you best believe she was never looking back.

Mo cut her eyes at her Mum as she got the right hump. As soon as she'd clocked her Mum's killer's expression, she knew that Hurricane Precious was about to make landfall. Mo was in for the tongue bashing of the century. Taser-tongue, that's what Mo called it. Her Mother's tongue certainly knew how to electrify a body into submission. She was sick of her Mum getting on her case, taking potshots every chance she got. Nothing Mo did seemed to be good enough for her Mum these days.

They hadn't always had such a rocky relationship. Before Mo had jacked in school at fifteen, they'd been tight, her Mum fiercely supporting her every step of the way. Mo's chest squeezed with sadness thinking of the years her Mum always had her back. When had her Mum turned into the Wicked Witch of the East End?

'Out,' Mo answered with attitude. With a twist of her lips, she sauntered down the stairs. She knew she should zip it and walk away because once her Mum got started she didn't know to press the off switch.

With a nifty one-two move, Precious blocked her kid

from going past. And screamed, 'Out? Well, we all know you ain't be *out* looking for a decent job. Or *out* down the community college getting a better edu-kay-shun.'

Abruptly, Mo's chest heaved as she spluttered and coughed uncontrollably. Her Mother's breath reeked of whisky. Precious Watson had always been partial to a shot or two, usually laced with coconut water, but it was only every now and again, nothing excessive. All that had changed recently. She'd morphed into a proper booze-bunny. A bottle of Jack D had become her best friend.

The physical changes in Mo's Mum were stark and dramatic too. Once her good looks had made her the talk of the East End Town. A major league hottie with film star stunning looks. Few women could touch her in the looks department. Precious wouldn't be seen dead outside her front door unless she was decked out to the nines, false lashes accentuating her teasing brown eyes and slap applied with the knowhow of an artist's touch to her glowing, brown skin. A fashion puss with men lining up for miles to have a chance to be seen on her arm. Her policy with most of them had been simple: You can window shop honey, but don't touch the merchandise!

Now, who would want to touch her? Mo mourned. Her Mum's face was haggard. The pitiful condition of her straight weave-on was a slap in the face to any respectable hairdresser – tangled, matted, crying out to be redone. The curves she'd once proudly flaunted had dwindled to a pitiful example of size minus zero. And stuck to her, like the shadow of her former self, was a nasty-green, wrinkled dressing gown that even Oxfam would turn its nose up at.

Mo was cut up, heartbroken that her gorgeous Mum had let herself go. Precious looked like her sell-by date had come and gone. What left Mo most gutted, what she missed most of all was her Mum's laughter. As bright as the sun shining over the river her smile had been. What a contrast to the way she now walked about with a face full of misery. In her heart Mo knew something had happened to her Mum. But what?

Mo pushed her sorrow aside as she stood her ground. 'I don't need this earache or a load of verbal. All I want to do is get some brekkie…'

Precious dressed her down with her knowing eyes not budging an inch. 'You need to buck up your ideas and find a job—'

'I don't know how many times I have to tell you, there ain't nuthin down the job centre that fits my skills.'

Her Mum scoffed with a humourless, grating laughter. 'What skills are those then? Knowing how to ponce off the state? Getting up to no good with that gang of worthless hood rats you knock around with?' Suddenly the older woman's face crumbled, eyes tearing up. 'What would your Dad say if he could see you now? I'll tell you what, he'd feel ashamed, that's what. Ashamed.'

'My Dad?' Mo's eyes widened with livid disbelief. The audacity! Her Mum had really gone and pushed her button now. Unleashed a skyrocketing temper she could barely control. 'You mean *the Dad* I've never clapped eyes on?' Her tone was sarky to the hilt. 'The Dad you won't tell me sod all about.' Her rage pushed Mo closer. 'Go on. Tell me all about him. I dare ya.'

Her Mum's mouth wobbled with uncertainty. 'I… I…'

Precious looked like she wanted the ground to eat her up, but no way was her daughter letting her off the hook. She'd opened this stinking can of worms and Mo was about to make sure that they dived right in.

Face flushed, breathing shallow and noisy, Mo let her Mum have it with both barrels. 'All I know about my ol' man is he's some white guy.' Her voice quaked with emotion. 'Feel ashamed of me?' She kissed her teeth, long and drawn out. 'Let me tell you, mommy drunkest, he's got a fecking nerve. If he was any sorta man, he would've been a proper Father to me.'

Her expression twisted to pure malice. 'Or is the reason he ain't around no more coz you drove him away? He get tired of that out-of-order tongue of yours constantly bitching and witching?'

Precious reared over her much smaller daughter, eyes glittering wildly and raised her hand ready to strike. The slap never came, instead the blow came hard and swift from the words she lashed Mo with. 'You don't wanna get mouthy with me, Little Miss Lady. You're not too old for a round of licks with the back of my hand.'

Mo stretched her neck ready to take on anything the world threw at her. 'Bring. It. On.'

'Precious! Leave the girl alone,' a voice cracked sharply with authority over their standoff.

Mo's gaze darted up the stairs where she found her grandad. Bertram Watson was aged somewhere in his sixties. He was always sketchy about how many years he'd been on this earth. People called him Brother Bertie because of his easy-going style and calming, carefree nature. Indoors and out, his trademark were two things – he sported a black pork pie trilby hat and moved with the aid of a walking cane that had a silver top with the Lion of Judah engraved on it. He was a blatant charmer, and not shy about flaunting it. Mo suspected that Brother Bertie had been quite a ladies' man back in the day. It was easy to see where her Mum inherited her stunning looks.

Mo's anger vanished in a heartbeat replaced by a sensation of such all-consuming love it made her heart ache. Mo loved her gramps to heaven and back. He felt exactly the same about her. There wasn't a thing he wouldn't do for his beloved granddaughter or baby-gal as he affectionately called her. Any time she needed a shoulder to cry or lean on his was always available. They had a very special bond. Mind you, he'd be hopping crazy, stamping his cane into the ground if he cottoned on to her plans for the future. Criminal plans.

Precious directed a disapproving, withering glance her Dad's way. 'I should've known you'd take her side. You always do. You need to stop sugar-coating everything for her. The girl needs to learn that life isn't made of sugar and spice.'

Brother Bertie used his cane to walk downstairs. He took his time, which had nothing to do with age slowing him down. He was a man who didn't believe in rushing life. 'I don't like seeing my two best ladies in the world at each other's throats.'

He winked at Mo, which kicked up a tiny smile on her lips.

As he reached the bottom, Precious kissed her teeth and stomped off to the sitting-room. At the door she turned back and gave Mo the evil eye as she stabbed a warning finger at her. Her lips twisted meaningfully with each word. 'I meant what I said. Stop sitting on your jacksie all day long and find a job. And find it quick-time.'

'And if I don't?' Mo spat provocatively, knowing full well it would royally wind her Mum up.

Precious didn't disappoint, as she showed her displeasure with a thorough twist of her lips. Her finger swivelled like a worm towards the direction of the front door. 'You'll be outta here, with your shit packed up in a black bin liner, quicker than you can say, *Job Seeker's Allowance.*'

The colour drained from Mo's face. 'What? You're gonna kick me out?'

Brother Bertie intervened, rounding, grim-faced, on his daughter. 'You losing your mind, girl?' His tone hardened. 'You are not putting my grandchild out of this house.'

Her gramps and Mum started to go at it big time just as Mo's phone pinged with a text.

Aladdin's cave in a van.

Right up your street.

Plump pickings

The location of this van full of goodies was attached. The text wasn't signed off with a name. That was something Mo had instilled in her crew. Never use names if you didn't have to.

Mo pulled her puffer jacket off the rail in the hallway and slung it on. Only then did her Mum and grandad realise she was off out. She'd had enough of this second-rate domestic bollocks. And the opportunity to do another dodge was too tempting.

When Mo opened the door, her jittery gaze checked the length of the communal balcony. She might have a target on her back as a result of the raid on the Bentley. And nabbing the gold-handled gun.

Mo cautiously stepped out making sure she had eyes in the back of her head.

Chapter Six

Mo realised too late that she'd been set up. There was no van in this alleyway. And three blokes materialised out of the shadows. Shit!!

In a flash, Mo weighed up her options. Leg it or stand her ground. She decided to tough it out.

'You alright, lads?' she hailed, bright and breezy, not breaking her stride as she tried to brazen it out.

No answer. That was not good. Not good at all. As the men closed in Mo soon got the lay of the land. It was actually two granite-faced toughs flanking one guy. And, Mother Mary, what a guy! Leonardo DiCaprio eat your heart out! Getting ready to take a possible caning from the most clit-trembling man she'd ever set her eyes on, now if that wasn't an example of Sod's Law, Mo didn't know what was. Then again, it all depended on what sort of caning he had in mind!

When they finally reached her, he took out a wallet and flashed it briefly in front of her. 'We're plain clothes cops and need to take you to the station so you can assist us with our enquiries.'

He must think she'd just fallen off a Christmas tree. If

they were cops, Mo was Madonna! The badge in his hand he hadn't given Mo enough time to checkout if it was legit. Of course, that was his intention all along. Probably the membership card of a snooker hall he belonged to. If he thought he was putting the frighteners on her, he didn't know Big Mo.

She looked Mister Gorgeous up. And down. OK, she might've looked a bit too long in his lunch box department.

'What station's that then? Mile End train station?'

A muscle ticked with displeasure in his jaw. He hadn't been expecting her to see-through his bogus credentials. Nevertheless, he still persisted with, 'We will have to ask you to accompany us now.'

Mo started to enjoy herself despite the stench of big-time trouble in the air. 'If you're looking for naughty girls, you wanna start with that Goldilocks. Word is she can't stop breaking and entering. A spell in Holloway should set her straight.'

She'd needled him too far as he now wore the very painful expression of someone with a parsnip hanging out of their backside. The pretence fell away. He double clicked his fingers.

Run!

Mo dodged to the side, but steel solid arms clamped about her waist and lifted her high. The other goon grabbed her feet. Mo struggled for all she was worth when she clocked Mister Gorgeous take out something from his pocket. A bag. A plastic one.

Mo's heart plummeted to the soles of her feet. He wasn't

going to put the bag over her head? Her struggles intensified with manic fury as he advanced towards her with a malicious grin. In a state of complete and hopeless disbelief and panic Mo knew it was game over. All her dreams of making a name for herself would never come true. Her life was about to be snuffed out.

The bag was rammed over her head and Mo's world turned completely black.

Mo was strung up like a smoked ham in the butchers at Christmas. The tips of her toes barely touched the ice-cold floor. She grimaced sucking back the sharpness of pain. The sensation of her arm muscles stretched so taunt was pure fire. At least it hadn't been a plastic bag that a-hole had shoved over her head, but a pillowcase. They'd dumped her into the boot of a car and unceremoniously dragged her to this place.

Mo couldn't be sure, but she'd bet her life it was a cellar. Dark and murky like the bowels of hell. The stench turned her tummy. It reeked of rotting wood and mildew and was chilly enough to freeze Satan's bollocks off. Mo figured that the particulars of her current deadly dilemma concerned yesterday's smash and grab job on the Bentley. Just as she'd suspected after she'd examined the gun that the flash motor was probably owned by some well-known bruiser who was royally pissed. Now he'd sent his hit squad to teach her a lesson she'd never forget.

But would that lesson involve killing her?

Mo wasn't going to lie; she was petrified from the top of her head to the tips of her frozen toes. But, you know what, as long as she had breath in her body no way on this earth was she letting these three gorillas witness her distress.

Mister Gorgeous stood with his feet braced apart in front of her. Cocky sod! Mo pursed her lips. He was somewhere in his twenties with the golden hair and blue gaze of painted angels seen in churches. Every last one of his features seemed to have fallen perfectly into place. And he was tall, an inch or two over six-foot. Evil sometimes comes wrapped up in the most beautiful wrapping paper.

One thug stood behind him, the other stationed near the door.

Gorgeous spoke. 'You have been a naughty girl.'

'I'll show you how naughty I can be if you cut me down.' Mo tossed back with a nudge-nudge wink-wink attitude.

A huge, harsh guffaw exploded from his mouth. 'We've got a sharp one on our hands here lads.'

Just like that, the humour died on his face. Mo caught the depth in his baby-blues. Cold. Killer eyes. Not gorgeous at all. She swallowed convulsively. Drops of sweat ran down the curve in her back. If she didn't figure a way out of this mess soon moron here was going to do her some serious damage. She could feel it in her bones.

He calmly continued, taunting, 'Mind you, I don't think you can be that sharp. Anyone with half a brain cell would've known not to put their tea leafing mitts on that car.'

Mo played dumb. 'What car? I don't know dick about no wheels. You've got the wrong, sharp little lady, bruv.'

He crossed his arms observing her closely. 'Do you know what really gets up my nose?'

It was blatant he was getting his rocks off relishing the power he held over her. Screw him! She wasn't playing knobnut's game. She stayed schtum.

He answered his own question. 'I hate midget slags who try to piss in my face with a lie.'

Mo kept up the smart-mouth routine. 'Talking of taking a leak, any chance of a visit to the khazi? I developed a bladder full in the boot of your motor.'

The gorilla guarding the door growled, 'Want me to shut the bitch up?'

Mo waited with bated breath as Gorgeous thought over the menacing request. Eventually he waved a dismissive palm in the air. 'Nah! There are plenty of other ways to teach someone manners.'

Mo was sticking to her story. 'I'm telling you bruv, you've got the wrong person—'

He cut smartly over her. 'Maureen Watson. That's your name.' He wasn't asking, he was telling.

Mo shook her head emphatically. 'The name's Watson, alright, but it ain't Maureen. Name's Charity. It's my first cousin who's called Mo.' Her eyes did the rounds of their sockets dramatically as she shook her head with mock sorrow. 'That girl's on the path to ruin. Her poor Mum cries herself to sleep every night for her daughter's lost soul. Mo won't listen to no one, not even me. You don't know how hard—'

His mocking slow handclap shut her up. 'I think you've missed your calling, darlin'. You should be playing some scrubber on *Corrie*. I'm sure they can find a part for a mouthy mot like you.' His arms dropped to his side, but they weren't limp, the muscles bunched and pulled inside his jacket sleeves. 'If you think you're going to find any sort of charity here, you've come to the wrong place.'

Mo refused to let it go. If she kept up her fable long enough, chances were a seed of doubt might take root and flourish inside the bastard's single brain cell.

'I'm telling you, over the grave of my beloved Mum – bless her dearly departed soul – you've got the wrong Watson.'

His tone dropped to a husky, hard whisper. 'What if I told you that in less than five minutes, sex traffickers are going to come through that door?'

Mo sagged with shock against her bonds. The bottom fell out of her world. She faltered. 'Sex ... Sex ... Traffickers?'

'Albanians,' he casually threw back, a tiny grin of delight tickling his lips. 'I hear they're rough on the merchandise. Like to shoot their stable up on smack. Keeps the girls nice and docile. At least twenty geezers a day spunking off between your legs. You're going to need the smack to numb the mind. You get me?'

With more drama than George Clooney, he suddenly slapped his forehead. 'Silly me, I got that totally wrong. This particular crew specialises in punters whose kink is getting off via the backdoor, know what I mean?'

Mo was chilled to the bone. A horrifying image rose in her mind. She was lying naked on a filthy mattress on the floor. The room was a pigsty, stinking to high hell of urine and the foul odour of sweaty stale sex. In the doorway a man stood with a potbelly openly playing with his cock. With a nasty leer he closed the door and advanced towards her. Mo screamed. Cried for help. But no one came.

Mo pulled her terror-stricken mind back to the present, almost gagging.

Fuck this! The time for playing nicely was over!

Her next words were precise, clipped and ever so slow in order to burn them into his thicko skull. 'Heed my words. Heed them well. Every time one of those filthy fuckers touches me, it won't be their faces I'll see, it will be yours. And when I get away – and you better believe it I'm going to escape – I'll come gunning for you. So, you better sleep with one eye open, matey.' Mo added, with a spine-chilling laugh, 'Nah! Even with both eyes open, you won't see me coming.'

His cheeks scolded red with rage, jaw jutting out with indignation. He was needled. Mo almost laughed out loud. The stupid numpty had fallen for her carefully planned dirty trick. She had deliberately goaded him to ensure he lost his cool. Split-second anger made people act on impulse. Tipped them off balance. And that's when you strike.

Gullible prick!

Mo tightened her fingers around the ropes ready to spring into action.

'Threaten me, will you?' he cracked, his words a firestorm of fury. Vengeance darkening his eyes, he pulled off his leather belt. 'I'm going to whip your gob till it's bloody. Then rip you a new one in that lying mug of yours.'

He went for Mo in a blind fury. Raised his belt. What

happened next, he didn't even see coming. Mo used her toes to spring high off the ground. Once in the air she swung her legs forward. The dope walked in between them. Gotcha! Triumphantly, she locked her legs around his neck. And squeezed. Now who was the fly in the spider's web?

Going to school had never really been Mo's bag, except for gymnastics. It had been right up her street due to her being so small. Now she used what she'd learnt to her criminal advantage.

Gorgeous wore a stupefied expression like he'd just been decked in the kisser by Mike Tyson. Shock twisted his features leaving that tasty mug of his very ugly indeed. The belt crash-landed to the cold ground, coiled like a snake that had breathed its last.

Mo sussed that the two other cretins would go for their shooters, so sternly cautioned, 'I wouldn't go for your hardware if I was you, gentlemen. If you do, his neck's going to go snap-snap and look like the Leaning Tower of Pisa.'

To underscore her deadly words, she pressed into her captive's windpipe. His face turned scarlet as he fought for air.

Mo allowed herself a moment of pure, sweet fun with Gorgeous. She couldn't help her snide dig. 'All your talk of blokes between my legs gave me ideas.'

Mo didn't care for all that chat about sex traffickers. A pox on men who did that to women.

'Right,' Mo ordered, her voice echoing off the bare brick walls. 'I want the goons to buzz off.'

No one moved. Electric tension crackled in the air. Grim-faced, Mo increased the pressure of her legs. The sooner they realised they were dealing with Big Mo and not some dopey schoolgirl, the quicker they could part company.

Gorgeous nodded frantically. Without hesitation his men left them alone.

But then Mo was the one who was in for a shocked surprise. The door crashed open, banging violently against the wall.

A big man ominously filled the doorway.

And thundered, 'What the fuck's going on here? I told you to bring her to me, not get your rocks off on some kinky sex trip.'

Chapter Seven

'I should fucking rip your guts out and then serve 'em up to you like sausages on a plate.' The older man exploded in the face of the younger man who had held Mo captive.

The older man had introduced himself to her. Said his name was Barker. Mo had never heard of him so had no idea she was in the presence of gangland royalty. That the man who had come to her rescue was the legendary villain, Barker. Barker wasn't his real name, but he'd been known by his nick for so long that most folk couldn't even remember the name he'd been born to. He was called Barker on account of him being a barker at the funfair when he was in his youth.

What Mo did know was that the man he was currently slamming into the wall for the umpteenth time was his nephew, Josh. Her kidnapper.

Barker was no oil painting with pockmarked cheeks, a bushy tash and brows. Barrel-chested and stocky with the muscle mass of a much younger man. He certainly didn't possess the stunning, hottie looks of his nephew, but Barker had something that seized Mo's attention immediately.

Power.

She could smell its intoxicating scent rolling off him. Wave after wave after glorious wave. The scent of the knock off perfume her Mum got off a guy with a stall in Chrisp Street Market wasn't a patch on the aroma of power coming from Barker. Mo dreamed of the day she'd be smothered in it. It reminded her of the powerhouse of a man she'd met all those years ago.

Mo keenly watched proceedings as she sat at a table in the deserted country pub with a cellar. Turns out Josh had been a very naughty boy indeed and not followed his uncle's instructions.

'I told you not to harm a hair on her head.' The older man roared, hot and low. 'The only reason the barrel of a shooter isn't buried between those Colgate gnashers of yours is you're my sister's kid.'

Not five minutes earlier, Barker had gone bat-shit ballistic when he twigged it wasn't a touch of BDSM he was observing, but Mo attempting to escape his nephew's clutches. He'd stormed in like Attila the Hun, yelling like a loon on steroids.

Despite Barker's profuse apologies, once they were above stairs Mo had fleetingly considered sprinting to safety for all she was worth. That's what any sane person would've done. But she hadn't. She couldn't put her finger on why that was, all she knew was some sixth sense compelled her to stay.

Barker released his nephew with a contemptuous shove and strode towards Mo. Raising her chin she glanced defiantly at him. 'It's a fine day when a girl can't walk the streets of our fair city without being molested. You want to enlighten me as to what I'm doing here?'

She was taking an almighty chance being ballsy because this bloke was a proper heavyweight. The way he held himself, the manner in which his gaze assessed his surroundings, it was as clear as a reflection in glass that Barker was a man accustomed to overseeing his own empire.

His bushy tash twitched like a cat preening its fur as he smiled down on her. 'We'll get to the whats and whereafters soon enough. First, let's wet our tongues with something from the bar. What's your poison?' He scrapped back the chair opposite and sat. 'Bet you're a white wine spritzer lady. A touch of class with a splash of fizz.'

Was he having a giggle? White wine? Who did he think she was? Lady Muckety-Muck parading her pearls on a day trip round the East End? And that's when something startling clicked into place in Mo's mind. This guy was trying to impress her. Now why would he be trying to do that? He looked the picture of an old school, seasoned villain while she was nothing but a new kid on the criminal manor still in the starting block.

What could this geezer want with her?

'A voddy and coke. A double.'

As he clicked his fingers at the bartender, beneath lowered lashes Mo's gaze slid to Josh who had by now peeled himself off the wall. He was patting down his clothes putting himself back to rights. He sensed her scrutiny and zeroed in on her. Their eyes tangled, held, leaving a breathless tension swirling within her. Some folks went through life lying to themselves. Not Mo. She admitted what that tension was.

Sexual attraction. Mo wanted a very raunchy portion of steamy lovin' with Josh. The guy was a bona fide hottie. Her nips grew pert and pebbled enough to hang a coat on. Because Mo was a run-around type of girl, most assumed she'd had a string of boyfriends by now. She was no virgin, but she wasn't putting it about either. She didn't take the giving of her body lightly.

Josh must've sensed her mind was frolicking in the gutter because his heavenly lips stretched and curled into a Hollywood A-lister smile. Mo arched an innocent brow like she hadn't a clue what he was playing at and kissed her teeth lightly with disdain, cutting her eyes at him for good measure.

Thankfully the arrival of the drinks drew her attention back to Barker.

'My real name's Freddy Morgan,' he informed her. 'But only my dear Mum calls me that. Everyone calls me Barker.'

She drank deeply from her voddy as she considered what he'd told her. Then cocked her head. 'You already introduced yourself. Is your name meant to mean something?'

Barker didn't appear offended, although any other time he'd have taken it as a blatant diss. If anything, he was lapping up the fact she didn't know about his stature.

'The reason you know sod all about me, Princess, is I keep my head below the radar. Only those in The Know, the important people, the guys and gals that matter are allowed a glimpse inside my world.'

'For all I know you could be chatting out of your back

hole, trying to impress some poor girl from the East End.'

He chuckled softy and then turned his shadowed gaze to his nephew. 'Josh, why don't you tell Little Miss Doubter here all about me and my organisation.'

Josh sauntered over with an easy, relaxed stride that left Mo in no doubt that he thought he was all that and a bag of chips. He stopped behind his uncle as if they were posing for a family portrait.

He flicked and patted the cuffs of his shirt and stretched his neck. 'Any racket that goes down in my uncle's manor only gets green lit with his say-so. Cross him and on a good day he'll give you a slap that will put you in a ward down the The London. On a bad, he'll put you in the ground.'

Mo swallowed, nerves kicking in. Cold sweat popped out on her skin, drops running down the back of her neck. If this was the real deal, this bloke was a living legend. A dangerous man. Mo was more scared now than she'd been strung up in the dank cellar. Whatever was going on here she suspected she was done for.

Kaput. Finished. Curtains.

Mo immediately went on the offensive, leaning forcefully across the table. 'Look, Mister Barker, I'm real sorry if it was your flash motor me and my mates—'

'The Bentley ain't mine.' He informed her.

Mo breathed in a harsh, shocked air of confusion. Her heart was beating like the clappers. 'If this isn't about that motor, what do you want with me?'

He leant back in his chair as he took out a very fat, chunky cigar from his pocket. His nephew took out a gold lighter and lit his uncle up.

Barker's cheeks ballooned as he puffed a few times. Then he let the smoke breeze across the table towards Mo's face. She wasn't even sure she was breathing anymore.

Barker pulled the cigar from his lips and told her the last thing she expected to hear. 'I want to offer you a job.'

'A job?' Mo parroted, stunned. 'I … I don't get it.'

He enlightened her. 'Any organisation runs on new blood, so I've always got my mince pies on the lookout for something new sprouting up on the manor.' He surveyed her closely. 'And I've had my eye on you girl for quite some time now. You're confident, sure of yourself. The blag on the Bentley shows you've got plenty of bottle, babe. Bloody brilliant. Not many people would have had the brass to do that.'

Mo couldn't believe it. This man was opening the door to a world she'd prayed for entry to for such a long time. She didn't kid herself that she'd be a major player at first in his organisation … However, in time, there was no reason why he wouldn't pass her the reins of running one of his operations. Mo imagined others kowtowing to her and calling her boss.

The Queen of Crime.

Mo frowned. There was something about his offer that sounded too neat. Too polished. Who'd ever heard of a bossman plucking a nobody like her from the backend of nowhere and giving her a starring role in his show?

So, she told him straight. 'Let me go away and think on it.'

Josh scoffed with snarling displeasure, turning the beauty of his face into something truly nasty. 'She's as dumb as day-old shit. The nerve on it. You take time out of your busy day, Uncle, to give Eliza Doolittle here a leg up in the world and she spits your generosity back in your face.' He moved threateningly around the table. 'I say you let me finish what I started downstairs.'

Mo reared out of the chair so suddenly it crashed to the floor. She wasn't taking that type of BS from no one. No one. Thinks he can put the frighteners on her? No chance!

She spread her arms wide and wriggled her fingers in a 'bring it on' gesture. 'If you mean go back downstairs so I can finish strangling your arse, then yeah, I'm up for that, bruv. Just say the word from those pretty-boy lips of yours.'

His expression turned to something scary at the mention of his looks. Ouch! Obviously, his God given looks were a touchy subject. He crowded close into Mo until they stood toe to toe. His eyes smouldered. All Mo could think about was snogging the hell out of his face. For pity's sake, what the heck was wrong with her?

Barker's command slashed between them. 'Children! Behave!'

Mo sucked her teeth as she moved back. She took in a few deeper breaths to settle down. Fixed her gaze on Barker. 'I thank you for your offer, but like I says, I need to think about it.'

Barker pleasantly answered, 'Quite right too. A wise decision. In business never jump in with both feet. Always give yourself some space so you can see your options.' He gestured at his still fuming nephew. 'Now, you get Miss Watson here safely back home. Back into the loving embrace of her Mum.'

As Josh led her towards the door Barker's mocking voice interrupted their journey. 'Blimey! Forgot to impart some info that would've no doubt helped you make the right decision.'

His tone froze her. Forgotten to give her information? Nah! This was a man who operated with aces tucked up his sleeve. And if Mo was right, he was about to reveal one to her.

She slowly turned on her heel to face him. 'What do you mean, the right decision?'

Barker had shed the cloak of a businessman and replaced it with the armour of a proper villain. 'A wrong decision could mean a little birdie might chirp in the ear of the man who owns that Bentley. And the birdie might tell him all about the little chick who obviously must have a death wish coz no one in their right nut would've put their slag hands on his motor.'

Mo's heart kicked up again, sensing something dreadful coming. 'Who does the Bentley belong do?'

Barker didn't answer her terrifying question. Instead he turned the screw on the offer he'd laid before her. 'Now, if you were a member of my family, you'd be covered. Protected if retribution came your way.'

Mo asked again, voice visibly shaking this time. 'Who does it belong to?'

Barker leant menacingly forward. 'What on earth possessed

you to try to steal a man's property while he was grieving for his lost son? Throwing dirt graveside.'

Mo's knees wobbled because she'd figured out whose name he was going to say.

'Jimmy Southpaw.'

Fuck me! Mo's knees almost buckled. Jimmy Southpaw ran the East End. He had a fearsome reputation. Didn't take any prisoners. If Jimmy Southpaw found out it was her who had left her fingerprints all over his Bentley and thieved his gun while he was burying his son, there was no doubt what would happen.

Mo was a dead girl.

Chapter Eight

Jimmy Southpaw was a by-the-clock man, so he turned up on the dot of midday at the betting shop on Commercial Road. As usual, he entered via the rusty door round the back. 'Odds On' was supposed to be one of the last independent bookmakers left in London. But everyone and their granny knew what it really was. Jimmy Southpaw's HQ. In the small flat upstairs, Jimmy held his business meetings, dished out judgements and punishments to those who were foolhardy enough to cross him.

He climbed the ancient, creaking wooden stairs to what had once been a granny flat but now served as his makeshift conference room. He opened the warped wooden door and went in. Apart from the installation of a kitchenette Jimmy hadn't touched the place. The wallpaper curled and was stained with age in places. The ceiling cracked and bowed. The green carpet had become a feast for moths leaving it threadbare. Of course, Jimmy could have had the place tarted up to look flash and fresh. But he didn't because it was a reminder that what goes up may one day come back down again. A reminder to always keep his eye on the ball and never take anything for granted.

The only concession to his current status as a premier gang boss was the long mahogany table. His family sat around it waiting for him. Kristal and Damien on one side and Harry on the other. They were already hitting the booze. At least they all had the decency to appear shamefaced and sheepish about turning Robbie's funeral into some type of new Olympic contact sport.

He took his seat at the head of the table. Next to Violet who he'd told to get here ahead of time. Violet was his true first born. Maybe it wasn't right that he'd given Robbie the title of heir but Violet being a girl that wasn't how things were done. Tradition. Boys always came first. At least that's what he'd thought back in the day. He'd once thought he might be able to find a modest place for Violet in his organisation, but the kid made a wallflower look like a live wire. She'd once come home from school crying her eyes out that the other girls were picking on her. To Jimmy, it seemed a waste of breath to tell her to knock these kids over. If someone doesn't understand that by the time they reach the playground, when will they?

Violet had never married and seemed content to continue to live with him, taking care of his household and domestic needs. Truth was, there was not much going on in the ol' brain cell department with Violet. Lights on, door open, but deffo no one at home. Jimmy would not have anyone calling her a thicko though. That would earn the offender a swift kicking to the family jewels, big time. Violet was Violet. Just like her name, a wallflower that lived on the sidelines staying well out of the limelight.

A stuttering Harry cleared his throat and avoided his Father's eyes. He spoke what sounded like a pre-prepared statement. 'On behalf of all of us, Dad, can I just say we're all very sorry about what happened at Robbie's send off. Totally out of order. Won't happen again.'

Kristal was avoiding Jimmy's unnerving narrowed gaze too. Her face looked like a slapped arse. 'Can I just second that? It was…'

Jimmy jumped in, glaring hotly, fed up with their sucking up excuses. 'Shut up! Do you hear me? Shut up! I don't want to hear no more about it except to say that if I get shown up like that again, I'll be taking names. Understood?'

Everyone shut up.

'Listen up and listen good because I've got a couple of important announcements to make so I want everyone to lend me their ear-holes…'

Cursing a blue streak under his breath Jimmy stopped when he clocked that his grandson was more interested in cruising his mobile than listening to him. Furthermore, hadn't he told that bloody Mother of his not to bring the boy along? Thoroughly pissed, Jimmy reached over, wrenched the phone out of Damien's hand and chucked it onto the floor. The kid was lucky he didn't crush it beneath his heel. Damien angled his neck in that odd way, levelling Jimmy with a blank look with his creepy, beady eyes that reminded Jimmy of the guys he hired to beat seven bells out of people. You could poke the kid with a flashing dildo and he'd still be wearing that moronic expression.

'You need to learn some manners, young man. When you're around this table, you only have eyes and ears for family business. Family always comes first.'

That was Damien's cue to apologise. He didn't. Nor did he show any fear. The kid might be a weirdo, but he had some bottle. Jimmy studied the kid. There wasn't a mark on him from the bust up with his uncle at the funeral which spoke well for his talent for rucking. Perhaps he had something about him after all. The trouble was when Damien kicked off, he didn't have any restraint. In this business you always had to have control.

'Right. Here's the deal,' Jimmy cracked on. 'We're taking Barker down, root and branch. I want him and his people wiped out. Burnt down. Destroyed.'

Excitement and tension fizzed in the air. Jimmy's eyes flamed with burning hatred for his enemy.

Jimmy added a proviso. 'I want to make one thing very clear. I don't want any harm to come to Barker. I'll be taking care of him myself. That's a personal thing for me.'

Harry eagerly offered, the force of his words pushing him forward. 'Just say the word, Dad and I'll tear him apart…'

Not to be out done Kristal put in her two pence worth. 'Two heads are better than one. Mine and Damien's. We'll—'

'Harry and Kristal, I want you both to get the job done together.' Jimmy butted in.

'What?' The warring members of his family responded together, astonished and stunned.

'You heard.' Jimmy wasn't in the habit of repeating

himself. He'd made his decision and they needed to abide by it. 'You take down Barker together. I want you both to carry out a raid on his club and put it and most of his crew out of action.'

Barker's base, Club Class, was a legendary nightspot Up West, located between Leicester Square and Soho. Most nights it had a queue around the block.

Harry played the dutiful son. 'Whatever you say, Dad.' He glanced at Kristal, arching a brow. 'We can work together on this. Isn't that right, sister dearest?'

Kristal bit her tongue. When she'd tied the knot with Robbie, Kristal had gone out of her way to be all cheerful-chummy with her new brother-in-law. Always had his fav cake, lemon drizzle, ready to slide on those fancy side plates of hers when he came a-calling. Always overdid the laughter like her sides were really splitting when he dropped one of his naff jokes. Always. Always. Always. She'd rolled out the red carpet for him, welcomed him with open arms into her home. And what did he do? Treat her with maximum contempt. Like a nobody. Not even worth the oxygen needed to say hello.

Now she hid her smug smile. Harry would soon find out who was calling the shots in this family and when he did she'd make sure he came crawling on his knees to her over broken glass.

Kristal put a good dose of saccharine sweetener into her ready response. 'O' course. Nothing would please me more than me and Harry – together – teaching Robbie's killer a lesson he'll never forget.' She snarled. 'We'll deliver him to you trussed up in a suitcase, Dad.'

Satisfied that they both understood who was boss, Jimmy sensed it was time to drop his other bombshell.

'I'm getting ready to plan my retirement.'

Kristal gasped. Harry's jaw hit the floor. Damien's gaze remained steady on his Grandfather. Jimmy rose from the table and went over to the bulletproof window. He lifted the dingy nicotine-stained net curtains and peered out onto the street outside. Out onto his beloved East End. The Commercial Road was one of the most iconic roadways in this part of the capital. He knew the streets here like the back of his hand. This was his home. And now he was preparing to give it all up.

He sucked in a light thread of air before he turned back to his gobsmacked family. 'It was always my intention to retire when I reached the big six oh. It's no secret the plan was to hand the reins over to Robbie when I stood down.' The heartbreak of losing his precious son was a stone in his throat making it impossible for him to speak.

Jimmy coughed the sorrow away. 'But he's gone. Time to make other arrangements. We all know that I'm not talking about a couple of savings accounts or a few rings and cufflinks. No doubt you're all wondering what arrangements I'll be making about the management of the firm when I hang up my swag bag?'

Kristal clucked her tongue and said, 'Well, I for one am very sad to hear that, Dad.' The only problem was she looked as sad as a lotto winner scooping the jackpot. She hadn't seen this coming and could barely contain her glee.

This meant she was going to have to move fast if she was to secure Damien's position.

Panicking, witnessing his brother's widow clawing her way into his Dad's good graces, Harry staggered to his feet. Held up his glass of vodka, awkwardly saluting his Father. 'I just want to say, on behalf of all of us, that we all want to thank you for all you've done for this family over the years. Building up the business and what-not. I won't let you down! None of us will.'

This was Kristal's cue to rise to her full height and lean over the table into Harry's face. 'You what? Who says you're taking over anything? Plus, dick brain, can't you see that Dad's still grieving over Robbie? You've got the front to try to jump in my Robbie's grave when his body isn't even cold yet? The last person Dad's going to want in the hot seat is a soft-centred snowflake like you with a hole in his trousers where his balls should be.'

Harry sneered from deep within his throat. 'I didn't notice you arrive on your broomstick, babe. Let's face it, you're not even family really, are you? That's Dad, me and my sister Violet. And Damien, here.' He grudgingly added his nephew. 'And let's not even get into that mucky gossip about you scribbled on toilet walls around the area. I'm just glad my Mum's not here to have a butchers at it.'

His sister-in-law cut her eyes at him, giving Harry a thorough clawing over. Her reply was deceptively soft. 'You know, I really would love to be able to see things from your point of view but my head won't go that far up my backside.'

Damien was on his feet, fists clenched, waiting for

permission from his Mum to let fly at his uncle. Truth was Damien Steele was always keyed for a punch up. The boy didn't have a business-like attitude to violence. Damien enjoyed it.

Jimmy got in there before things got out of hand.

'Turn it in. The lot of ya.'

With the big prize at stake, they turned it in, resuming their seats. Kristal and Harry waited with bated breath for Jimmy to announce who he had anointed to run his criminal empire. But they should've been savvy enough to sus that the secret of Jimmy's success in gangland was he always liked to spring a surprise and turn the obvious on its head.

He took his position at the head of the table again, this time remaining on his feet.

'I haven't chosen my successor yet. I won't be for a month. I'm keeping my eyes on all of you. At the end of that time whoever impresses me the most will be the person I choose to fill Robbie's shoes.'

Chapter Nine

The gormless granny from next door was banging at her front door. Again. Kristal ignored her. She was too busy dumping all her dead husband's clothes in black bin liners ready for carting off to the charity shop. The only reason she wasn't turning into Kristal Scissorhands and slashing Robbie's shit into ribbons was out of respect for her darlin' boy, Damien. Her son had adored his ol' man. Cutting up Robbie's clothes would be like carving out her son's heart.

Nevertheless, Kristal relished every last moment of delight she got binning his clobber. It wasn't like he was going to need any of it where he was now – in the roasting fire pit of hell. Robbie had been a total fusspot about what he clothed himself in. He'd loved up his designer duds to the core. Armani, Gucci, in fact anything with an Italian label found a space hanging in his wardrobe. Her lips spread, smug and satisfied, imagining what he'd do if he could see her now. Scrunching up his clothes like they were rags.

The double doors of the mirrored wardrobe in the bedroom she'd shared with her husband were flung wide. Kristal had chosen every piece of furniture in the room.

Chunky, mock-marble bed with a huge mirror-headboard and leopard-print sheets. A massive bubble gum pink dressing table with light bulbs framed around its mirror. Green velvet chaise longue positioned to perfection so Kristal could relax back watching the flat-screen TV mounted on the wall.

His clothing was one of the reasons she'd noticed Robbie all those years ago. '81 it was. The day after Prince Charles and Princess Di had tied the knot. Kristal had been outside the pie and mash in Chrisp Street market, lounging about with some mates. Out of nowhere he roared up in this spanking, in-your-face, sports car. Out he vaults like a Swinging Sixties movie star, feathered mullet blowing in the breeze. Her mates were 'get a load of that' coo-cooing over his looks. Not her. What caught and held her attention were his clothes. Bomber jacket and stonewashed classic 501s. Not a speck of dirt on them, as pristine as they'd been on the clothes peg in the shop. Not that she'd taken him for an off-the peg type of geezer. His gear would be made to measure. Every piece of material tailored to perfection around those tight buns of his. Seeing the storm he was creating, he'd swaggered over – flash bollocks – and introduced himself as easy as you please.

Her girlfriends had been fazed and dazed by who he was – everyone knew who the mighty Steele's were. Kristal had played it seductively cool with a flash of come-hither eyes from under her heavily lacquered lashes, a tilt of her rounded hips and flick of her big *Dynasty*-style puffed out hair. Robbie had fallen for her like a ton of bricks. Kristal was flashing his engagement ring three months later and his wedding band seven months on from that.

Their first home had been a three-bed terrace with a cellar off Roman Road and Kristal had applied herself to the task of being a model housewife. Husband and home always came first. Kid added when Damien came along. But she should've known that happiness would never last. It never did in her life. What a thicko to think that playing house would get rid of the poison of her childhood. It turned out Robbie was incapable of keeping it in his trousers.

It all kicked off with the jeans shirt she now held clutched between her fingers. 1983. Six months bellyful with Damien she was, and Robbie comes weaving home on a skinful. Kristal didn't have a problem with that – a fella has to let off steam with his mates. What got her blue in the face with murder was this very shirt he'd worn that night stinking to high fecking heaven of some slapper's cheap, nasty perfume. She knew how it was in some marriages. A story as old as time, a married man getting his third leg over. But in the fairy tale world Kristal and Robbie had created ... She couldn't get her head around him doing the dirty on her. Then she'd clocked the skanky love bite on his neck. Some slag-vampire had been having her evil fangs away at Kristal's hubby.

Nah! She wasn't putting up with that. She'd show Robbie what for. Kristal had made a beeline for the kitchen to fetch the cast iron frying pan to whack him senseless about the loaf. Two-time her, would he? She'd teach that bastard ... Then she'd frozen with the handle tight in her fist. If she divorced Robbie, she'd become a figure of gossip. Even worse, a figure of pity. Forever known as the woman who couldn't hold onto her man. Then where would she go? She couldn't go back to her home. Her real home, not the one she'd made up and told everyone she'd grown up in.

If the truth about her got out … Kristal had hugged her baby bump instead and whispered to her unborn child, 'Gonna give you all the love your ol' fella obviously don't want to have.'

And that's how her marriage had played out. Her looking the other way while Robbie ploughed the field. True to her word, Kristal transferred all her love to her son. Spoiled her kid rotten. Smothered him to death with it. No one dared speak this to Kristal's face. Say a badness against her lad she'd clobber you to death on the spot. She'd use anyone and anything in defence of Damien.

She rammed the offending shirt into the black bag as the thump-thump against her front door grew louder.

'Mum,' Damien yelled from his room on the floor above, 'you gonna get that or what?'

Kristal smacked her lips together, irritated. By rights, Damien really should make the trek downstairs to answer the door by way of getting some exercise. He really needed to shift the flab and grow some muscles. When he took over his Dad's place in grandad Southpaw's criminal empire, he needed to look the part.

Note: *if* not *when*. Her boy was going to ascend to the throne one day and the sooner that tosser Harry got that through his bird brain the better.

Kristal let her son be. She was too soft-hearted when it came to that boy. Her backless, high-heeled pink slippers with the fluffy faux feathers clacked against the stairs. She was very proud of their leafy mock-Tudor house in Hertfordshire. When they'd moved here six years ago, she couldn't leave the East End behind quickly enough. Who wanted to live in a place full of poor people? More importantly, a grand lady such as herself needed to ladyship it over a fuck off home in the suburbs. Six beds, twin garage, pool in the back and one of the three reception rooms converted into a snooker room. Now, that's what you called class. Folks in the East End wouldn't know class if it jumped up and tickled their fancy.

'Hold your flamin' bloomers,' she called out in the spacious hallway.

When she got the door open Kristal artfully lifted an eyebrow at her neighbour. Belinda Merriwether. Plummy-gobbed, twin set and pearls madam who'd never taken to Kristal's kind living on the street. Having said all of that, Kristal laid on her best bib-n-tuck voice. No way was she allowing this starched skirt to carry tales of her being a fishwife to the other neighbours.

'Bell-lin-daa.' Kristal pronounced slowly in her best imitation posh accent. 'What may I help you with today?'

The other woman waved something long and bushy. Kristal jumped back with a yelp. 'This is what's left of my cat, Tabitha. Someone ch…' The word stuck in the old dear's throat as tears sprang to her eyes. 'Chopped her tail off.'

Kristal's palm pressed against her ample chest in slack-jawed horror. 'Who would do such a thing? When they find him, they wanna…' *Best bib 'n' tuck voice, babe!* 'Want to be chopping off his tail, if you get my drift.'

She pulled back the door in a welcoming gesture as she clucked her tongue in sympathy. Her neighbour was a proper busybody, no doubt about it, but Kristal was truly sickened to her stomach at the turn of events. Who would do such a thing to a poor, defenceless animal? They needed to bring back hanging for that type of stuff. No! The electric chair!

'Why don't you come in for a nice brew and tell me all about it.'

The older woman stiffened, ignoring Kristal's invitation, the amputated tail dropping limply by her side. 'This isn't the first time this type of murderous deed has happened on the street. A few months ago, the Wilkinson's dog vanished. A few days later, his front paws were nailed to their door—'

'You're bloody joking…'

Kristal's neighbour ran over her stupefied exclamation. 'The year before that the Hussein's rabbit was never seen again, apart from its floppy ears thrown over their garden wall.'

Suddenly a foreboding gripped Krystal. 'How comes this is the first time I'm hearing about this?'

Belinda tilted her chin with stiff upper-lipped pluck. 'I'll say what none of the others is brave enough to say because your deceased husband's reputation proceeded him.'

Woah! The woman was skating on very very thin ice

putting Robbie's name into the mix. Then again that was typical of her deceased old man. Only in the ground a week and already causing ructions.

Kristal's warning finger didn't let her neighbour go any further. 'My husband – God and all the angels bless and embrace his soul with everlasting love – was a respected businessman. Anyone who says different wants to watch their step come nightfall.'

But the other woman wasn't backing down. 'I've come here to say it on their behalf. My Tabitha and all the other pets have been a victim of your son—'

'You what?'

Nah! Nah! Kristal wasn't having this. The old girl was going too far. Really taking her life into her hands.

'One of the children saw him take Tabitha last evening.' Belinda Merriwether's voice cracked. 'And she's never been seen again. Apart from her tail.'

Kristal reared in her face, all sympathy at her neighbour's plight gone. 'My son ain't touched ya...' She ran a hot, scathing glance over the other woman. Kristal dropped the fancy pants accent in one second flat. 'Ya pussy? Now why would my boy wanna put his hands on your grey-haired pussy? I suspect it's all dried and shrivelled up now.'

While her neighbour gasped and spluttered in outrage, Kristal resumed with a scornful scoff. 'Whoever's been fingering your pussy, it ain't my son.'

And with that she slammed the door with righteous indignation. Kristal leant hard against the door. The sodding cheek! The nerve! Kristal was hyperventilating ... and something else. Something that scared her witless. Could her Damien be capable of doing that … that awful thing? Nabbing animals and butchering them? There was a violent streak in her son she couldn't deny. Sometimes he lost control of himself and took things way too far.

'Damien! Damien!' she shrieked up the stairs, gripping the bannister tight.

No response. Kristal called his name again. Nothing. Her son was lost in his own world sometimes. She marched up to his room with the intention of asking him point blank whether he was a pet serial killer. He'd retreated further into himself when his Dad died. He hadn't cried though, which was strange. What had happened was his violent temper had taken a turn for the worst. Of course, he knew better than to ever turn that temper onto her. But was he using it against the neighbourhood pets?

Kristal found her son engrossed in a very noisy computer game that involved the shedding of a lot of blood to win points.

'Mum?' He looked up at her with surprise as if he hadn't heard her stomping up the stairs.

Kristal came over all dreamy just looking at his face. How could anyone with a sweet face like his do what that batty bitch next door claimed? He was the light of her world. The best son there ever was. He might be lightning fast with his temper and fist, but she knew in her heart of hearts her son would never torture defenceless animals. Never.

Kristal silently took a stand. It was time for her to sort her son out. Get him to stop throwing those fists of his around like some maniac. Get him to understand that violence was all about wielding control. Plus, they were going to have to outwit Harry in coming out top when they took down Barker at his club. It was Damien's right as Robbie's son to be sitting beside his Grandfather as his rightful heir and God help anyone who told Kristal any different.

Kristal's mouth set into a grim, firm line. She knew exactly what to do. It was time for her to take Damien for a visit to a very special lady.

Chapter Ten

Sister Agatha grabbed the man's fist before it connected to the woman's face for a second time. His poor victim, his wife, cringed and cried, her face bruised, an eye swelling fast. What a brute!

Silence fell like another blow in the foodbank, which was located in the back of Poplar High Street. The couple were regulars at the foodbank, the bloke a well-known piss up artist. Today was no different. Sister Agatha wrinkled her nose with distaste. He reeked of the overpowering sourness of beer. The people present didn't voice it, but they were all thinking the same; this fool had chosen the wrong nun to tangle with. Sister Agatha was kind and generous, but step on her habit, a body would find themselves on the lightning bolt end of her wrath. Sister Agatha took no prisoners where right and wrong were concerned.

Aggi, that's what the East End community she served called her. Sister Aggi. She was considered an institution, a beacon of light and goodness when times got rough. No matter the incident or the hour, Sister Aggi was always there to hold a hand, offer a shoulder to lean and cry on, say a prayer in the darkest hour of need.

'You don't want to be doing that, sonny,' she warned in a deceptively soft, saccharine-coated voice. 'In the *Bible* it tells us, "*Man who raises his hand against his wife will be dammed for all eternity to the heathen fires of hell*".'

The Good Book said no such thing! She'd made it up. It wouldn't be the first time and it certainly wouldn't be the last. Doing The Lord's work in the heart of the East End sometimes called for scripture from The Book of Sister Aggi. In her black and white habit, she looked more like an avenging angel of Christ. A wimple hid her hair making the bony angles and ridges of her face standout. Except the reality was, as a nun, no one really took much notice of her face. Her lips were compressed together, the premature ageing lines on her forehead more pronounced. How old she was no one really knew.

The man wrenched his fist away and staggered back, almost tipping over the table with the plastic cups of orange squash lined up in rows.

He levelled a bloodshot, bleary eye on the nun, features stamped with the promise of hideous violence. 'Who do you think you are?' He shook his bear-like fist at her. 'Touch me, will ya? I'll blacken both of your eyes.'

Sister Aggi moved fearlessly closer. If he thought she was scared of him he had no idea who he was dealing with.

Her lips dipped at the sides as she tore a strip off him. 'You and whose army, Roger Ainsley? I remember when you were seven and I chased off that group of numpties who were giving you a right, royal pasting. Look at you now, a bully-boy yourself. Folk come here to fill up their bellies and fill up their hearts and souls. Now, I want you gone from here before I get a broom and sweep you out with the rest of the rubbish.'

He was about to give her another gobful when he noticed some of the guys in the room, younger and packing more muscle, positioning their bodies in a threatening manner. Put a finger on their Sister Aggi and they would drag him around the back and annihilate him. Roger Ainsley might be as tanked as a sailor on the last day of shore leave but he wasn't stupid. He left as quickly as his drunken legs could carry him.

After a collective sigh of relief, everyone went back to their food as the nun turned to the battered woman. It broke Sister Aggi's heart but the last thing this beaten woman needed was pity. What she did need was support and referring to an organisation that helped women in her situation. The nun got into action, cleaned her up, popped a hot meal in front of her and left her in the company of a group of local women. Bless these ladies who were volunteers at the foodbank. Women who had been through their own trials and tribulations who would see this woman right again.

After that, Sister Aggi went for a much-needed breather in the alley round the back. She gave it a couple of seconds before furtively looking about. No one in sight. Lickety-split quick she whipped out a pack of ciggies from the pocket of her habit. When she'd taken her vows, renouncing all worldly pleasures, Sister Aggi hadn't been able to get rid of the taste of nicotine. If Mother Superior caught her at it there would be hell to play.

Hell to pay. That made her chuckle as she lit up. Pulled hard on her fag. Heaven! Her eyes flutter momentarily closed with the pleasure of it. When she opened them again, mid-way through her forbidden vice, she noticed a familiar figure on the High Street. One of the former pupils from the school who had been in Sister Aggi's needlework class. Sister Aggi had got to know those kids inside and out, including spotting when they were up to mischief. And the person her gaze was glued to now had the swagger of misdeeds if she ever saw it.

The nun dropped her ciggy. Ground it out with her black flats and steam walked onto the street until she caught up with the mischief-maker.

She called out, 'And what has got you moving as if the Devil were at your heels, Maureen Watson?'

Mo took the steaming cuppa offered by Sister Aggi. She sat at the sturdy wooden table, which was the centrepiece of the kitchen of St. Philomena Convent on a quiet street off the Commercial Road. Rumour was in a past life the Victorian building had been a brass house catering to the ungodly needs of the men of the parish.

Mo was here under sufferance. The only reason she'd taken up Sister Aggi's invitation for a cup of Rosie was the last thing she wanted to do was disrespect her. The nun had gone out of her way for Mo when she was a young one. There was a special bond between them.

Mo took a sip and then asked, 'So, how's it going, Sister Argy Bargy?'

That was Mo's special name for the older woman because the nun and her elbows were always getting stuck into stuff that needed sorting out, including a fight or two in the playground when she'd volunteered up at the school.

The nun squinted her eyes knowingly at Mo. 'What have you been up to?'

Mo averted her gaze from Sister Aggi's X-ray vision that seemed to drill right into her, unlocking all her secrets. 'Oh, the usual. You know, looking for a job. A proper Dick Whittington I am … Walking the streets of London with my knapsack over my shoulder.'

The nun laced her slim, work-hardened fingers together. 'Why don't you come down and help out here, at the foodbank until you snag that job? We're always looking for a pair of extra hands.'

Mo pursed her lips. Help the downtrodden? Nah! That wasn't a good look. All very worthy and all that, but why would she want to be around people who reminded her of her crap life at home with her whinging Mum? Best to leave that to the do-gooders. The ones who wanted the weight of a halo over their heads.

'I've got plans,' she finally revealed.

Sister Aggi gave her a straight-talking stare. Mo prided herself on not being scared of a soul, but those all too knowing eyes of this wise woman were enough to get her running for the hills.

The nun asked, 'And why do I get the impression these

plans will be taking you to the wrong side of the street?'

Mo worried her lip. She couldn't decide whether to tell her old needlework teacher the truth. Blimey, how could she deal with the inevitable disappointment she would see written across Sister Argy Bargy's face? The last thing she wanted was to let this God-fearing and giving woman down.

Still, Mo wasn't one to dodge the truth. And anyway, what did she have to feel ashamed of? Choosing a life of ducking and diving was as traditional in these parts as your ol' Mum's apple pie with Bird's custard.

Mo puffed out her chest. 'I'm considering working for this geezer called Barker—'

'Barker?' The nun turned ashen faced. Then she leant in close, alarm bringing colour storming back to her cheeks. 'Are you off your rocker? That man is involved in Satan's work. There isn't a bad thing that man doesn't have his filthy fingers in. Last year a couple, only married a couple of months, turned up at the foodbank, her with a belly out here.'

Sister Aggi's hand came out to indicate someone who must have surely been carrying triplets. 'That evil man turfed them out of one his properties because they couldn't pay the rent anymore. A rent, I might add, he'd hiked up by a hundred pounds a week overnight. Is that the type of man you want to be working for?'

Put like that, it did sound bloody bad. Sure, Mo had figured out working with Barker would involve a wagonload of naughties ... But the sort of naughties that kicked a pregnant lady swiftly in her dreams? Sick climbed nastily up

Mo's throat. She didn't want to be party to that kind of carry on, did she?

Mind you, what she couldn't afford to forget was Barker said he would protect from Jimmy Southpaw's fury if the most feared gangster around began to hunt her down. Looking back Mo could've kicked herself in the proverbials for pulling that stunt. She so wished she'd never done it.

The scrapping of Sister's Aggi's chair brought her back to the present. The other woman walked to stand by the bay window with the pretty criss-cross lattice pattern on it. The daylight hit her features in a way that Mo could see every year imprinted on her skin, the burden of year upon year of slogging and helping others to put their lives right.

'I've seen things in my life.' Sister Aggi swallowed deeply clearly finding it hard to get the words out. 'Things that will live with me for all my days on God's green earth. Things that lodge in my stomach like a hot stone.' Her face turned completely towards the window as her shoulders hunched. 'Do you know what I do sometimes? I try to rub my tummy to make the hot stone feeling go away. But it doesn't matter how hard I rub, that terrible sensation won't leave me alone.'

Mo was transfixed by the raw emotion in her voice. She was ashamed to say that she'd never considered that the nun felt things like ordinary folk did. She thought the Sisters were programmed like religious robots without emotions to crack on with God's work.

'Sister—' Mo began, desperate to say something that would make this woman who was so special to her feel better again.

Mo never finished, holding back the gasp in her throat when she saw the other woman's face. It was awful. As if someone had gutted her with a serrated knife.

'I don't want you to end up like me, with painful things growing in your body.' Her face brightened slightly. 'You were the best seamstress in my class. I've never met anyone who knows their way around a needle and thread like you do.'

She was right. Mo was gifted when it came to making clothes. None of the other kids had been able to touch Mo. Behind her back some the other girls had nicknamed her, Stitch Up, as a laugh, but she knew they'd been as bitchy jealous as heck.

With a purposeful stride, the nun left the window and when she reached Mo she hunkered down. Gently took Mo's small face into the palm of her work bruised hands.

'Promise me you won't see Barker again. Promise me you'll go to the Community College in Whitechapel and check out the courses they have.'

Mo didn't answer as her mind spun. Maybe Sister Aggi had a point. She could always go up the college to see if they had clothes designer courses. Or she could go down Commercial Road, the Petticoat Lane end, where the rag trade had once thrived and ask around to see if she could be taken on as an apprentice. Maybe … Maybe Jimmy Southpaw didn't give two monkeys about her and his flash car.

Mo nodded once. 'I promise.'

Mo's promise went out the window as soon as she stepped through her front door. Her Mum went spare as soon as she saw her, yakking and barking about Mo being a layabout, bringing shame and despair to their front door. On and on and effing on. The trouble with her Mum's mouth was it didn't have any brakes. Needled beyond endurance, Mo stormed upstairs to her room. Slammed the door. Whoever had dreamed up, 'Home is where the heart is,' had never lived with Precious Watson.

Truth was Mo was tired of feeling powerless. She wanted to be somebody.

Mo pulled out her mobile. 'Mister Barker, when would you like me to start?'

Chapter Eleven

'Whatcha want?' Twinkle's Mum, Sheena Brodie, nastily cracked, speaking around the ciggy drooping limply from her dry, cracked lips. Her talon-red nails gripped the front door.

Her saggy-skinned face rippled with disdain at the person parked up on her doorstep. Mo Watson. Her girl's so-called best friend. There was no love lost between Mo and Twinkle's Mum and neither of them was afraid to show it.

Twinkle lived with her Mum on an estate where it was whispered the council housed the families with a history of disorder, rank badness and gigantic rent arrears. It was on the part of The Island where the wind seemed to blow at its harshest and bleakest.

Mo almost, almost, gave it back to her bestie's Mum in spades. Instead she asked, 'Is Twinkle in?'

That royally ruffled Sheena's feathers, her back stiffening with outraged disapproval. 'I'll remind you, young lady, that when the Priest poured water over my daughter's head it was to the name of Priscilla not frigging Twinkle, Wrinkle or Dinkle. Got it?'

Mo had to hold herself back. The only reason she didn't give this excuse for a human being a proper mouthful was out of respect to her friend. Sheena Brodie was as notorious as the estate she'd lived on her whole troubled life. Blokes in and out of her gaff like a revolving door up Piccadilly Circus. Lying flat on her back was her business. *That girl has seen more ceilings than Michelangelo* was one of the kinder things people sneered behind her back.

Who Twinkle's old man was was a matter of local debate. Maybe that was why Mo and Twinkle had bonded so hard back in school. Neither of them knew who their Dad was. But that's where the comparison stopped.

The back-fence story goes that when Sheena found herself in the pudding club she could only scrape together enough for a sleazy back alley abortion. So off she goes, only to discover someone had cut the abortionist's throat the day before so she hightails it back home as fast as her legs can carry her. For anyone else that would've been a sign that her baby was meant to be born. But, oh no, not Sheena Brodie. This time she found a well-known back alley butcher called, Knitting Needles Nelly, who drops dead of a heart attack as soon as Sheena lies down on her filthy kitchen table. Number three chokes on a chicken bone as she's giving Sheena the full SP on her services and cash only price list. Number four refused to open the door because by then word had spread, far and wide with the speed of fleas on a cat that the Brodie girl was death appearing at your door.

Poor Twinkle had been birthed by a Mother who refused point blank to suckle her at her breast and hated her for life.

Mo was getting mighty pissed at standing on this doorstep like a day-old bottle of milk. 'Is she in or ain't she?'

Sheena cut her eyes at Mo, stubby fingers tightening on the door. 'She ain't in, curly top.'

Twinkle's Mum was about as subtle as a flying brick that she also didn't cotton to Mo because she was black. She wasn't one of these in-your-face racist. Her way was a snide dig every now-n-again that was hidden under the guise of 'I'm just having a joke'.

Yeah, fucking Ha! Ha! Flipping ha! Not funny. But Mo didn't give her the time of day. She was well used to the dirt this cretin slung in her face.

'Tell *Twinkle* I was looking for her.'

She didn't hang about for an answer, eager to get away from the stench of Sheena Brodie. Mo turned and was about to walk away when she abruptly froze. Was that a noise coming from inside the flat? A whimper?

Alarm bells ringing, Mo spun on her heels to face the older woman again. 'What was that?'

Sheena stiffened, shifty-eyed and defensive as she positioned her body to block the entrance. 'Dunno what you're chatting on about.'

Mo didn't even think, she just did. Mo motored forward to get inside the flat.

'Oi! Oi!' Sheena cried, trying her best to hold onto the doorframe and the position of her body. 'You can't barge … Ouch!!!'

That shriek of agony was courteously of Mo stomping on her toes. The woman lost her footing, crashing into the wall.

Mo elbowed her hard in the ribs for good measure as she rushed by. Nothing was stopping Mo from helping Twinkle if she was in some type of distress. Her heart beat like crazy at the thought of what was going on.

There were all types of tales of what went on inside that Brodie Woman's home when the front door was closed. She provided the sort of services even a brass house wouldn't have on its menu. Mo shuddered at what her poor Twinkle must've seen growing up within these walls. Lately, Mo had a terrible suspicion what was really going on here.

The witch who was Twinkle's Mum screamed, 'Get out of my house. Get out...'

Mo didn't give her the time of day, her only purpose to continue her frantic search for her friend.

'Twinkle!' she shouted.

'Mo.' Twinkle's reply sounded muffled and weak like she was having trouble catching her breath.

Anxious and alarmed, Mo wasted no time in checking the rooms. The place made a pigsty appear like a palace. Dirty carpets, stained settees, a pile of dishes and ashtrays stashed with stale fag ends all over the shop. Mo knew that Twinkle hated pity, but hell, she couldn't help feel it pinching deep in her soul. That her mate, who was always turned out to perfection, had to live in this dump was beyond the pale.

She finally found Twinkle in her tiny bedroom. What Mo saw made the bottom drop out of her world. A man stood beside Twinkle's bed doing his flies up. Her beautiful best friend lay curled on her side, her skirt round her waist and knickers about her ankle. Mo didn't need to ask what had gone on here. A ball of red-hot rage mixed with fury mixed with outraged dynamite shot up inside Mo.

Sensing they weren't alone, the scumbag who had had the audacity to put his stinking hands on the best friend there ever was turned his head.

Seeing Mo, he leered. 'You another one? Tell Sheena one's been enough for me today.' His thumb gestured in Twinkle's direction. 'I've still got the scratches of this one all over me—'

Mo sprang at him with the cry of an avenging banshee, teeth bared, fists ready to do significant damage. Caught off guard by her attack, as soon as Mo's body slammed into him, he went down like a ton of bricks. She used this to her advantage to dish out a series of hard knuckled blows to his face. She caught him good under the eye, the side of the mouth and his nose. Mo knew how to deliver a memorable bunch of fives. Her grandad, Brother Bertie, had taught her well. And the fucker couldn't hit her back because her knees dug into his arms holding them immovable against the carpeted floor.

She snarled into his face, 'Attack innocent girls, will ya?' Smack! Belted him a right across the face.

'You ever lay a finger on her again and I'm gonna rip your dick off.'

Smack! Smack!

A distraught Twinkle cried out from the bed, 'Please stop, Mo. Pleeeeeeze.'

Mo didn't want to, but seeing how distressed her friend

was she reluctantly jumped off him, her chest heaving. 'Get out of here.'

Only after she'd issued her warning did she recognise who the toerag was. Eric Brown. Scumbag Number One. Last year a fourteen-year-old girl had accused him of raping her. Of course he'd denied it till he was blue in the face. It was his word against hers and because his older brother was a well-known thug round these parts no one would speak against him. But the whispers said it was him alright, creeping up to her and dragging her off into an abandoned warehouse near the riverfront. And apparently it wasn't the first time he'd done it.

Eric Brown was fuming and bloodied when he got to his feet. He stomped over to Mo and got in her face. Let him hate on her, she wasn't scared.

Words tight and threatening, he promised her, 'You better watch your back—'

'Or what?' She chucked in his face. 'You gonna drag me into an abandoned building like you did Flora Williams?'

He scoffed licking his wounds and left. Mo followed pretty quickly after, witnessing Twinkle's Mum making a big production of trying to apologise to him as she hung onto his sleeve. He wrenched free, looked back at Mo with evil retribution blazing in his eyes and without a word slammed the door behind him.

Sheena targeted her flashing, hate filled glance towards Mo. 'You interfering—'

Mo barrelled into the passage taking Twinkle's Mum by total surprise. She must've read the intent in Mo's eyes because Sheena nearly trip over her feet trying to run for it. No chance! Mo caught her by the hair and dragged her into the disgusting kitchen. Frogmarched her to the sink piled high with unwashed dishes. Thrust Sheena's head under the tap. Turned the freezing water on. The other woman gasped and choked as the water ran in her face and inside her mouth.

'Let … Me … Go,' she wheezed.

Mo only increased the pressure of her hands on her head. 'I swear on my life you better listen to me or I'm going to finish you off.' Mo was so riled up she didn't even recognise her own voice. 'Listen to my words and listen good. You ever let another monster touch Twinkle and I'm going to come here at night, while you're snoring and drooling in your bed and do things to you you couldn't even imagine. Got it?'

Mo didn't even wait for an answer, simply let go of the disgusting woman's head and stormed out. She found Twinkle in the tiny bathroom trying to cleanse the filth from her body. Mo's heart nearly broke in two. She should've realised what was going on here.

Why didn't you tell me?

I could've helped you?

All these and other questions she wanted to ask Twinkle, but she didn't. What her friend desperately needed was the support of her bestie. And that's what Mo did, helped her wash up with no questions asked. Dried her skin and hair. Moisturised her gorgeous freckles and face with the pads of her fingers.

Only later inside Twinkle's room, as Mo held her best

mate in her arms as they lay on the bed did Twinkle's chocking voice weakly say, 'Do you remember last year when I went with Gary Cook? And you couldn't understand why?'

Gross Cook was what they called him behind his back. Tubby and tall, a mountain of a lad who had far too much gristle on him. Mo didn't get what Twinkle had seen in him. Surely, her bestie could do better than that?

Mo remained closed mouth to allow Twinkle the space to explain. 'Since I turned fourteen, Mum's being saying I was old enough … you know.' Mo knew and she'd thump Twinkle's Mum a solid one right in her mouth if she were there. 'I managed to dodge it for a couple of years, but knew she was going to set me up with one of the filth that comes through the door.'

Twinkle pulled in a shaky breath, tucking her head deeper into the comfort Mo provided. 'So, when Gary starts asking me out, I gets to thinking if I do it the first time with him at least I chose it. It weren't forced on me. And, know what Mo, it was really sweet. He made me feel like a princess.' Suddenly her voice changed. 'It's only been a few times, Mo.'

The fury stoked scorching and dangerous within Mo again. 'It should have been *no* times.'

Twinkle's palm rubbed Mo's arm in a soothing motion as if it was Mo who'd been wronged. 'You've scared the stuffing outta her. She won't do it again.'

How could Twinkle be so calm about it? It made Mo want to howl and tear the world apart. Mo might have her problems with her Mum, but Precious Watson would never,

ever do what Sheena Brodie had done to her own flesh and blood. Not in a trillion years. Precious Watson loved her daughter with every fibre of her being.

'She wants putting down.' Mo shook as the words flew out. 'Call herself a parent—'

'I've heard the stories about how she didn't want me. Tried her best to flush me down the toilet,' Twinkle softly interjected. Mo winced as her mate continued with a voice that was surprisingly strong. 'I ain't a Dumbo and I've got a pair of ears, so I've heard all the talk about what she tried to do when she found herself in the family way.' She pulled in a shaky punch of air. 'But it don't matter. I love her. She's my Mum. I pity her because I think something bad happened to her when she was a kid to make her this way. If I go, she'd have no one.'

Weren't life a bitch banging on about honouring your Mother and Father? Well, two fingers to that was how Mo saw it. Respect wasn't floating around for free. You had to earn it. And that included Mum's and Dad's. It was at times like this Mo couldn't help wondering if the Father she'd never known had loved her. Had he ever taken her in his arms? Held her lovingly to his chest? Whispered nonsense baby lingo as he stroked her cheek?

Mo shook off the gut-wrenching scenes as she enfolded Twinkle in her arms and squeezed her real tight.

'East End Girls Forever,' she whispered.

'East End Girls Forever,' her bestie trembled back.

Chapter Twelve

The TV presenter of the talk show on the flickering screen of the portable telly inside the sitting-room in the prefab could barely contain his excitement as he dramatically pronounced: '*Next up: Is your husband having an affair with your Mum? We ask the questions you want answered.*'

Eileen Dripsey settled her solid bulk into the armchair and popped her swollen ankles up on the zebra-print pouffe. Then she proceeded to stuff her face full of cheese and onion crisps from the bowl in her lap as she watched the show with heart pounding anticipation. Eileen didn't get why some folk slagged off daytime telly. She couldn't get enough of the stuff. No better morning spent than with her fav reality TV host, Floyd Plunker and a studio filled to the rafters with talon-ready wives and Mums, itching to scratch each other's eyes out in a no holds barred cat fight.

Is your hubby knocking off your Mum? This episode should be a right old ding-dong,

Suddenly, the tune 'I'm Too Sexy' began playing in the passage. Eileen groaned. That was her doorbell. What Herbert was calling at this time of the morning? Then she noticed her mobile had an alert that she had a client booked. Oh heck, she was really getting forgetful these days. Her stubby fingers grabbed her mobile and checked out the client's name.

Kristal and son.

Her clients didn't like giving their surnames, which was all okey-dokey with Eileen as long as they left their cash. Eileen's brows pleated together as she thought long and hard. Wasn't Kristal the woman who'd asked her to put a curse on her husband a couple of years back? Or a hex on her Father-in-law? Kristal was the big brassy bottle-blonde with a lot of front in every sense of the word. And a fearsome temper to match.

Eileen struggled out of her armchair and switched the telly off in a huff. In other circumstances she'd have pretended to be out, but truth was she needed the money. She also had the distinct impression if she didn't answer Kristal would boot the door in.

'Who is it?' She called in an airy voice as if she was leading a séance. Eileen knew perfectly well who it was, but her clients paid for a mystery, so she gave it to them from the off.

'Kristal and her boy,' came back the impatient reply. 'We've got an appointment.'

'One moment, my dear.'

Eileen heard Kristal warning her son. 'Right, this is serious, OK? Don't take the piss or I'll box your ears into the next bank holiday.'

Eileen picked up speed back into her front room. Drew

the curtains across so everything was dark. Lit a few scented candles she'd got for a song down Whitechapel Market. Last, and most important, she changed into her work clothes. A long purple kaftan-style gown that was patterned with golden suns, moons and stars. She plonked on a matching hat. Eileen had bought the set from a closing down sale at a magicians' shop in Manor Park.

Taking deep breaths through her nose to get herself in the mood she made her way to the front door. As soon as the door was opened, she clasped her hands together as if in prayer. 'My children.'

Kristal said, 'Madame Amon-Ra, I can't thank you enough for seeing us on such short notice. It's about my son, Damien here. He's got a problem.'

Eileen caught an eyeful of surly Damien. He looked like he had more than one problem and by the looks of things the lad wanted to bolt for it.

She sweetly intoned, 'My house is your house, my children. May I ask you to remove your shoes?'

While her clients followed her instructions, Eileen re-entered her sitting-room and stood on top of a box in front of a makeshift altar to add extra height to her small frame. Inwardly Eileen sighed with blessed relief that she hadn't knocked back a couple with her porridge as she usually did in the morning or she'd have had trouble keeping her balance on the box. Tumbling off and falling flat on her face was not a good look in front of a client. The altar was covered in colourful cloths she'd gotten from a sari shop down Brick Lane. A thick black candle flickered in the darkness.

As Mother and son entered, Eileen distinctly heard Damien mock with an air of laughter, 'Blimey! Has there been a power cut?'

By way of an answer, his Mother grabbed him by the arm and shook him like she had him clamped between her teeth. When the boy looked like he was about to up sticks, his Mum gave him such a killer stare the colour drained from his face. Mother shoved son to his knees before the altar and swiftly followed him.

Madame Amon-Ra waved her open palms meaningfully before Kristal. No response. She waved her hands again and got the same response. Chrissakes! She fluttered her hand practically in the other woman's face, so she took the hint.

Kristal Mumbled, 'Oops,' and took out a bulging brown envelope. Knowing the darkness shielded her expression Eileen drooled with greed as she practically snatched it. She stashed it deep in the kaftan's pocket.

Eileen rambled, 'How may I help you today?'

A distraught Kristal explained. 'My boy here, the thing is, I think he's possessed.'

Eileen looked at Damien whose face was shrouded in shadows. It hardly mattered if she could see his face or not; she couldn't spot evil from *Snow White*. What she did was put on the show the clients paid her handsomely for.

'Possessed?' Eileen hid her groan. Possessions were the worst. She had to put on a belter of a show to earn her fee. Afterwards, she always felt completely cream crackered.

'Yes!' Kristal practically shouted. Her voice quivered. 'An unclean spirit or something. There's deffo something not right in there. I mean, I don't want him turned soft or nothing. He's got to be able to look out for himself. The problem is, every now and again he loses it. If you could drive out whatever it is that makes him go nuts, I'd be very grateful. Just pour something on his head and chant a few words. You know the drill.'

Eileen waved her hands and slightly rocked her body. She mumbled unintelligibly as she swayed. Abruptly her body went rigid as she dramatically gulped. 'I sense an unhappy spirit has taken residence in your son's heart. But I have many methods at my disposal that date back to Ancient Egypt and Babylon that will soon make this unwelcome guest depart from its unhappy home. Please stand back and be still Kristal.'

Kristal struggled to her feet and shuffled back. Eileen laid her hands on Damien's head. She stood as stiff as a statue for a few moments before raising her hands again. 'I'm sorry, Kristal, but there's nothing I can do for your son. He's resisting. You see, he doesn't believe in me and without belief, there's nothing I can do.'

Kristal took a few steps forward and hissed through her lips, 'He doesn't believe? Can you excuse us for a few moments?'

She dragged Damien to his feet and frogmarched him into the passage. Their row was whispered but was still more than loud and biting enough for Eileen to hear the Mum giving the son a choice selection of verbal.

'I'm warning you, Sonny Jim, I've forked out two hundred smackers for this. My bird in there can't do anything for you because you don't believe?' She poked him angrily in the chest. 'You'll believe soon enough if I belt you a fistful of smackers across your moosh.'

Damien wasn't giving in. 'Of course I don't believe. She's a fucking con-woman. You're so fucking gullible. That get-up she's got on? Looks like she's going to saw a woman in half and pull a rabbit out that stupid hat on her head. I've seen better magicians down the boozer.'

Eileen heard a clump and a yelp before Kristal dragged her son, who now sported a large bruise on his cheek, back to his knees at the altar. Eileen stole a brief glimpse at her watch. If she got this over with in a jiffy, she might still be in time to catch the end of: *Is your husband having an affair with your Mum?*

Hands back on Damien's head, she chimed, 'Ah! That's better. Your son believes now.'

Damien winced as Eileen liberally sprinkled rose water on his shoulders and face. She made some strange noises as her shoulders jerked. Then chanted, over and over:

'Baray-e-meharbani kiya aap isay dhra saktay hean'

'Baray-e-meharbani kiya aap isay dhra saktay hean'

The words meant, 'I'm sorry, can you repeat that please?' which she'd learnt from an 'Urdu for holidaymakers' tape she'd picked up in a travel shop for a trip to Thailand. She'd only discovered later that they didn't speak Urdu in Thailand.

Eileen's voice speeded up, becoming agitated as she whipped herself up into a right royal lather. She began to gasp and shudder as if she were having sex with her husband's Mum. Finally, with a shriek, her hands flew off

Damien's head. Her body tilted backwards; arms wide open as if she was about to take flight. Her bulging eyes were fixed on the ceiling as if something had departed heavenward.

A gobsmacked Kristal searched the ceiling too for some evidence of what had happened. Even an alarmed Damien was looking.

An exhausted Eileen lowered her arms and head and climbed down off her box gasping. 'Your son is at peace now Kristal.'

A concerned Kristal hurried over and took the healer by the arm. 'You alright there, love? You look like you've had a funny turn.'

Eileen pretended to catch her breath. 'My work is done. Children, I must rest. Please depart.'

'Of course, of course,' Kristal agreed. 'But are you sure you're good to go?'

Eileen slumped into her armchair. Why didn't this woman and her dopey kid piss off so she could turn the TV back on?

Kristal turned to her son. 'Are you at peace then?'

Damien was shaken. 'I feel a bit weird as it happens.'

His Mum kissed Eileen's hand. She walked backwards so she was facing Madame Amon-Ra as she headed for the door. 'Thank you so much! Thank you so much!' Even Damien bowed to the healer as he went. It seemed he really did believe now.

When they were mercifully gone, Eileen dragged herself out of the chair, blew out the candles and popped the telly back on.

Her eyes lit up with glee. Two women were slogging it out in the studio while beefy security staff tried to separate them. Floyd Plunker, the presenter, looked on with 'sure to raise ratings' satisfaction. Eileen reached under the chair for her bowl of crisps and started stuffing her face again.

There was nothing she enjoyed more than a good performance.

Chapter Thirteen

'Where's gramps?' Mo couldn't hold back the excitement she felt as she stepped inside the sitting-room with her new jacket.

After the horrible event at Twinkle's, Mo had cajoled and coaxed her bestie to accompany her on a trip down Fontill Road in Finsbury Park so Mo could buy some new clobber for her first day working for Barker. Usually they clothes shopped down The Roman but if you wanted to be kitted out a touch more upmarket Fontill Road was the place to be. Mo had ended up buying a powder blue lightweight jacket, its brass buttons giving it that touch of bling.

Mo couldn't wait to show it off to her gramps. He'd be truly made up for her, although probably not when he discovered what her job was. Not that he knew anything about the goings on in London's underworld.

Precious was watching *The Weakest Link* with a half-gone bottle of fruity Vodka Taboo.

'Huggy Bear!' Her Mum hurled at the telly literally on the edge of her seat as she watched the quiz show.

Confused Mo shook her head. 'You what?'

Her Mum absently turned to her. 'The answer to the question. Huggy Bear from *Starsky and Hutch*.'

'Starsky and who?'

Precious rolled her eyes in consternation, shaking her head. 'You young people have got no sense of culture.'

Culture? Where did her Mum think she was? Up Whitechapel Art Gallery?

Precious caught sight of Mo's bag. Her lips drooped with accusation. 'You been on the rob again?'

Oh! Here we go-go! Mo clamped her jaw so tightly her teeth hurt. She huffed and puffed. 'Why are you always having a go? Always want to see the worst in me?'

Her Mum's features were strained and for the first time Mo saw that her eyes were bloodshot. Her Mum had been crying. Again. Some nights she heard her Mum weeping pitifully into her pillow. Why was her Mum so sad these days? Crying her guts out like her life was over? Something was going on with her.

Feeling a tug in her heart Mo offered, 'Want me to make you a brew?'

Precious' grateful smile brought life back to her face. Mo's heartstrings caught as she witnessed the beauty her Mum had been known for. 'That would be lovely, sugar. I'll have the dinner on soon when your grandad gets back.'

'He's out?' Mo was surprised. Gramps loved a stroll with his flash walking stick but most evenings he could be found in the living room waiting for the evening news to pop on. 'Where's he gone?'

'The allotment. He's putting one of his pumpkins into

the council's allotment competition. Think he's digging it up today.'

In horror, the bag slipped from Mo's hand. Bloody hell.

Jimmy Southpaw's gun.

She ran out of the flat as if the cops were chasing after her.

'Are you going to help then? Or are you planning on just sitting there on your bony backside sunning yourself?' Brother Bertie complained as he rested on a spade at his allotment, his spare hand rubbing his aching back.

He was taking a potshot at his closest friend, Nora Baxter. People called her Ruddy, short for 'Ruddy Nora' because when folk saw her coming, instead of swearing they'd groan, 'Ruddy Nora.'

The story goes that during the war a Luftwaffe V2 rocket missed her pram by inches, which many took to explain why she'd grown up knowing how to use her fists. Trouble her and she'd deck you in a second flat. Back in the day, she was known as a gal about town. Her era the Swinging Sixties. Her manor shady Soho. Her hustle primarily card games. That's where she'd met Brother Bertie.

Tittle-tattle claimed they'd once been an item. Then they'd been torn apart by their families' disapproval on account of him being black and her being white. Looking back, it's hard to imagine that there was that type of carry on because nowadays everyone is hooking up with everyone else. Back then it was a massive No-No. Whatever their history was, Brother Bertie and Ruddy weren't telling.

Ruddy sat on a deck chair by his shed, sporting '50s vintage polka dot framed cat-eyed sunglasses with a knotted hankie over her outrageously crimson-red beehive wig. Her skirt was daringly raised above her knobbly knees like she was sweet sixteen. And she had her face on, of course. Ruddy never went anywhere without being plastered to the nines. A dusting of face power, ruby-red lipstick that was drawn over the top of her lips to plump them up and false eyelashes so long they could have a second job raking the leaves near her feet.

'Help?' Ruddy shot back at Brother Bertie. She took no offence at how he'd spoken to her. It was all part of their good-natured banter that characterised their relationship. 'Cobblers to that. I'm a Londoner, love, not a swede basher. We don't plough the fields and scatter. We do all our farming down the mini-mart.'

But perhaps the glow of the sun made her remember. 'Apart from hop picking, of course. Used to head down to Kent when I was a nipper to earn a few coppers on the farms. That was a good laugh, apart from the fresh air, obviously. A right relief, it was, to get back to the East End and get some decent smoke in your lungs. And it was too quiet for my liking. Apart from the odd cow mooing in the distance, you couldn't hear nuthin' at all. I thought I was going a bit mutton as it happens.'

Bertie slammed his spade into the ground. 'So that's a no then?'

But Ruddy was off on one. 'Oh, and scrumping. Nothing like pinching some fruit. Had to bunk a bus ride out of town of course, not much in the way of fruit trees down our way. I think the local vicar might have had one in his garden, but we had everything off that before the blossom fell.' She shook her head at her memories. 'Dunno know why we bothered to be honest. None of us could stand the taste of fruit anyway but me ol' Mum liked an apple or two.'

Brother Bertie gave up. He shoved his spade deep into the earth, left it there and picked up his silver-topped Lion of Judah engraved walking stick. He looked at his precious allotment and felt proud. Row after row of different types of vegetables, including this year's ginormous pumpkin. It was backbreaking work keeping up an allotment, especially at his time of life but the thing was he had the land in his blood. Back in Jamaica when he was a youth, tilling and looking after the land and livestock had been the only life he'd known.

Brother Bertie had had the allotment since the seventies. Not many people were interested in farming a tiny strip of inner-city land back then. Now people were falling over themselves to get one, the Council's waiting list a mile long. He also came from a generation that held onto anything valuable whether you wanted it or not. You never knew when you might need it again.

Ruddy clucked her tongue. 'Dunno why you need to grow vegetables, anyway. You go down the grocers and it's all laid out on the shelves. And they don't come in funny shapes either like yours do. Have you seen some of the things they dig out of the earth on this site? They're obscene. Last autumn, the bloke on the lot next door had a carrot that looked like a gentleman's privates. You couldn't dish that up for your ol' Mum, now could you?'

Even after fifty years in London, Bertie was still married to the land and defended it. 'That's what vegetables are supposed to look like, you silly, old woman. And what they did look like before they started fiddling with their genes, spraying them with poison and injecting them with chemicals called oxy-moron, mono sodium gyrate and satanic acid. No wonder everyone's sick these days.'

Brother Bertie shook his head in sorrow as he made his way to his shed. Inside he opened a banged up wooden cupboard with shelves packed to the brim with bottles of Brother Bertie's special white rum. He grabbed a bottle, a couple of glasses, his portable radio and carried them outside. He dropped into the deck chair beside Ruddy with a blessed sigh. His deckchair was designed with the Jamaican flag and Ruddy's the Union Jack.

Her eyes lit up when she clocked the bottle. Brother Bertie's own home-made special blend of rum. It was Wray and Nephew Overproof Rum with marijuana leaves soaking in it. Brother Bertie grew his own weed in a secluded patch behind some improvised wicker fence to shield it from prying eyes. They'd christened his special drink, 'Lord Have Mercy Rum Punch' because when you tasted it all you could say, in a daze was, 'Lord have mercy.'

Ruddy took a sip. Her body convulsed from head to toe with a shiver of utter pleasure. That stuff could make your eyes spin for a good hour.

Brother Bertie popped on the radio. Patsy Cline's 'Crazy'

was playing. Soon they were lost in a heady fog of wacky-baccy rum, sun and music from a golden musical age.

Ruddy suddenly tapped his arm with excitement. 'Get this. Some young kid tries to mug me last week. Comes up to me and says,' she put on a daft voice, '"Here, lady, give us your purse".'

Brother Bertie kissed his teeth savagely. 'Them young kids have no respect.'

Ruddy continued. 'I says to him, "You want my money, sonny? I'll give it to you, don't you worry".'

She grabbed her bag and pulled out a blue plastic carrier bag very heavy with copper coins. She proceeded to demonstrate how she'd given the thieving toerag her money.

'I wrapped this around my hand.' She demonstrated, which made all the coppers bunch up together at one end of the carrier bag. 'Then I swing it around like David against Goliath. And, bish-bosh! Bullseye! Whack him in his loaf. There's my money, you tea leafing prat. That'll teach you to try to rob vulnerable old ladies going about their everyday business.'

They both clung to each other, shoulders shaking with laughter and cracking up until their bellies hurt. Ruddy was clever that way. If the Old Bill stopped her, they couldn't classify a bag of coins as a weapon, now could they?

Brother Bertie took another sip of his special rum. 'Talking of youth, I'm worried about my baby-gal.'

Ruddy could see how serious he was. 'Big Mo? What's up with her?' She knew how much he loved his granddaughter. Would do anything for her.

He shook his head, very troubled. 'Don't know what's going on with her, but all of sudden she's different. Like she's moving in different company. She's always been a bit fly, but not like this…'

The feather-light touch of Ruddy's fingers against the back of his hand halted the rest of the words.

She whispered, as she peered suspiciously into the distance, 'Talk of the Devil. Looks like some young help might be at hand for old farmer Bertie.'

When he followed the direction of her gaze, he saw his granddaughter running through the allotment entrance.

'Girl! Over here!'

Mo heard Ruddy call out before she spotted her gramps and his close friend parked in deckchairs like sunbathers on the beach. She knew it was going to be difficult to recover the gold-handled gun with these two looking on. It was a tossup which of the pair was the more suspicious character – her Gramps or Ruddy. They weren't going to fall for her claptrap of this being a social call.

She was right.

Ruddy peered over her sunglasses with a piercing, puzzled stare. 'What are you doing down here then, young Mo? I didn't know you had green fingers.'

Mo did her best to put on an innocent show. 'Mum said grandad was up here doing his growing, so I thought I'd drop by and see how it was going.'

The suspicion was leaden. 'Is that so now?'

Ruddy could make a vicar's prayer sound like an effort to

wriggle out of something. Mo pressed on. She had to get these two off the site. 'Yeah. Well, Mum doesn't think you should be doing this anymore, what with your bad back and everything.'

'Probably true,' Brother Bertie agreed. He arched slightly in the chair to relieve the creaking in his spine. 'Maybe I should hand this place back to the council. Let someone younger take it over.' Then he looked at Mo with a twinkle in his eye. 'It's the digging that's the problem. I can still sow seeds. Now if you was to turn the earth over for me, I could roll out another season.'

Mo's heart sank ... Then pinged back into action. Maybe ... She looked over at her grandad's spade. 'Tell you what, Gramps, why don't I turn the earth for you starting now. I'm going to kick-start near your pumpkin. What a beauty.'

Before he could tell her 'yes' or 'no' she was off. Clothes soaked in sweat, Mo dug away for nearly an hour before she reached the carefully marked spot where the gun was buried. Suddenly, a sound like snorting pigs filled the air. Mo faintly smiled, she knew that sound so well. She looked over and confirmed her gramps was fast asleep snoring for England in the warm sun. Ruddy was also in La-La-Land, her mouth catching flies, her skirt hiked indecently high.

Mo gently loosened the earth around the gun and picked it up. Crept past the snoozing pair and went into her grandad's shed. Inside she found a loose plank in the floor and re-buried Jimmy Southpaw's weapon. She was new to the business of hiding shooters. But she was learning.

Seconds after Mo left the allotment Ruddy's eyes snapped open. So did Brother Bertie's. They'd been pretending to sleep. Beneath hooded eyes, they'd observed Mo digging frantically away at Brother Bertie's best pumpkin.

'You thinking what I'm thinking?' she asked him.

'That whatever she'd buried with my pumpkin has got something to do with…' Brother Bertie momentarily paused voice trembling, '*That man.*'

Ruddy noted her friend's frail hands were shaking. She took Brother Bertie's hand in hers and squeezed.

'You leave this to me,' she promised with steely determination. 'If he's got anything to do with Mo I'll find out.'

Brother Bertie's grip tightened. His features were eaten away with dread. 'It's too dangerous. If anything—'

She stopped him with a tender kiss to his weathered cheek. 'We've been through hell and high water together and we're still here while others are long gone.' She cupped his face between her palms and made him a promise:

'You leave that bastard to me.'

Chapter Fourteen

'You want me to do what?' Mo croaked at her Mum in utter disbelief the following week.

Mo stood in the kitchen doorway in her new business jacket ready to set off for her first day on the job with Barker down his HQ, the popular West End nightspot, Club Class. Her Mum was busy making a cuppa for her grandad, who sat silently at the small table minding his own business.

Precious Watson repeated as cool as they come, 'I want you to pick up your cousin from the airport. She's just arrived from Jamaica.'

Had her Mum been having a tote on the ol' wacky baccy? *I need this like I need a hole in the frigging head!* Anxious about her first day on the job with Barker, Mo had woken up as jittery as a junkie facing rehab accompanied by an urgent sensation of her insides wanting to splash out. Being nervy wasn't her go-to style. Ultra-confidence and not being fazed by new things were her trademarks.

In the end, to bolster her mojo, she'd stood in front of her bedroom mirror and waited until her reflection had switched from Maureen from the block to Big Mo of the future. And what a sight to behold Big Mo of the future had been. Decked out in a sharp DKNY trouser suit, leopard-print heels and sunglasses with lens tinted the same shade as her startling grey eyes. She held a large dog on a leather leash, studded with diamonds. Behind, on either side, stood two men. Born fighters, big and tough to protect her. That was her destiny, right there in front of her.

The Underworld Queen of London Town.

It had done the trick, bolstering her confidence again … Now her Mum was doing her best to derail her.

Mo was incensed. 'Cousin? What cousin?'

The only cousins she could recall were her aunt's kids up in Sheffield and they were a troubled lot who her grandad did his best to keep her well away from.

Precious turned fully to face her daughter. 'Delilah's my cousin's daughter's kid by her first husband who it turned out was still married to someone else. The girl wants to make a new life in England, so I agreed to put her up.'

Cousin's daughter's kid by her first husband who it turned out was still married to someone else? Why do Caribbean families have to be so bloody complicated? Mind you, those same Caribbean communities prided themselves on looking after their own. That's how they'd operated in the fifties and sixties when they came over to the Mother Country. The first to arrive would earn enough money to send for someone else and then the new arrival would do the same.

Mo squared off with her Mum, hands jamming onto her hips spoiling the line of her jacket. 'I don't care if she's the first cousin of Ali G. I'm starting a new job today.'

Her Mum's eyes narrowed dangerously, for the first time really seeing Mo's jacket. Spanking new clobber. 'You never said nuthin' 'bout no new job.'

Mo shifted nervously. 'Yeah, well, you've been giving me grief long enough about me getting one. So, I found one.' She could hear the high-pitched panic in her reply.

'Where's this place you're working at?' Precious' nose twitched like she could smell the stink of something fishy in the air.

Mo could've kicked herself where it hurts the most. She should've figured that her Mum would demand the full SP on her new job, and so, accordingly, Mo should've cobbled together a ready-made BS story all primed and ready to go. If her Mum caught on that she was working for a villain in a club, Up West, there was going to be holy hell to pay.

Mo quickly and vaguely muttered, 'A firm in town. Needed another body on the front desk. Pay's decent too.'

Her Mum stared her out for a few seconds. Then, 'You're going to have to give your new boss a bell to tell him you're going to be late. Because you, young lady, are going to pick up Delilah.' She checked the white clock on the kitchen wall. 'In fact, her plane should be touching down within the next hour—'

'No can do.' Mo wasn't budging an inch. It would be career suicide to turn up late for her first day on the job with Barker.

Precious slammed the cup down. 'Haven't you got a heart? That poor girl will be waiting with her suitcase scared out of her wits and bewildered when no one turns up.

Besides, I told you last week she was coming.'

Her gramps joined the discussion in a gentle and persuasive tone. 'Do it for me, baby-gal. I know what it's like to turn up in a new country with only your grip for company and no one to meet you.'

Mo rolled her eyes heavenward. For pity's sake!

Mo had never stepped foot in Heathrow before. Her first reaction was she didn't like it. Way way too choc-a-bloc for her liking. People everywhere. So much was going on a body didn't know where to put their eyes. Gramps had told her to find the arrivals lounge, so she bustled her way through the crowd and stood with the people waiting for relatives and friends.

Mo's nerves bit into her. She'd cautiously phoned Club Class to be told that Barker wasn't around so she'd left a message saying she was going to be late. It had crossed her mind to tell a porkie about having to go to the quacks, but that had sounded so lame. In the end she'd gone for a half-truth. She had family business to attend to. Not the best way to kickstart her entry into London's criminal fraternity but there was sod all she could do about. Truth was she could never refuse a request from her darlin' gramps.

After an hour, Mo cursed beneath her breath when Delilah was a no-show. Where the hell was the girl? Mo gave it another fifteen mins before changing tack and heading to the information desk. The woman behind the counter held fast to one of those robotic fake smiles, whereas her eyes shone with a veiled bitterness that proclaimed she was way better than the job she'd landed.

'How may I help you?' she asked.

Mo shuffled her feet. 'I'm here to meet someone on the flight from Jamaica. It should have landed a good while ago by now.'

'Jamaica,' the woman muttered checking her computer. Less than a minute later she turned back to Mo. 'There are no flights from Jamaica expected today.'

'What?' Mo was stunned. 'That can't be right.'

The woman's smile slipped slightly. 'Maybe you got the wrong day.'

Mo began fuming. What if her Mum had indeed got the wrong day? Sent her on a fool's errand on one of the most important days of Mo's young life? Right, she'd had enough of this malarkey. Time to jack it in and trot on out of this madhouse.

With forceful determination Mo twisted about. Stopped dead. Less than a metre away stood a woman who looked more like a teenager than the twenty-years-old she was. She held a beaten-up square-shaped piece of cardboard with 'Mo' scrawled on it in thick, black pen. Mo's eyes bugged out. Crikey! What was she kitted out in? A straw hat with a shiny-satin blue ribbon with a bow tied on the front. A pinafore style dress that looked like it belonged in a '50s Littlewood catalogue. Her surprisingly muscular legs ended in white ankle socks and black, flat shoes that were polished enough to reflect Mo's gobsmacked face. Her hair was styled in two chunky plaits finished off with red ribbon bows.

Good grief! The young woman looked like she was on her way to St Trinian's.

Mo moved guardedly closer. 'Are you Delilah?'

The other woman nodded. Her thick plaits and ribbons bounced like a wild tropical parrot about to take off.

One of Mo's brows arched suspiciously. 'The lady at the info desk said there weren't no flights from Jamaica today.'

'I came on the flight from Miami. My poor Mother didn't have enough money to send me on a direct flight.'

Well, that made sense. Still, it wouldn't have hurt her Mum to have informed her before she set off instead of Mo waiting like a prized plonker for a flight that didn't exist.

Suddenly her cousin clocked a woman walking past with a pair of shorts on. Delilah's mouth turned down; her nose tipped up in the air. 'These woman have no SHAME. Parading around with all that flesh hanging out. DAUGHTERS OF SATAN! The good scriptures say: *"You may clothe yourself so that the shame of your nakedness will not be revealed"*. I will say a prayer for their lost souls tonight.'

Mo's jaw slackened as she gawked at her cousin. Mo had never heard the like in her life. Had her cousin been drinking the Kool-Aid? Dumfounded, she realised that her cousin was a full-time Bible basher. Most of her Jamaican relatives were respectable types but they also loved a taste of fun and letting their hair down especially with a bottle of Wray and Nephew or Cockspur rum nearby. Delilah looked as if she'd fight fun off with a specially anointed sword.

To underscore this, her cousin shouted after the object of her evangelical passions. 'The Devil will get you, sister. He will sink his fangs into your bum-bum hanging from that shameless tiny piece of material you call a pair of shorts and never let go.'

People were openly gaping at them and whispering. Mo wasn't turning into the laughing stock of Heathrow Airport. In two strides she grabbed her cousin by the arm and marched her willy-nilly out of the airport. She noticed Delilah had a single piece of luggage, a battered suitcase that she wheeled behind her. On her back was an everyday rucksack.

'Do you want me to do that?' Mo pointed at the suitcase as they waited for the Piccadilly Line train to roll in.

Delilah shook her head as her hand tightened on the suitcase handle. That's when Mo noticed a wicked looking scar across the back of her hand.

'How did you get that?'

Delilah's dark eyes seemingly turned even darker. 'Hard work.'

Hard work, eh? Well, if hard work left those types of marks Mo could do without it. It cemented her resolve that she'd made the right decision in the path she'd chosen.

'Cousin.' Delilah addressed her. 'I am looking forward to you taking me to church on Sunday.'

Mo restrained from laughing out loud. The day Mo went to church was the day her family was getting ready to put her six feet under.

A ditzy grin suddenly appeared on Delilah's face. 'I have come to England to find a husband. A godly man who will work hard to put bread on the table and give me at least five children.'

Mo sniggered. She couldn't help it. Her cousin might be as boring as a dog taking a snooze on a Sunday afternoon, but she sure knew how to tickle Mo's funny bone.

'Well, good luck with that,' was what Mo told her.

On the journey home, her cousin took out a small black Bible to read. Thank God for that. Mo had had enough of the sermonising to last her all the days of her life. When the train hit Leicester Square, Delilah quietly closed her *Bible* and started singing, 'In the Sweet By And By' in an ear mangling, scratchy voice. The other commuters moved to the far end of the carriage. Some even chose to stand up which is saying something for a London commuter. Mo had had enough and sank low into her seat, pretending that her square, stiff cousin had nothing to do with her.

When they finally reached Mo's home, she dumped her cousin on the doorstep and fled for her life.

Chapter Fifteen

Was that a scream?

Mo abruptly froze, shivers skating up and down her spine. She was inside Club Class, in the lower ground floor corridor that led to Barker's office. Club Class stood on the border of Leicester Square and Soho in the heart of London's groovy, non-stop West End. Mo wasn't feeling groovy. Four hours late, she was. Four bloody hours. Barker would be well within his rights to show her the door. Mo prayed she hadn't blown her chance.

She got her ears into gear, listening carefully for anything remotely resembling a scream. Nothing. Must be her imagination doing overtime. Mo finally reached Barker's office door. When Mo had entered the club, the lippy, ice-maiden receptionist had proceeded to fling out a roll call of directions to Barker's office that Mo found hard to keep up with. Right. Left. Up the stairs. Down the stairs for two flights. A corridor. Probably have to do the Hokey Cokey at the end at this rate.

'Come on in, Mo.'

Barker's booming command snapped Mo out of her

thoughts. A twin set of security cameras mounted on the wall observed her every move. Mo stepped to it, picking up pace towards the door at the end of the corridor. Smartly and without hesitation she opened the door. What she saw inside the room stopped her dead in the doorway, chilling her to the bone.

'Don't be a stranger,' Barker, well … barked.

He waved her impatiently inside. It was a room that would have usually filled her with wonder with its modern furnishings. It had one of those cute, personal bars, sexily lit up in glam blue-purple lighting. Mo had always dreamed of owning a bar like that.

What got in the way of her displaying any open admiration was the poor bollocks scared out of his pants bound and gagged in a wooden chair like last year's Christmas turkey. A wet patch stained his trousers from the crotch to the inside of his leg. Josh, Barker's henchman and nephew, stood over the terrified soul with a pair of lethal looking pliers.

Barker casually sat in a large overstuffed exec style swivel chair with a fat cigar clamped between his lips. Mo quickly shut the door and then hesitantly moved towards her new boss. Blimey! She hadn't expected this sort of carry on on her first day. She knew violence came with the territory but to be confronted with it in such a blatant manner made her question her career choice.

Something told Mo that her first day on the job was going to be a baptism of pure fire.

Mo got in there quickly with an explanation for her

lateness. 'Mister Barker, I'm sorry—'

Her new boss cut over her with the sharpness of a blade slicing into flesh. 'See that bag of shit over there?' He waved his cigar at the bloke in the chair. 'He seems to be under the miscomprehension that he can take my money with one hand, splash it around with the other. And, get this, not have to pay it back when the due day comes a-calling.'

If there was one thing Mo had learnt at her grandad's knee it was to keep it well and truly shut at certain times. This was one of those times. Her gaze flicked to the man in the chair. Tears streaked and dirtied his horror-struck face. She wouldn't be human if she didn't feel pity for his situation. Nevertheless, if you took money from a Top Geezer like Barker you better be ready with your wallet when the piper wanted to be paid back.

'Whatcha think I should do with the wanker?' Barker asked her, his busy tash stretching as if just waking up.

Oh heck! That blindsided her.

Mortification rose up within Mo that she was being put on the spot like this. Mo shoved it back. Think treble fast on her feet that's what was needed. Mo got her brain into gear. Barker was deffo not expecting her to say give the sod a scolding and then send him on his way with a flea in his ear back to his dear, ol' Mum.

The last thing Mo wanted to come across as was a soft touch, so she reasoned, 'Mister Barker, the first thing to consider is what crime has he committed. He's taken your hard-earned dough and not paid you back. Did you send him a reminder of sorts before you brought him here?'

Barker mashed his cigar out in the thick glass ashtray. Then pinned his hot gaze right through her. 'You think a man of my stripes should be sending warnings to the likes of Noddy over there, like I'm the council wanting their overdue rent?'

Mo stuck to her guns. 'Sometimes, a man in your position wants to let it be known that he's a bloke of fairness.'

Barker angled his head like he'd never seen her before. 'Like I'm a gent?'

Josh sniggered as his grip on the pliers tightened. 'Next, she'll be telling you to pop on your top hat and spats.'

'I'll top you in a minute,' Mo furiously lobbed his way.

Mo might have to take orders from Barker, fair dues. It didn't mean she had to take shit from man-child over there.

Josh insolently smacked his lips and blew her a kiss. Yuk! Mo turned her disgusted face away, although, if she was being honest, her nips and vag were playing silly buggers again as soon as they spotted him.

Barker's voice grabbed her attention again. 'Let's say I gave him a warning and the sad fucker still didn't cough up what he owed? I brings him down here. Now what do I do?'

Mo thought hard. 'The size of the debt don't matter coz if someone takes your money they take your money, no matter if it's large or small.' She cast her gaze to Barker's victim whose terrorised gaze pleaded with her. 'It seems to me that you could batter him black and blue, but would you get your cash back that way?' She shook her head. 'I don't think so.'

Mo turned back to her boss. 'Now, if you beat the stuffing out of his missus he might have a mind to pay you back quicker than the blink of an eye. Or, at least, threaten to do something to his wife. Sometimes all that's needed is the threat over a loved one.'

Barker eased out of his chair and walked over to Mo and didn't stop until he crowded her space, looming down at her. 'Is that what you think I should do to your Mum, Mo? Or what about that grandad of yours who puts himself about with that fancy stick of his?'

Mo's heart dropped to the floor, as her tummy tipped sideways. She'd walked with the innocence of a lamb to the slaughter straight into Barker's trap. This heart-to-heart had never been about the tosser who'd spat in the eye of Barker's generosity. No! There was only ever one unfortunate in the spotlight. Her. Sick rose in her throat at Barker's threat. Had she brought danger knocking at her family's door?

She remained schtum as Barker continued to sprout off. 'I don't like people who try to screw me over a debt and I don't like *my people* taking the piss out of me thinking they can waltz in here whenever they can be arsed.'

Josh jumped in with glee. 'I say we start with her grandad and use his stick—'

The fury coursing through Mo's blood didn't let him finish. 'You touch a hair on my gramps' head and I'm coming after you. I'll shove that plastic dick of yours straight down your gob to shut you up for all eternity.' Her chest heaved with the convictions of her threat. And she meant every last word of it.

He advanced on her, the pliers tapping menacingly against his palm. 'Wanna play with the big boys? I'm about to teach you this ain't no place for some tiny tot who thinks she's got a pair between her legs.'

Abruptly, Mo's mind flashed back to her childhood. To the bullies circling her.

'Titch.'

'Short-arse.'

'Pint-sized dwarfy.'

Mo saw red and went for Josh. But she bounced back when Barker lunged and caught the collar of her new powder blue jacket. The atmosphere sizzled as she and Josh hissed at each other, shooting daggers that were more deadly than the weapon in his hand.

Barker released her when she'd settled down. Mo smoothed her jacket back into place, although, by now, it resembled something she'd picked off the rail in a charity shop.

Her boss told her, 'You're lucky I'm feeling in a charitable mood.' He stabbed a warning finger her way. 'Don't ever be late on my watch again. Next time won't be so pretty.'

'Yes, Mister Barker.' The words had the texture of gritty sand in her mouth.

Barker strode purposefully to his desk and took out a package from a drawer. It was the size of a cake box, neatly wrapped in brown paper.

He gave it to her with a slip of paper. 'I want you to deliver that pronto to an associate of mine. You'll find him at the address on the paper.' An added warning fired up his eyes. 'Of course, it goes without saying it's to be delivered unopened.'

Mo briskly nodded and turned to go, but not before she witnessed both her boss and his wannabe tasty nephew advance with menaces towards the man hog-tied to the chair. She heard the tape on his mouth ripped off with a sticky rasp.

Josh said with gleeful drama, 'Now open wide.'

Mo couldn't get out of Barker's office fast enough. She hurried along the corridor, the screams of Barker's victim echoing against the walls as his tooth was wrenched out.

Chapter Sixteen

Mo was being followed. It didn't take her long to figure this out soon after departing Club Class with Barker's package tucked under her arm. A pair of likely lads, about her age. She wondered if they'd followed her to the club, waited outside and were now about to roll her over and grab the parcel?

With a snide eye she caught their reflections in shop windows as they kept pace with her. They wore classic street thief gear. Pumps and hoodies with no labels. Clothing all a forgettable black. Their faces and features obscured in the shade of their hooded tops, hands in the pockets. Nothing that would help the cops identify them later. Not that it would cross Mo's mind to call the Bill.

The people traffic on the Dilly was thick, but that didn't seem to be holding these two cretins back. They didn't appear to give a crap about who saw what they did. Questions started racing in Mo's mind. Who'd told them to follow her? What was inside the package she was carrying that was so important?

Mo dived into a vintage clothes shop and watched the

youths stroll by. But of course they weren't going far. They were loitering nearby waiting for when she reappeared.

Mo turned her attention to the package. The obvious thing to do would be to tear it open, drop the contents down the front of her top where at least the boys would have a fight on their hands if they thought their scummy mitts were going anywhere near her thrupenny bits.

But Barker had been explicit. The package must be delivered unopened. This was her first job and she was already on the cusp of blowing it. Frustration kicked Mo in the gut.

Mo fortified herself. No way on God's green earth was she ballsing up her maiden job for Barker.

Mo looked down the rows of classic clothes and took her chance. On the wall was a fisherman's smock with lots of buckles and belts. Her eyes bulged when they clocked the price: One hundred fifty nicker. A bargain apparently.

Mo grabbed the smock off the hanger and did a runner. The shop attendant got wise to what she was up to and stupidly tried to get in her way. Mo pushed her in the chest and over the woman went like a skittle at a bowling alley. Mo belted down and across Shaftesbury Avenue straight into incoming traffic. Car brakes screeched in the air as motorists veered to avoid her accompanied by very ripe shouts of abuse. Mo scrambled over the hood of a car and made her escape down a side street.

Chest heaving, Mo spun around. There was no sign of the two following her, but Mo wasn't fooled by that. She knew they were lurking around somewhere. In the shadow of a rusty fire escape, she got down to business. Yanked on the fisherman's smock. Positioned the mystery package under it to make it look like she was pregnant. When she'd finished tying the belt, pulled up the heavy cast iron zip at the front, she was good to go.

Mo hit the West End streets again. Cautiously, doubled back to the Dilly. Kept her eyes front and back as she waited for the bus to take her to East London where the package had to be delivered. When the bus arrived, she did one more spot check before boarding. At Stratford she caught another bus down to Forest Gate. She found the address Barker had given easily enough. It was a boarded-up pub on a quiet street that was slated for conversion to flats. Just like so many other pubs in the East End. Mo's features creased slightly in confusion as she checked the place over. It looked empty. If there was no one around who the fecking hells bells was she meant to hand the package over to?

Then it all happened in a flash. So fast, that if the cops had wanted a description for an e-fit, Mo would have had nothing to give them. She was grabbed, hands twisted and pinned behind her back. Mo didn't need to be the Brain of Britain to suss that the two fuckwits had caught up with her. How they'd done it she didn't know. While she struggled with one the other bastard tackled the iron zip on her smock. Mo leant forward and sank her teeth into his hand. As he yelped with pain she kicked out at his shins.

Fury rising off him like the stink floating up from the gutter near them, he belted her one across the face, snarling, 'Poxy bitch!'

Although her face was on fire, Mo took another go at the lad's digits with her teeth while trying another kick, aimed at his goolies this time.

Despite himself, the guy behind her was impressed. 'She's a live one.'

The response from the other was a derisive snort. 'She's gonna be a dead one if she keeps this up. Grab her neck.'

A vice-like arm hooked around her throat and squeezed. Blood flooded hot and unnatural in Mo's face as her airway was choked off. The air rasped loudly in the back of her throat, her eyes bulging.

Can't breathe! Can't breathe! Can't breathe!

All her thoughts fled when he pulled out a blade. A wicked looking thing with a razor-sharp jagged edge. If she was going down Mo wasn't going to behave as if she was on her knees. She glared boldly into eyes that were bloodshot from way too many nights smoking weed.

Tension coiled inside her as Mo waited for him to stick her. And stick her again. But instead he took his knife to the front of the smock and sliced and slashed from the top down. The parcel fell neatly into his hand.

'Bingo!' he announced with cocksure triumph.

The stranglehold on her neck was released. Mo tumbled to the pavement, gasping and gulping desperately for oxygen. The bastards were a blur as they scarpered down the street.

Fuck! Fuck! Fuck!

Mo felt like pounding her fist to the ground. The first job Barker had given her, and she'd bolloxed it good and proper.

The taste of failure was bitter in her mouth. She struggled to her feet pulling out her phone. What really rankled was being rolled over in the street as if she were a rank amateur. Mo, of all people, knew up close and personal the types of dodges played out on the street. What she couldn't understand was how they'd followed her from Up West? Then another idea came to her … What if the two who'd roughed her up weren't the same pair from the Dilly? How did they figure out where she was dropping off Barker's package?

Mo's head began aching with answers she didn't have. She found Barker's number but hesitated. If he knew his parcel was gone for a burton that would put the kybosh to her notorious career in the underworld. Plus, it would also appear that she couldn't handle herself on the street. The phone went back into her pocket.

Mo steadied her breathing to help her think this through. Those fuckers may or may not have been the same ones as before. Just say they were … and went back Up West? What if the surprisers could be surprised themselves? Mo's eyes cooled as her lips tightened with vengeful determination.

Mo swung into action. Armed with a short, stout leg off a lopsided bench that was in what had once been the beer garden, secreted up her sleeve she headed back on the bus Up West. Once back in the Dilly she had to decide where to look; knowing she was at a strong disadvantage because this wasn't her manor. Too many people figured you know one part of London you know it all. Wrong!!! East London was different from West, North different from South.

Nothing for it but to do the best she could. An hour later, Mo was exhausted. It felt like she'd checked every nook and cranny in Piccadilly through to Soho. No sign of those dick brains anywhere. Perhaps they'd gone. Perhaps they'd caught the Tube. Perhaps... Suddenly a light bulb lit up in her head. What did she and her former crew do after jacking Jimmy Southpaw's Bentley? Go off to a burger bar to celebrate.

With renewed purpose, Mo set off again, peering into kebab, pizza and burger joints, fast food places that tried to pull the wool over the eyes of tourists with their fancy names. Mutton dressed up as cheap fried chicken.

Mo struck gold in a chicken and chips eating hole where her assailants were stuffing their faces full of French fries and wolfing down chicken nuggets. Sitting between them was Barker's package.

Mo retreated, hood up, to shelter in the doorway of the building next door. She needed to figure out her strategy. Taking them on in the chicken joint was a fool's game. They'd see her coming a mile off. Now, out in the open was different. The advantage of surprise would be on her side giving her the time she needed to dish out a proper caning with the table leg.

Mo bided her time.

Ten minutes later, when the youths emerged, Mo pounced. One of them took a heavy blow to the belly and doubled over while his mate took a resounding bash to the head. He fell back against the windows, groaning with shock and pain. A final blow to the first across the neck put him down on the pavement. She rifled through their pockets, grabbed their wallets. Picked up the package and got out of there like a bat outta hell.

Mo found a bench in a local park to examine the wallets. She wanted to see if there were any IDs so she could pass onto Barker the identities of the youths who'd been sent to jack her. But all either of them contained was exactly fifty quid each and a couple of travel cards. Obviously, the money was cash in hand wages for the job. They might have looked like just another couple of street hoods, but they were obviously professionals.

It was an hour before she decided to risk going back to the disused pub in Forest Gate. The boys might have recovered and be waiting for her back at her destination. And this time it would be personal. She thoroughly scouted the area around the defunct boozer before going up to the boarded door and striking it hard with the table leg. Footsteps echoed on the other side before the door swung open and a heavy beckoning her in.

Inside what was once the saloon bar, were two tables. At one table sat…

WTF!

Barker. Mo couldn't believe what she was seeing. But it was all too real. And if that wasn't enough of a sucker punch to the gut her two attackers sat at the other table. One clutched a bloody hanky to his head wound.

Barker burst out laughing. 'It's Mo! With my parcel!'

Bewildered, dazed and most definitely confused Mo

headed for her boss and handed him the package. Mo nearly let loose with a 'What the fuck was all that about.' But she sucked it back because going off on one at Barker was not a good idea. He was Barker, legendary villain.

Nevertheless some emotions churning inside her must have shown because he observed, brow arching along with the side of his tash, 'You look like you wanna knock my block off.'

Mo could feel the stillness of the lads at the other table, their tension as they watched the play between her and Barker.

Mo shifted her stance to the way she learnt from the Big Man all those years ago. 'Normally, Mister Barker, I wouldn't question the particulars of an order you gave me.' Mo pulled in a deep, long punch of air. 'But seeing as how I've been up and down this city and taken a licking in the bargain it would be' – *Don't get his dander up by choosing the wrong word, girl!* – 'helpful to know exactly what the mission was today. Seeing as I'm new and all that.'

Barker tossed the package over his shoulder onto the floor. 'There's nothing in it, babe. It was just a little test to see what you've got balls wise.' He looked at the two wounded parcel thieves on the other table. 'And I must say, I'm impressed. You've certainly got more than them two losers.'

Mo pulled the hundred quid out of her smock. 'This must be theirs then.'

Barker looked at the money and then threw his head back and laughed. 'You keep it treacle. You've earned it.'

He got up off his chair, came round to where Mo stood. 'I like you. I think you're going to go a long way in this business. I think you could go right to the top.'

Chapter Seventeen

Ruddy popped on her broadest smile, patted her wobbly beehive wig and then proceeded to enter The Docker's Return. It was a pub at the Aldgate end of Commercial Road. She spotted who she was after straight away. Dottie Donavan. A woman who went way back with Ruddy. And, more pointedly, also happened to be Jimmy Southpaw's charlady down his bookies. Jimmy being 'that man' she and Brother Bertie had discussed in such hush-hush tones at the allotment.

'How's tricks, chick?' Ruddy asked Dottie as soon as she reached the table in the snug in the back. She parked herself down without waiting to be asked.

Dottie stared at Ruddy over a glass of Pale Ale. Dottie was a woman of average height, but she looked so much smaller bent by years of manual labour. Age and hard work had worn down the skin on her face to the texture of fine paper, so thin in places that tiny blue veins were visible.

'Wotcha, Ruddy.' Dottie answered, shifting her lips like someone who'd forgotten to put in their false teeth. 'Me back's playing havoc with my constitution as per usual. Sigh-a-tikka is what the quack calls it. Trapped nerve. Tell you what, pushing out a kid don't have a patch on this pain.'

Ruddy clucked her tongue and made all the right sympathetic noises as Dottie carried on telling her tale. About ten minutes in Ruddy got down to business.

She lowered her voice, gaze darting about. You had to be careful what came out of your mouth in The Dock. The place sometimes seemed to have ears. 'Why don't you give that back of yours a rest? Eh? Let me do your shift down the bookie's tomorrow bright and early?'

Being a cleaning lady had been Ruddy's former stock-in-trade. Most folks treated cleaners as if they were invisible. Stupid! You can keep secrets from your right-hand man, your lawyer and your accountant but your cleaner knows the works. They see the notes you meant to throw away but left on your desk. Know what you've thrown in the bin. Hear the rows in the office. The furtive phone calls to your piece of skirt or shirt you keep on the side.

Ruddy knew full well that Jimmy Southpaw wasn't a first-grade pillock like some of these other faces who ran criminal enterprises. He would've vetted his cleaner right down to knowing what Dottie watched on the box on a Saturday night. The gossipvine reported that if he was holding one of his meetings the charlady was given an extra tenner and told to take the rest of the morning off. He was a firm believer that curiosity killed the cat. And he wasn't above taking cats to the vet and putting them down when necessary.

Dottie knew this, so was understandably very wary about Ruddy's offer. 'Oooh! Dunno about that, Nora. Jimmy's mighty particular about who he has on his premises. If he finds out I've had someone fill in for me, he's likely to turn nasty. You know what Jimmy's like. Everyone does.'

Ruddy cosied up to friend. 'But he ain't gonna know, now is he? I won't tell him if you don't. Anyways, he's got his hands full with this feud with Barker, so I hear. Hardly likely he's going to be checking out who's shining his door knobs down his bookies, know what I mean?'

Dottie wet her lips with some Pale Ale, shaking her head adamantly. 'If it was anyone else but Jimmy, I'd do it in a heartbeat, a heartbeat. But The Southpaw? He's lethal when he's upset.'

Ruddy threw a deceptively friendly arm around Dottie's neck. Then tightened her grip. 'I know he is. But you're forgetting, so am I. Look, I don't want to turn nasty here, but I need the money. Come on chick, just this once. He won't find out I promise.'

Ruddy got the key to Jimmy's bookies. Just this once.

Next morning, Ruddy scuttled down the High Street at half past six. Dottie told her that she started at the bookies at seven, pronto, because Jimmy turned up on the premises at exactly nine on the days when he made an appearance. That would give Ruddy at least two hours to turn the place over while giving it a good buffing at the same time.

As a veteran in the Mrs Mop business, Ruddy knew how to find things in the places she worked. Trouble was that depended on knowing what you're looking for and she didn't. Not exactly. She'd boiled it down to anything that made mention of young Mo. She wasn't leaving here until she found something, or nothing, that would put Brother Bertie's mind at ease.

Once inside, Ruddy collected all the cleaning stuff from a cupboard under the stairs and headed to the upper floor. There was the room that Southpaw used as his boardroom with its long table, chairs, kitchenette and not much else. Then there was his office behind a door with glazed panels. If she was going to find anything, it would be in there.

Ruddy got to work with her polish and duster, giving Jimmy's furniture and fittings the best going over they'd had in a long time – she took a pride in her work – while at the same time examining all the paperwork on the desk and in its drawers.

There wasn't much to find. Obviously, Southpaw was supremely careful about what he left lying around. A wise man if the Bill ever came calling.

Ruddy emptied the bin on the desk and began rummaging through it. Nothing. Not a sausage. She moved onto the pictures on the wall, which she took down and cleaned. Almost all the photos were of Jimmy Southpaw himself. Jimmy as a teenager, in his boxing shorts, gloves on, fists up, menacingly leering at the camera. A much older Jimmy handing out trophies to youngsters at boxing competitions he'd organised. Jimmy feeding sugar to a racehorse he'd once owned. All the photos were Jimmy, Jimmy, Jimmy.

'The bloke's so far up his own arse, he can see his own fillings,' Ruddy muttered.

Behind one picture she thought she'd struck gold. A safe. But the safe was open with sod all inside. Nora was running out of options...

A creak sounded beneath her feet. Ruddy froze. Looked down at the threadbare rug she stood on. She'd cleaned enough properties in her time to know what that noise might mean. A loose floorboard. And what did folk sometimes do with loose floorboards? Hide their secrets beneath them. Ruddy got on her knees. Rolled back the rug. Tucked the pads of her fingers into the aged floorboard and lifted.

Bingo! Inside was a large padded envelope. She wasted no time picking it up and peering inside. A stack of stapled papers. She took them out and started reading. The blood drained from her face.

Suddenly the light in the room seemed to change from dark grey to yellow. Ruddy's head shot up and found out why.

The door to the office was opened allowing bright sunlight to flood in. In the doorframe was a figure silhouetted like an angel in the light.

But this was no angel.

Jimmy Southpaw.

He wore pumps, trackie bottoms and a hoodie top. A film of sweat coated his forehead. He'd been out jogging by the look of things and this was an unplanned visit to his HQ. He glanced down at her, manner unhurried as if she was a dust ball of dirt he'd forgotten to sweep away. He took note of what she was holding.

His voice was quiet and controlled. 'Well, well, well. If it isn't Nora Baxter. I didn't realise you were popping in for a chat. You should have rung ahead. I'd have popped on a pot of Rosie and got some Rich Tea bickies in.'

He closed the door ominously behind him. 'I must say, this is a very unusual kind of burglary. The geezers in stripy jerseys don't usually give the place a good clean while they're nicking your gear. I suppose I should be grateful really.'

This is where most would've lost their nerve. Not Nora 'Ruddy' Baxter. She was as steely and as bold as brass as they come. 'Wotcha, Jimmy. I know what you must be thinking but there's a perfectly good…'

Jimmy Southpaw cut her short, his voice and features hardening. 'Shut it, you old crone. I'd expect you not only to have more self-respect but more respect for me than to try to blag your way out of this visit. There's only one thing I can do in a situation like this.'

He clenched his fists and raised them to his chest as if he was back in the ring. 'I'm going to have to shut you down.'

Chapter Eighteen

'Do I look like the Jobcentre?' Mo raged at her Mum.

Precious pursed her lips. You'd think she'd asked her daughter to thief the Crown Jewels. So she repeated, 'All you've got to do is take your cousin to work with you and ask your boss to sort her out a job. Always look after your family.'

They were in kitchen, the view of the calm, soothing river a strong contrast to the tension building inside the room. Reggae legend, Dennis Brown's, iconic tune, 'Money In My Pocket' pumped from the mini hi-fi system with surround speakers. Precious adored Dennis Brown. Sweetest voice in the universe. She loved her music. Loved to groove, especially to a down-n-dirty old-stylee bump-n-grind with that special somebody. Mind you, there hadn't been much to dance about in her life lately.

Today was the first day she'd finally started feeling her old self again. The nasty dressing gown had been ditched down the shoot at the end of the landing. The manky weave-on replaced by super skinny, golden-bronze extensions that fell down her back. She wore a figure-hugging pink T-shirt with rhinestones and jeans that made her booty pop.

Now her girl wanted to spoil it by giving her a mouthful of backchat? Nah! Not happening! Precious' mouth flattened into a line of disapproval. What was the world coming to when you had to repeat yourself within the four walls of your own home? And what got her dander up, good and proper, was when the repeating had to be done to the kid she'd carried and nurtured in her belly for nine months and laboured for eleven hours straight to bring in to this world at Mile End Hospital maternity ward.

Precious hung onto her surging temper. She was fed up to the back molars of her only kid thinking she was the big woman of the house. That role was Precious's, and Maureen Watson best believe it. There was only one Mum in this family.

Precious stood at the cooker rustling up some solid brekkie for young Delilah. No sausages or bacon, mind. The girl said it was against her beliefs to let the flesh of dead animals pass her lips. This had only come to light after Precious had proudly placed a plate of her mouth-watering home-made jerk chicken on a bed of rice and peas in front of Delilah at the kitchen table her first evening here. Delilah had politely and quietly informed her what the problem was.

See, that's what Precious loved about the girl. No OTT dramarama. Delilah hadn't made a face or turned her head away from the steaming pile of meat, she'd simply and quietly explained why she couldn't eat it. Bless her heart, she'd even suggested that she put it in a container and take it down to the foodbank run by Sister Aggi.

Just thinking about Delilah lit up Precious' face. She had already taken that girl into her heart. Already shortened her name to Dell. The girl was respectful, understood the meaning of, 'thank you' and 'please'. And – get this – not one curse word passed her fucking lips. And the girl wasn't afraid of *honest,* hard work. She'd pitched in with the housework off her own back. Precious sighed heavily. Now why couldn't her Maureen be like that?

'No can do.' Mo flatly refused her Mum's request. Again.

Precious gulped down her irritation and tried being nicey-nicey instead. 'I'm sure there must be some type of work for Dell to do at this club?'

Mo's brows slashed together, a cagey expression setting on her face. 'Who says I'm working at a club?'

'Do I look like I was born under a cabbage patch?' Out of her pocket Precious produced a fancy matchbox with 'Club Class' written on it in fine gold lettering. 'I knew the place well back in the day. That's where I met....'

Realising where her reminiscing had nearly led her, Precious snapped her mouth shut mentally kicking herself. Merciful heaven! She'd almost spilled to her daughter that's where she'd met Mo's Father all those years ago. Her heart started racing. Her hand shook as she flipped over the fried egg.

Thank God, Mo didn't seem to have picked up on her slip up.

She kept her face averted from her daughter. 'Please, baby, do this for me. There must be something Dell can do down the club.'

Mo threw her hands despairingly into the air. 'She's a religious nut job, Mum. Should've seen her up the airport, telling all and sundry that they were going to burn in hell's fire for all eternity because they were showing a bit of leg. She'll be preaching to the punters at the club to repent their satanic ways on the DJ's mic.'

'Nothing wrong with having standards,' Precious retorted, although she conceded that Mo had a point. Nevertheless, she wasn't shifting. 'If you don't take her, I'll march her down there myself.'

Mo gasped and reached her Mum in three strides. 'You wouldn't—'

'You watch me.' Precious waved the egg flipper in Mo's face.

Delilah's chirpy-cheery voice interrupted them. 'Blessings be upon you Cousin Precious. Blessings, Cousin Mo.'

Dell was still decked out like a fresh-faced teenaged private schoolgirl in a pale-blue summer dress, the whitest ankle socks and black buckle shoes that looked like something out of an Enid Blyton story. Mo couldn't see her lasting around here. Way too innocent. The East End would gobble her up in no time at all.

Dell held her arms up and wide. Looked to the heavens. 'Father, thank you for listening to my prayers last night when I beseeched you for hours on my knees to find me a job. Praise be! Cousin Mo has found a job for me—'

'Woah!!' Mo was shocked beyond belief. 'Now hang on a min—'

Dell shot across the room and smothered her and her

objections in a huge embrace. 'Thank you! Thank you! I will do anything you ask. No work is too lowly for a servant of the Lord.'

Dell didn't freak out. Didn't run screaming out of the coven of sin that was Club Class. Mo's brows crashed together in confusion as they stood in the club. Delilah and the small rucksack on her back she never seemed to be without, took in her surroundings with a turn. Then her gaze narrowed and stuck like quick setting glue to the shelves of the most corrupting booze behind the bar.

Dell's expression was one of absolute, mouth-tightening displeasure. 'In the words of St Peter: *"This is a place of debauchery, lust, drunkenness, orgies, carousing and detestable idolatry".*' Abruptly, her cousin pulled in a sharp, shaky breath as her face fell. 'But I need a job. I can't stay at your Mother's and Brother Bertie's and not pay my way. It's not right.'

A voice interrupted, calling out, 'Did I hear someone's say they were looking for paid work?'

A very chipper and cocky Josh stood behind them. As per usual his duds were an impeccable, tailor-made fit. And Mo's private parts couldn't help salivating over him. *I wonder what he looks like without all that gear stripped off him?* Her tongue came out of its own accord and teasingly touched her bottom lip. *Someone get me a fan coz I'm Hot! Hot! Hot!*

So distracted by her filthy thoughts, Mo couldn't stop Delilah when she stumbled forward and practically threw herself on Josh's mercy. 'Yes, sir, I am in need of a job. I will work from sunup to sundown if I'm called upon to do so.'

Josh told Delilah, 'You're just in luck, sweetheart. We've got an opening in our disposal department—'

'Otherwise known as cleaning,' Mo tartly filled in.

The expression on Dell's face was as dazzling as the sun coming out. 'I'll be the best cleaner this place has ever had.' She straightened her back, making her small rucksack stand to attention. 'I won't let you down.'

Then Josh went and misjudged the situation by taking Delilah's eagerness to please as an invitation to slap on the charm and try it on. He tilted his head and flashed his baby-blues, supremely cocksure of his seductive self. 'Anytime you wanna work … overtime, you come and see me, doll.'

The sunshine vanished from Dell, her face visited by an expression of dour and sombre intent. 'St Peter says: *"Your beauty should not come from outward adornment, such as'* – she took in his head – *'elaborate hairstyles'* – the rings on his fingers – *'and the wearing of gold jewellery'* – his duds – *'or fine clothes"*.'

The 'You what?' expression on Josh's face communicated that he wasn't sure if he'd been complimented or dissed. Before he figured it out, Mo bundled her cousin over to Linford, who managed the main floor, to show her the ropes.

Mo spent the next couple of hours doing jobs for Barker about the club and keeping half an eye on her cousin, who seemed to be quite content with a mop and bucket or broom humming along to some hymn. Wherever she went so did the rucksack on her back. Then Mo got word that she was needed in Barker's office in the lower ground floor. Inside Barker's office it wasn't her boss who waited for her.

It was his nephew. Josh sat with his feet crossed on his uncle's desk as he lightly stroked a gun in his hand.

'You ever seen one of these before?' Josh pointed the gun at her.

Mo didn't flinch. She suspected he was trying to get a rise out of her. The dope wouldn't ask her questions like that if he knew what she had tucked away on her grandad's allotment. Jimmy Southpaw's shooter. Mo strolled confidently to his side of the desk, her gaze checking out the gun. She didn't know much about them, but this one appeared pretty bog-standard against the beauty of the gold handle of Jimmy Southpaw's.

What Josh next told Mo took her breath away. 'Barker wants me to teach you how to handle one.'

Mo was struck dumb. Finally found her words, although they came out in a disjointed pattern. 'What...? Why...? Why would he do that?'

Josh stood up, the gun hanging by his side. 'If my uncle sees potential in something, he puts his money where his mouth is and invests in it. And obviously he thinks you're worth putting his hand in his pocket for.' He smiled, long and easy. 'So? You up for it?'

Mo couldn't believe her luck. To have the opportunity to really handle a piece of hardware. 'Two hundred per cent, mate.'

'Follow me.'

Josh took Mo to another room in the basement corridor

where a gun range was set up. For the next couple of hours he showed her the ins and outs of how to use a piece, including holding and moulding her body as she fired at targets.

Josh leant in even closer, his heat meshing with hers.

'You done good, girl.' He breathed in her ear as he expertly plucked the gun from her fingers and laid it on a long wooden bench.

Mo was on fire, pure and simple. A volcanic heat rose in her blood and bones. His lips brushed against the curve of her neck. Oh, fecking horny hell! Mo couldn't stop the groan that escaped her. The way the lower region of her tummy started to spasm and ache. Her head fell back. Eyes closed. Mo wasn't one to sit around and let stuff happen, so she did a one-two twist that had her straddling his lap. Mo was a woman who finally understood those that succeeded in this life were those who took. Those who reached out and grabbed.

'Do that again,' Mo ordered as his fingertips did magic tricks against her clit.

He laughed softly. 'Bossy boots, ain't ya?'

'That isn't all I am,' she whispered, then nibbled his ear, her hips swaying against his tight cock.

After that there was no more talking. Only the feel of her legs around his waist as he pressed her up against the wall. Mo's throaty moan as they finally fucked. As they … Mo snapped out of sexy wonderland with a wince. Josh was pounding into her like he had the Liverpool Street to Southend Express to catch. Talk about 'Wham bam, thank you mam.' The geezer didn't have a clue where to find her G spot. He probably thought the G spot was the name of a club down South London way.

To say she was bitterly disappointed was the understatement of the year. It just goes to show that all that glitters isn't always gold. Mo inwardly sighed, deflating like a balloon. She played the hard girl to the hilt, but underneath that tough exterior she dreamed about what all the other young women fantasied about – finding Mister Right. A guy who'd get into her sexual groove and understand her to the tips of her toes. He'd bloody know where her G spot was!

Josh's jabbing away at her was becoming very uncomfortable indeed, so Mo cried out, going into fake orgasm mode to get him to come off.

'That's the spot, baby!'

It did the trick. Josh finally sagged against her, coming deep inside her. Thank the Lord that was over!

She forgot all about his lousy lovemaking, her gaze locking with the gun sitting on the table. When the time was right, she now knew exactly how to use Jimmy Southpaw's shooter she had hidden away.

Chapter Nineteen

Harry strutted his cocksure stuff with the authority of lord of the manor in front of the assembled men. He stood in front of a chalkboard in the function room of the Dockers Return pub outlining the raid on Club Class. He was making a big production of being a gangland boss-in-waiting. The C he'd snorted awhile back added to his puffed up ego.

'To sum up, gents, I'll be hiring two ladies of the night to create a distraction with the door staff. Then you lot pile out of your motors and in the club you go.' Excitement pulsed through his veins with every word. 'Then you tear the place apart. I mean max-eee-mum damage. Shooters plugging massive holes in the ceiling. The bar area riddled with lead. Punters running and screaming for their lives.' Cold steel hardened his voice. 'I want that crap hole put out of business for good.'

Harry was getting a hard on just thinking about what he had in store for Barker. Oh yes! This was what it was all about, alright. Harry congratulated himself on how clever he'd been, choosing heavies from around the country. None of them were Londoners. This was an old gangland trick

Robbie had taught him. Want a big job doing and the trail never leading back to you? Choose out of towners who don't know who you are. None of the gathered crew knew who Harry was or who Barker was. In fact, they knew sweet FA about the reason for the raid on the club.

All of the guys had come highly recommended from contacts with his Dad's firm in Liverpool, Manchester and Glasgow. They didn't have criminal records or clean skins as it was known in the trade and were vouched for by some seriously tough men. Crucially, if they were nabbed by the law there was nothing they could say that would put the Steele family in the shit. Harry had thought of everything.

His Father was soon going to find out who the rightful heir to his empire was. And it wasn't that dumb bitch crazy-Kristal with her knockers hanging out and skirt up her arse while her son sat on the throne.

'Can we expect much opposition?'

The sharp question lifted Harry out of his thoughts and back to the room. He found the asker, a thickset Scouser with a peanut-shaped shaved head and face of a psycho.

'The wank-job who runs the club has got a bit of a rep. Fancies himself a tasty geezer so there might be a bit of gunplay in response to our visit.' Harry deliberately downplayed Barker's notorious standing. The last thing he wanted was to put the wind up his temporary crew. He smiled showing all his teeth. 'But you don't look like the sort of gentlemen who'd be bothered by a bit of handbags on a Saturday night. You wouldn't be here if you were, now would you?'

Someone else chucked a question. This one was a little difficult to decipher. It sounded like, 'Wha aboot wahpons?'

'What's that?' Harry's features screwed up in confusion. Blimey, it was like being back at school. And Harry had hated school with a vengeance.

The guy mimicked the shape of a gun with his hand.

'Gotcha!' Harry nodded his understanding. 'What about weapons? Sorry, mate, I don't speak Scottish.'

Harry chuckled away at his own little joke. As soon as he clocked the guy's humourless expression, he cut the laughter short. The fellas in here looked like they dispensed thug-love every day of the week and were capable of selling their grannie if the price was right.

'Weapons will be provided on the evening. They'll be the latest in hi-spec, deadly firearms and totally untraceable.'

A bruiser with the physique of a farmhand but sounded like an actor in an ad for West Country pork pies. 'I've got a question.'

'Where do you hail from, young man?'

'Somerset originally.'

Harry cracked another of his lines to prove how confident he was in his role as a gangland boss. 'Somerset born and Somerset bred? Strong in the arm and thick in the head?'

The cold, deadly silent stare he got in reply suggested that while his Father might be able to josh with the staff, he wasn't quite at that level yet. 'What's your question?'

'Word is this raid is a double hander and there'll be

another team involved? But you haven't mentioned them?'

Harry was rendered speechless. When he finally found his tongue, he spluttered, 'Where did you hear this 'word'?'

'My guv'nor told me there's a lady in town looking for recruits for the exact same job as this one. Only she seemed a bit confused about the details, so he told me to take the gig with you instead.'

Kristal. Fucking Kristal.

Harry thought he was going to burst a blood vessel. She'd promised him – crossed her heart, hope to die – to leave recruitment until they had their planning meeting together. Then again, he reminded himself of his own plans. Plans that involved hooking up with his sister-in-law never seeing the light of day. He was planning to do this job on his own. It would be the only way to show the old man that he was capable of fitting in to Robbie's shoes.

Harry tried to pacify the man, a malicious grin hanging off the corner of his mouth. 'Don't you worry yourself about any ladies in town, mate.' He winked knowingly. 'Unless you're planning to hire one for the night with your winnings after the job. Know what I mean?'

That elicited sniggers from some of the others. Harry puffed his chest out with pride. If he could get this pack of cutthroats eating out of his hand, skies the limit when it came to what he could achieve as his Dad's successor.

'Why don't you lads pop on downstairs and get yourselves a jar or two. On the house o'course.'

Barely were they out of the room when Harry's phone went. It was his Father.

Harry swallowed convulsively. 'Alright, Dad? What's occurring?'

'Just checking in to find out how the plans for your *visit* to Barker's is going?'

The coke in his system pumped Harry to the brim with false confidence. 'All pukka, Dad. I've put a nifty team together. Top guys, the lot of 'em, totally reliable. I've worked it all out to the last detail. You put your feet up and enjoy the snooker on the telly. I've got this.'

'That's good to know, boy.' There was a long pause before Jimmy added, 'And Kristal? You've sorted out her end of the operation?'

Harry was fit to spit. The idea that pampered lady-who-lunches could play any role in a major league oppo like this was lol. But of course, he was under his Father's orders to plan things with Robbie's widow, so he was obliged to play along.

'Truth be told, I've left her messages a-plenty but she ain't got back. Don't wanna know. Probably topping up her tan in a beauty salon or getting her nails done. You know what birds are like.'

Jimmy Southpaw came back terse and adamant. 'I want her involved. I want to see how she handles herself. So, you'd better get on the ol' dog and keep trying.'

'You want the straight up truth, Dad?' Harry went in for the kill. 'I don't think Kristal can hack it. She's a bottle job.'

'He's not going to call, is he?' Kristal succinctly announced in the beauty salon.

She was indeed having her nails done. Tips attached, then glossed over with a classic French manicure. She was living the life of Riley, laid back on a recliner at her health club. One hand was being attended to by the nail technician while the other cradled a Pina Colada. The recliner's mechanical massager bucked and groaned emitting a sound like a man being choked to death. Kristal wasn't interested in all that BS about massages making you feel relaxed. Relaxed? Ha-fucking-ha to that! Nah! Getting her muscles plucked and pummelled made her feel amped up. Ready to take on the world.

Damien sat on a chair nearby, legs spread out, nursing a half pint. 'Who's not going to call?'

Gimme strength! 'Your Uncle Harry, ya lump. Who do you think I meant? The Dalai Lama?'

'Oh! Right.'

Kristal carried on as if she hadn't heard her son. 'Slippery little sod. He thinks if he locks me out, he can do Barker's place over all on his tod and get all the credit. That's why he ain't returning my calls. Why he's always *busy* 24/7. Planning to get the whole shebang done-n-dusted before I can get a look in. Then he'll be teacher's pet with the ol' man. He gets to be son and heir when the ol' boy retires, and we're left out in the cold.'

Damien could do little else but sigh. He was bored out of his box. Should've brought his latest digi gadget for company. He knew if he didn't answer his Mum, she'd go spare and probably attack him with one of the nail technician's very, very sharp implements. 'Better give grandad a bell then. Bring him up to speed with what's going on. Make him lay the law down to Uncle H.'

Kristal snatched her hand away from the manicurist. 'Alright, love, that's enough. I'll be down to me cuticles at this rate.'

When she was gone, Kristal turned on her son with a furious glare. 'Oh yeah, that's a cracking idea. Grass Harry up. Go bitching and moaning to Jimmy Southpaw, that's really going to make me...' She coughed to cover-up her slip up. 'I mean *you*, darlin', look like leadership material.'

Kristal let out a relieved sigh under her breath that her boy hadn't noticed her slip up. Once Damien became heir, she became the power behind the throne. The *real* power.

Damien took a slug of his beer and shrugged. 'What other choice have you got? Uncle H is disobeying the ol' fella's instructions. Just point out he's being disobedient and dissing you. You know where Grandad Jimmy is on that. Grass Harry up.'

Kristal hopped off the lounger and hunched down by her son's side. Somehow, she needed to get through his slow mind how important this was. She was doing this for his future. Her darlin' baby. Didn't he understand that?

'If Harry gets the job done and Barker's joint is a smoking ruin, do you think Grandad Southpaw's going to worry about how he did it? Do you think he's going to give your uncle a slap because I didn't get a starring role in the oppo? He ain't.'

Kristal drew in a deep agitated slug of air. 'He's going to give Harry a pat on the back for showing some initiative, slapping his balls on the table and taking the bullocks by the horns.' Her tone stiffened with fortitude. 'I ain't gonna let him get away with it. If your Dad's baby brother wants to play silly buggers, he'll find out I'm a bigger bugger than he is and no mistake.'

As Damien considered her words, that strange way he held his head sometimes become more pronounced. Finally, he gave his Mum his thoughts.

'Uncle H knows his onions. He's been in the loop for years. He knows where to find guys. Knows how to source shooters and plan an operation like this. Not being funny or nuthin', Mum, I'm sure you picked up a few tips from Dad over the years but a raid on a guy like Barker is a serious undertaking. Barker ain't gonna simply roll over and let you tickle his tummy. Say what you like about the geezer, but he's a fighter. If you try to get in and work him over before Uncle H, it'll be a shitshow for sure.'

Kristal looked around for something to hit her boy with. When nothing was available, she lunged up and cuffed him round the loaf.

'Ouch!' Damien held his head. 'Whatcha do that for?'

'You're a bigger tosspot than Harry.' Kristal was tempted to grab him and shake some common sense into him. 'I don't know how to plan? I don't know how to get guys? I don't know where to find shooters? We'll see about that. You'd be surprised who I know and what they're capable of.'

She stared off into the distance, her gaze seemingly fixed on the other occupants, ladies in bathrobes, bathing costumes and gym gear. Kristal saw none of that. Her imagination ran riot with scheme after scheme of getting one over that interfering, conniving, flash numpty Harry.

Kristal hissed, 'I'm going to knacker Barker before Harry gets the chance. I'm going to have your uncle's trousers down and spank his bare behind.'

Chapter Twenty

Even before he opened his mouth, Mo could see as plain as day that Barker was in a foul mood. He stalked across the club floor towards her, lip curled, brows snapped together and eyes bursting with a raging fire.

'Where the hell have you been? I've been on the blower to you for the last couple of hours.' The words hissed between his teeth. His face darkened alarmingly when he spotted Delilah. 'And what the four X is she doing here?'

Obviously, Barker had forgotten that Dell was his newest employee at the club.

Mo knew full well she had to keep a civil tongue in her head when it came to this man. Nevertheless, she got the proper hump coz she'd done sod all wrong. It wasn't in Mo's nature to end up doing the whole 'yes, Mister Barker, no, Mister Barker, three bags full, Mister Barker' routine. Deffo not in her nature. It had been a couple of weeks since the package and him testing how valuable she was, and she'd come up trumps.

Despite the brewing resentment Mo kept her response above board and respectful. 'I was on the Tube. You don't get any signal down there.' She absently added, jerking her chin in the direction of her cousin. 'And she works here. Cleaning…'

Her voice dribbled away as she finally took in the scene around her. The place was empty of customers and the staff were building barricades out of tables and chairs. What the double bubble toil and trouble was going on here? And why was the official music video for Craig David's 'Fill Me In' blaring from the huge wall-mounted screen if there were no punters around? Add to that Mo had never seen Barker looking this frazzled before. Something was clearly up. Very badly up.

'What's going on?' she demanded. 'Why aren't there any clubbers in the house?'

Barker shrieked at one of the guys across the room, 'Not there, ya plonker. Over there.'

He twisted back to Mo, mouth grimly compressed, a muscle ticking in his cheek. 'Jimmy Southpaw's people are paying us a visit for some high jinks.' Mo and Dell shared a meaningful look and sharp intake of breath. Barker looked at his watch. 'They'll be darkening our door in about thirty mins, so we need to be ready for them.'

The blood drained from Mo's face leaving her skin an ash-shaded brown. 'Half-hour?'

'I was expecting them next week but there's obviously been a change of plan. That's Jimmy Southpaw for you. Always trying to mix it up and catch you on your toes.'

Mo might still be on the bottom rung of learning about the bizz but even she knew the only way her boss would have an in on his deadly enemy's plans was if he had a snout in Southpaw's camp. There was no way she could ask Barker. Mo wasn't far enough up the pecking order for that.

Barker took Mo by the arm out to the foyer. 'About a dozen of them are coming. Southpaw's git, Harry, is the front man although he'll probably stay put in a motor somewhere in the vicinity.'

Mo rapidly blinked, soaking up all the info. If she was going to make it to the top tier of the underworld it was imperative that she remember and store all the dirty tricks of the trade that came her way.

Abruptly, she suggested, 'When they turn up, they'll probably have a wrinkle on hand to get past the door staff. Probably a couple of girls to put something in the window to distract the guys on the door.' She tilted her chin thoughtfully at him. 'If that's the plan there's two ways you can swing it boss. Either lure Harry Steele's mob deep into the club. Or take them out as soon as their jack boots step foot in the building.'

Barker was impressed and showed it. Mo restrained the smug smile from coming through. Her boss wasn't the only one with a bagful of dirty tricks.

'We want them in the palm of our heavily armed hands on the dance floor. That's why the music video's on, to create the illusion that it's a regular night here.' He placed his large hands around her arm, the gravity of the situation showing in the heat coming off his flesh.

'I'm putting you in charge of a small crew here in the foyer, all nicely hidden away. When Harry Steele's mob come steam rolling through, you jack-in-the-box them and start caning them from the rear. That will push them into the dance floor—'

'And we give them the hiding of a lifetime from the back and front.' Mo expertly finished off, adrenaline pumping like crazy through her veins.

Barker's fingers dug deeper into her skin, no doubt leaving bruises. 'This is an important job, Mo. Don't fuck it up, girl.'

He let go of her and produced a set of keys. 'In the top drawer of my desk in my office you'll find a pistol.'

The air sharpened and caught in Mo's throat at the mention of a gun. She'd only had that one opportunity to get familiar with a shooter doing target practice with Josh. She didn't want to acknowledge how hard and fast her heart was suddenly beating against the walls of her chest. The weight of hard metal in her hand. A finger on the trigger. Pull. Bang! Bang! That would change her life forever. Mo toughened her spine. She was prepared to do this. She had to be.

But what if she killed someone? Took a life?

Before she could grapple with the terrifying question, Barker was telling her, 'Don't use it unless you have to. It's always a drag having to get rid of dead bodies. Let's move!'

Mo rounded up her cousin, Dell, and hurried down to Barker's basement office. She felt terrible about putting her innocent, church-going cousin in harm's way and if her Mum ever found out she'd put Dell in danger … Mo shuddered.

And that's why she instructed her wide-eyed relative, 'Park yourself in the boss's flash chair. Sit tight in here. I'll catch-up with you later.'

Mo rolled her eyes when Dell did exactly that but with her small rucksack on her back. What was it with her and that bag? Mo swiftly put it out of her mind as she focused on the job at hand. Dell gasped in heart-stopping horror when Mo took the gun out of the drawer and found a length of lead pipe in another.

The words shook from Dell's mouth. 'Cousin Mo! What are you doing with Satan's plaything? And that other tool of the Devil?'

'Stay put. Lock the door after I've gone.'

'Keep your heads down and your mouths shut and don't move till I give the order,' Mo ordered the four men concealed with her behind the cash desk in the foyer.

Although she spoke with the natural command of a general to her soldiers, Mo still expected at least one of them to get stroppy and start bitching about taking orders from a woman. Men needed to get with the programme and realise this was the twenty-first century where that kinda backwards shit was yesterday's news. She waited, a dare-ya expression gleaming in her eyes. And relaxed when Barker's boys nodded.

It was ten minutes till kick off.

Five minutes.

Two.

But then, at the last moment, Mo realised all of them

hiding left the front of house looking suspiciously deserted. Southpaw's thugs would know something was up. Mo jumped up and took over the register just in time. Harry Steele's heavies booted through the entrance. Padded and tooled up, masked and ready to take care of business. Obviously they were skipping the lovely ladies of the night diversion plan.

Mo threw her hands up in mock terror nicely carried through with a hysterical scream as she took refuge beneath the register. Her hand pressed the button for the automatic lock to open the door to the main dance room. Like lambs to the slaughter Harry's men stormed past her straight into the trap waiting for them in the other room. The gang rushed inside, waving their weapons, screaming and shouting.

Mo called her squad of men to arms. Pushed through the door to attack Harry's people from behind and block their line of retreat. She didn't wait to see how things were going although it was obvious Barker's people were in retreat under the banshee onslaught of Harry's crew.

Mo wasn't having that! She swung her lead pipe, catching one of the enemy across the back of the head with a sickening crack of heavy metal against bone. Dazed, he sank to his knees mumbling in a Scottish accent. Finally, he tumbled unconscious on to his face.

The fight ran pell-mell across the dance floor with Mo in the thick of it. Josh materialised by her side fighting for all he was worth. In the melee no one noticed the door swing open again and another dozen masked and hooded figures joined the battle. But Mo did. Not only did the new arrivals seem to be led by a curvy woman who was intent on taking no prisoners, the new gang, togged out in overalls and masks seemed to be an all-female crew.

Mind buzzing as she kept up the fight, Mo tried to unravel what was happening? Did the new arrivals mean that Harry was commanding two different gangs? If that was the case, whoever was Barker's leak in Southpaw's outfit hadn't done their homework too well.

It was a three-way gang battle now but no one was quite sure who was fighting who or where these women had come from although they were putting on quite a good show with their weapons. The dance floor was littered with the wounded and broken. Harry's men kept pressing forward winning new ground. The gang of women kept pressing forward winning new ground. Mo and Barker's men were almost pinned up against the back wall. Angry tears burnt the bottom of Mo's eyes as she sensed defeat. No way was she going to be taken.

Her ears began ringing, buzzing with the dehumanising insults of the school bullies:

'Titch.'

'Short-arse.'

'Pint-sized dwarfy.'

No! No! No! Mo shook her head. The memories of every time those evil girls knocked her down and how she'd staggered back on her feet gave her strength. Her foot thrust out to kick someone. Her lead pipe went up and down. But it didn't matter how brave she fought, Barker and her were still losing. The wall was almost at their back...

What happened next was one of those events Mo would never forget. In a blur, a figure leapt into the room, wearing a loose hoodie under a baseball cap. In a criss-cross motion this person flung their arms over their shoulders and unzipped the bag on their back. In a flash, from the bag they produced two brutally sharp-edged, gleaming, wicked looking machetes. The newcomer waved the huge knives high, let out a bellow and went after Club Class' attackers with the fury of a ninja, laying into the attackers with sweeping, cutting motions. Whoever this badass assassin was they gave Mo and Barker's men renewed energy. They started fighting back. Really fighting back.

Mo kept flicking sideways glances at the machete-wielding individual. Something about them was very familiar. She couldn't put her finger … Then it came to her.

No. Fucking. Way.

As she peered closer her gaze widened with incredulity.

Delilah?

Her ankle sock wearing, church-going, 'we must love each other' cousin? Mo couldn't believe it. *Is that why Dell keeps the rucksack on her back all the time? Because she carries machetes around with her?*

Before Mo could grapple with the unbelievable, Harry's battered gang and the gang of women, buckled, bent and finally fled towards the exit, chased by a triumphant Mo. On the busy street outside, masks were discarded, and Harry's gang and the women melted into the night-time crowds.

What had Barker said about Harry? Oh yeah! He'd be lurking somewhere close by keeping an eye on proceedings in his car. Determined to have a reckoning with him she hunted Harry down. It didn't take her long. He was stupidly easy to find because a furious row was going on by the driver's window of a Mercedes saloon.

The fearless woman who'd led the posse of women was giving him a severe tongue-lashing. 'You wait till your ol' man hears about this, Harry. You'd better book a plot next to my dearly departed husband, you're going to be needing it.'

Kristal Steele. That's who Mo sussed was doing the verbal.

Harry scoffed, a half-gone ciggy in his hand. 'My boys would have been fine if you hadn't brought the ladies gym class from your health club down here.' He knew full well Kristal's crew had been a gang of professionals to the core. 'What was the plan? To distract Barker's crew with handstands? Some aerobics? You dumb bitch.'

When Kristal saw Mo approaching, she hissed at Harry, 'Watch out, mate, here comes Barker's boss girl. Perhaps she's going to do a handstand for you? I hope your car's insured.' With that, she disappeared into the night.

Mo raised her lead pipe to smash Harry's windscreen. But she stopped short when he leant out of his window with a cocksure grin.

'Alright, babe. There's no need to smash my wheels up, now is there? That would be gratuitous.' He gestured at her with his cigarette while she stood with her arm still raised. 'You're good. I like you. I think you're going to go a long way in this business.' Mo was so shocked by his compliment she let him leave without doing a thing.

As he drove away, an exhausted Mo lowered her arm and walked back to Club Class. As soon as she entered, she heard the screams. She ran for it. Into the main room. And skidded to a halt at what she found. Everyone was looking up towards the ceiling. Mo's heart dropped into the abyss beneath her feet.

Hanging from the railings in the VIP lounge by the tips of her fingers into thin air was Twinkle.

OMG! Shattering shock held Mo immobile. Then her hand instinctively flew to her mouth in horror. What was her best friend doing here? None of this made sense.

'Mo! Help me!' Twinkle's plea was a high-pitched shrill, filled with fright.

Mo was already on the move as she shouted back, 'Twinkle, hun, you keep those fingers tight. I'm coming.'

Twinkle's right hand slipped off the rail. She screamed, desperately clinging to the rail with one hand. Everyone gasped as she swung in the air.

Mo had never run so fast in her young life.

'Don't move,' she yelled.

Twinkle moved. Her hand slipped. And she kept falling and falling.

Chapter Twenty-One

Mo was climbing the walls of the Royal London Hospital, known locally as The London. She was in the intensive care unit. And in despair. The deepest, darkest despair she'd ever known. Why wouldn't any of the doctors let her know how Twinkle was doing? After two hours surely, *surely*, they must have something to tell her?

Her earlier triumph at seeing off Jimmy Southpaw's crew had shrivelled up and died. Mo wanted to die too. She wanted to howl at the moon. How could the bestest best friend in the world be…?

Acid bile rose thick in her throat.

As long as she lived, the image of Twinkle's twisted body on the floor would remain with her. Especially one of her legs, sticking out at a crooked, ugly angle. Twinkle had been so still, eyes closed tight. And the blood seeping and spreading like thick, red poison. Mo thought her bestie was a goner, for sure. Then Twinkle had whimpered, the sound of a battered, defenceless animal crying for help. Mo had screamed her lungs out for someone – *anyone* – to get an ambulance.

Barker had put the kybosh on that. An ambulance was a no-no. A 999 call would bring the plod to their door too. Instead they'd got Twinkle down to the hospital in Josh's motor, with him driving. Once there, they'd shouted the odds for help. Mo understood when Josh told her that it would be better if he did a disappearing act and left her to it.

Mo came back to the present with a start when she heard her name being called. The butterflies in her belly fluttered madly when she saw the grave expression on the doctor's face.

Mo rushed over. 'Is Twinkle alright?'

The doctor smiled slightly at the use of her friend's nickname. 'Priscilla is comfortable for now.' She then appeared uncomfortable, reluctantly adding, 'But I won't be able to tell you anything else about her condition because you're not her family. I can only speak to her next of kin.'

That would be Twinkle's disgusting excuse for a Mother. The hospital had got on the phone to her after Mo had grudgingly given them Sheena Brodie's details.

Mo asked, voice so small even she could barely hear it, 'I can see her though?'

The doctor nodded, but warned, 'Not for too long. She's sedated and needs her rest.'

A shaft of pure pain stabbed and twisted inside Mo's heart at her first sight of Twinkle. It was so fierce she had to hang on to the doorframe to prevent her legs crumbling under her.

Oh God! No! No! No!

Her mind screamed each word with helpless heartbreak. Beneath the sheets, Twinkle was laid out like a corpse ready for its silent journey to the morgue. Her face was as white as chalk, her arms lifeless by her side. Mo couldn't hold the sobs back. They came harsh and hard and hurting. Tears gushed down her cold cheeks, her heart breaking into a thousand, tiny pieces.

Mo wiped the back of her hand across her runny nose and bloodshot eyes as she finally made the awful trek towards Twinkle. As soon as she reached the bed, Mo laid her hand over her best friend's. The cold, clammy feel of Twinkle's flesh went straight through her.

Mo broke down, head wretchedly bowed. 'I'm so sorry, Twinkle. So sorry. If I hadn't taken that job at Barker's you'd have never gone to the club in the first place. I don't know what you were doing there but I know you wouldn't have come to the club if it wasn't for me.'

Guilt. It burnt through every fibre of Mo as corrosive as acid. A part of her mind reasoned that she hadn't invited Twinkle up to the club. That her best friend had turned up out of the blue. But it still didn't stop Mo taking the blame for Twinkle's presence at Club Class. The fact of the matter was Mo would always feel responsible for Twinkle. The weight of her guilt was one of the worst things she had ever experienced in her life.

The door swung open with such force it crashed against the wall. Sheena Brodie staggered through doorway. Fecking hell! She looked like she'd just emerged from an all-night rave in an LBD that barely covered her Notorious VAG. The caked layers of slap only emphasised the hollows of her cheeks and crustiness of her lips. A potent rage seized Mo when she noticed the man accompanying Twinkle's Mum.

Eric 'Slime-ball' Brown.

The man who'd had his evil way with Twinkle and who a respected family accused of raping their fourteen-year-old girl. The way he had his arm possessively around Sheena Brodie's shoulder it was clear for all to see that he'd moved his evil affections from daughter to Mum. He leered at Mo, licking his lips with obvious malicious satisfaction at seeing her again.

How dare Twinkle's Mum bring him here! How bloody dare she!

Before Mo could create noise about it, Twinkle's Mum hysterically cried out, 'Where's my girl? Where is she?'

When she finally clapped eyes on her unconscious daughter she threw her arms dramatically in the air and let out a biblical wail of anguished agony that was enough to bring down the walls of Jericho.

'Lord above and all the saints and sweet Mother Mary. What's happened to my baby? Who did this to my beautiful little angel?'

She pulled out a tissue, stuffed her face into it, sobbing and wailing uncontrollably. It was an emotional performance, no doubt about it. If it had been delivered by anyone else Mo would have believed it. But this was Sheena Brodie. The worst Mum in the universe. Mo's mouth drooped with revulsion. It was all for show. Sheena didn't give a rat's bollocks about her kid.

It didn't take long for Sheena to prove her right. Her snuffling abruptly stopped when she tugged out a flask filled with the hard stuff and knocked it back. What a fake up drama queen. Un-fucking-believable! Sheena wiped the back of a hand across her mouth as she moved towards her daughter, swaying like a drunken branch in the wind. When she reached the bed, her fingers twisted in the blanket to stop herself from falling flat on her face. What a total show up.

Sheena shook her head, gazing down wildly at her daughter. 'My brave, brave girl. Mummy knows how to put you to rights.' Before Mo could intervene, Sheena tipped her daughter's head forward and thrust the flask of booze to her lips. 'Go on. Get that down you. This will sort you out.' Of course Twinkle's lips didn't move and the amber liquid dribbled down the sides of her mouth, dripping off her chin.

'Come on,' her Mum insisted, getting ratty. 'You loved the stuff when you was a nipper much more than a good guzzle on my nipples. A spoonful of it in your bottle and away you were with the fairies. Not a peep out of you all night long.'

Mo looked on in jaw-dropping disbelief. Was she hearing right? Sheena had boozed up Twinkle as a baby? Such a rage came over Mo she didn't quite know how to deal with it. How could someone as saintly, as pure hearted as Twinkle have come out of that bitch's belly?

'Get away from her,' Mo demanded, waving her arm over Twinkle to make Sheena back off as if she were warding off the most corrupt evil.

Sheena fixed Mo with a malevolent, accusing stare. 'As

soon as the ozzie calls me, I knew you would be involved in this. I says to Twinkle, I tells her, that darkie kid is going to drag you into the gutter one of these days. She'll have you mugging old grannies on the street before you know it. But she wouldn't listen to me.'

Mo wasn't shocked at the other woman's blatant racism. She had never cottoned to the colour of Mo's skin from the get-go. What did hurt, hurt Mo so bad, was that for once she thought Twinkle's monster of a Mum was right. This was all her doing. The only reason Twinkle had been at the club was because of her.

Mo stammered emotionally back, 'I didn't mean for any of this to happen.'

Sheena bared her teeth, rounding on her daughter's best friend. 'Look at her,' she screamed in Mo's face, ranting like a mad woman. All Mo could do was stand there, shaking and take it. 'The quack says her hip's all busted up. Probably gonna end up a cripple. And I tell you this for nothing, I ain't looking after no gimp.' She spat, 'Says she's gonna need help in the khazi. Well, I'll tell you this for free, I ain't wiping her arse.'

Mo wanted to slam her palms over her ears. Twinkle never being able to walk again? It can't be true! Can't be true! If only she could wind the clock back. Go back to this morning and start all over again. All she wanted to do was curl up and cry her guts out.

Sheena Brodie inched her neck into Mo's space in the motion of a snake hissing before it strikes. 'Is that why you're here? To finish my girl off?' She shoved her face so close Mo could see the blackheads peppering her skin and the river of red veins of an alcoholic woven into her nose.

A new voice thundered into the room. 'Lady, you better *shut* your potato trap and give your tongue a holiday. You best leave my baby-gal be.'

Brother Bertie stood in the doorway, leaning on his stick, an avenging angel ready to do battle. His porkpie hat was tilted to the side, half on, half off.

Sheena looked him up. And down. 'Who the fuck are you to come in here—?'

'I'll tell you who I am.' Brother Bertie didn't let her finish. He raised his stick and pointed it at her as he advanced in the room. 'I'm your worst nightmare, is what I am.'

Sheena Brodie's face paled, her gaze riveted on the tip of Mo's grandfather's walking stick. Her feet shuffled back as he kept pushing forward. The backs of her legs hit the armchair and she tumbled into the seat. At no point did Eric Brown wade in on Sheena's behalf. In fact, he stood there with his arms crossed. Coward!

Brother Bertie pointed the stick down at her. He was spitting mad. 'My grandbaby-gal is the only friend your girl has ever had. *Ever*. Do you hear me?'

Twinkle's Mum knew when to keep it zipped.

Brother Bertie went on in a furious tone. 'When she was eight, do you know what your daughter whispered to me? She tells me, "Brother Bertie, I'm so hungry at night I sneak to the kitchen and cram dry Cornflakes into my mouth and pretend they're crisps." You're lucky I never set the social on your skin, you evil woman.'

He leant down, the ferocity with which he dished it out making his porkpie almost topple off. 'I give Twinkle the biggest bowl of my home-made oxtail, yam and dumpling soup. I've never seen anyone eat food so quick. She licked the bowl clean. LICKED IT CLEAN!!! From that day forward Twinkle became my blood. You hurt Twinkle, you hurt me.'

Sheena yelped when he shook the stick over her. 'If I ever hear you running that filthy trap of yours again against my granddaughter, have the nerve to comment on the colour of her beautiful skin, being Twinkle's Mum isn't going to stop me hunting you down and showing you that my stick isn't simply made for walking. Got it?'

He kissed his teeth loudly and turned his head to Mo. 'We're off.'

Mo shook her head. 'I can't—'

'Now!' Brother Bertie wouldn't brook no backchat.

Mo pressed her lips with the lightest touch to her bestie's icy cheek. 'East End Girls Forever.'

For the first time ever, Twinkle didn't whisper back.

As soon as she made it to the corridor Mo collapsed into her gramps' secure, waiting arms and sobbed her heart out.

Chapter Twenty-Two

'It went tits up because numb-nuts here put in a late appearance.'

'Late? You pulled a fast one on me about what time we agreed to meet up.'

'Fast one? Anything quicker than a snail's jacksie crawling is fast to you.'

Jimmy barely held his temper in check, glaring with livid disdain at Harry and Kristal who went for each other's throats like gladiators fighting to the death. The friction of Steele against Steele made the sparks fly inside his office at the bookies. The Ping-Pong back and forth between them made his head throb. Set his teeth on a razor's edge.

He'd had enough.

'Shut. The. Fuck. Up. The pair of youse.'

His bellowed instruction reverberated around the room. He had ordered them both here for a post-mortem on what the naffing Nora had gone wrong with the raid on Barker's tonight.

Harry directed his gaze to the floor. He was ashamed and couldn't look his Dad in the eye. He should have figured out

Kristal was up to no good. Smiling with those bleached, double-decker's she called teeth in his face, while, all the time, plotting and planning how to lure him into her booby trap. The bitch had stolen his golden opportunity to demonstrate and convince his Dad, the legendary Jimmy Southpaw, that he was the natural heir to his empire.

Inwardly he seethed. How could his Dad even entertain giving his throne to that puppy Damien? You wouldn't even know the little shit was in the room right now because he sat as quiet as a beached whale letting his Mum be his mouthpiece. I mean, what kind of top boss does that? Eh?

Harry wouldn't forget what Kristal had done. Getting even with that brass was going to be his number one priority.

Harry observed his Dad ease back in his exec chair. As per usual Violet was close by his side. And, as per, she looked as vacant as the Bates Motel. Don't get him wrong, he loved his big sis, but when his day came he was going to shut her away in a residential somewhere on the Kent coast.

'Tonight's been a major league botch job,' his Dad started, tone balanced and even. 'Not much we can do about it now.'

Kristal and Harry snapped disbelieving sneak peeks at each other shocked at Jimmy's easy-going manner. His enemy, Barker, had just delivered a crushing defeat and Jimmy Southpaw looked like he was getting ready to slip on his slippers with a mug of cocoa by the fire. He should be cursing. Smashing the furniture. Shaking his fist. Vowing revenge.

'There's plenty of time to put Barker back in his box,

preferably encased in concrete at the bottom of one of those new developments on The Island,' he carried on in the same surprising, chilled out fashion. He got to his feet. 'Both of you get some sleep. Tomorrow's another day. We'll put our heads together and come up with a new plan.'

That fleeting, astonished look passed between his son and daughter-in-law again. Was this for real? Maybe Robbie's passing coupled with grief had truly pickled the old man's brain? Whatever the reason, Harry and Kristal breathed a collective sigh of relief that they'd escaped the executioner's axe.

He embraced them both and gave Damien an extra manly hug and slap on the back before they left.

'Robbie…? Stop it … You know the rules,' Kristal Mumbled and tossed and turned restlessly in her sleep at the feel of her husband's fingers tiptoeing inside her leg heading directly for her pot of treasure.

They had an arrangement. Her pussy was off limits. His prick was sweetened in honeypots outside the marital home.

'Robbie, I've flipping well told you…'

Kristal bolted up as if freezing ice water had been chucked over her. Realisation dawned. That couldn't be Robbie touching her up. He was dead.

Her eyelids punched open in chilling alarm. Her heart went into free-fall as she stifled a scream. Two hulking brutes stood either side of her bed. Their black clothing blending them into the shadows. She couldn't see their faces. Then she clocked another one. The bastard with his hand up her baby doll on her leg.

Kristal barred her teeth as she snatched her leg away. 'Get your filthy mitts off me, you perv. Whatcha doing here?'

One of the others answered. 'You need to come with us. Any dramatics and one of us will go upstairs and make sure your son never wakes up.' He shaped his hand into a shooter just in case she didn't get his drift.

Damien! Kristal couldn't allow any harm to come to her boy. Then again … her side eye slid to her bedside unit drawer…

'Looking for this?' the one who had dared put his hands on her lazily asked. Her handgun dangled from his finger. A nifty and deadly little piece that Robbie had presented her with on their honeymoon.

Kristal knew when she was beaten. But she gave them a chilling warning:

'You wanna kiss your wife and sweethearts real long the next opportunity you get because it's going to be the last time you do it. Jimmy Southpaw is going to put you and your bastard boss, Barker, six feet under.'

They gagged her after that. Slung her over a shoulder and took her from her house.

Harry didn't see trouble coming until it literally boshed him in the mouth. After leaving the bookies he'd indulged in some sweet lovin' and sweeter cocaine. He was humming like a lovesick idiot. Nothing like hot, hard coke-filled sex to restore his balance.

Unfortunately for him, it also meant that his guard was down. So he never saw the one-two combination that connected to the side of his head and jaw. He hit the ground like a lead balloon. A hacking cough seized him as he rolled in brutal pain. The nasty metallic taste of blood filled up his mouth.

'If you ever get jumped, make sure that your first blow inflicts maximum damage. That will cause a chink in their armour or make 'em scarper.' That's the advice Robbie had bestowed on him when they were growing up.

So Harry kicked out, hooked his foot around the ankle of one of his assailants to bring him down … One of the others was one step ahead of him and smashed him on the leg with a scaffolding pole filled with concrete. A piercing shriek shot out of his mouth.

Harry was no trouble after that. They bound him up the same way they had Kristal. Except, he was not given the luxury of a fireman's lift. He was dragged along the road like a hog being taken to the slaughterhouse.

Harry and Kristal were nearly pissing themselves with terror. They were chained to the track of one of East London's Docklands Light Railway Stations, which had closed down for the night hours ago. Petrified, they lay side by side like Penelope-bloody-Pitstop. The station was high above ground level, open-aired, which left Kristal and Harry exposed to the early morning elements. The wind was frosty and hostile, turning the temperature of the sweat coating their bodies to minus zero.

Suddenly one of the four thugs who stood at the edge of the platform keeping an eagle eye on them jumped down and yanked the tape from their mouths.

They both started broadcasting in stereo at once:

'Barker, you're gonna die for this, you scumbag.'

'My son's gonna hunt you down.'

The man put a halt to their noise with the help of a serrated-edged knife above their faces. Satisfied they understood the score he got back on to the platform.

Silence. Then footsteps. Coming closer. Out of the darkness.

Barker.

Except, it wasn't Barker who emerged from the shadows.

Jimmy Southpaw did. Along with his shadow, Violet.

He watched as the gut-sickening truth dawned on those two wallies. As they actually, for once in their pathetic lives, used their nut to put two and two together and not come back with five. Finally, they figured out that the earlier sit-down at his HQ was them being expertly manipulated into a false sense of security. His way of getting them to take their eyes off the ball. And they had done that BIG TIME. Morons, the pair of them. They should have sussed that his earlier reaction was out of character. Jimmy Southpaw forgive a trespass? No. Fucking. Way.

'Did you really think there would be no come back from the Barker balls-up?' He finally asked them, his words a cold, rasped whisper in the morning dark. 'That Jimmy Southpaw was going to let it go with a 'let's work it out tomorrow' holding hands therapy session?'

'Dad—'

'Dad—'

The last thing he was in the mood for was any interrupted, cry-baby nonsense. So, he pulled out a semi. Their gobs instantly snapped shut. Then Jimmy Southpaw took out a silencer attachment. Fastened it to the nozzle of the gun with excruciating, corkscrew slowness. Kristal and Harry's ragged and terror-stricken breathing rose high disturbing the air. They kept a lid on it though. Didn't try to reason or beg for their lives. No one needed to tell them that Jimmy with his finger on the trigger was a very dangerous man. A very dangerous man indeed.

He glanced over his shoulder to casually wave the shooter at the D.L.R station logo sign mounted on the platform. 'These trains were one of the best things to happen to the East End. After the docks closed, parts of the East End almost died. Became a wasteland. No one wanted to know them no more.'

His tone was jaunty, as if he was telling some kids a bedtime story.

'Then this railway comes along and changes everything. Connects places and people. Helps my beautiful East London breathe again. Everyone's as shaggy-dog happy as a mutt with two tails coz the train don't have a driver. It can steer itself without a human being at the controls. Like magic. Fancy that, eh?'

He swung his hard gaze back to them. 'Hopes were higher than a hippy on acid. But do you know what happened when they did a test run with one of the first trains on this nifty piece of railway?'

No response. Good. They were finally getting it through

their dense dumb noodles that he did not want either of them butting their whinging mouths in. He was silently flexing his power. Re-establishing who was boss. Who was the geezer with his finger on the control button?

'It goes chug-chug-chugging along, on its merry way. Guess what happens when it comes in the station? It keeps on chugging and chugging and chugging … Right over the bleedin' edge, it goes. Crash! Bang! Fucking wallop!'

In a heartbeat his tone switched to deadly serious. 'See where I'm going here? I decide to take my hands off the wheel of my organisation and hand over the steering to Sooty and Sweep here. And what occurs? My fecking business is almost derailed—'

Harry's mouth got in the way of his brain. 'Nah! That weren't my fault, Dad. She—'

Growling, out of patience, Jimmy Southpaw pumped two bullets into the tiny section of the railway track that separated Kristal from Harry. She yelped while Harry let out a strange, grinding noise from the back of his throat.

Jimmy Southpaw was in a proper rant now. 'I told you both to have a sit-down, put your loaves together and sort out the best way to shut Barker down. It's called fucking teamwork.'

Jimmy trembled with such fury it looked like he was about to lose the plot. 'And the way I hear it, Barker's got some girl, some kid who probably only came out of her Mum's womb yesterday in the maternity ward up at The London, who pissed all over you and run you off.' He spat on the track with revulsion. 'Maybe she's the one I should be asking to step into Robbie's shoes?'

Kristal was the one who finally said something her Father-by-law wanted to hear. 'You're right,' she responded calmly and, more importantly, respectfully. 'We loused it up. Robbie would've covered all bases. Planned it down to a T. Ain't that right?' She twisted her head as much as possible to her brother-in-law.

'Uh? Yeah. Yeah. Won't happen again, Dad.'

One of the most feared faces in London stared down at them in the choking silence. Nodded as he put his shooter away. 'You better make sure it don't. Because you better believe one thing: I ain't putting second best and second rate in Robbie's chair.'

His chest expanded as he breathed in the bracing, fresh air. 'You both decided to chuck each other under the bus and look where it's got you – nearly under a train. Talking of trains…' He took out a key and tossed it on to the gravel between them on the track. 'The only way you're going to get out of that chain is to work together to get that key. Then undo the padlock. *Teambloodywork*.'

Harry and Kristal's mouths slackened. Their heads turned and stared at each other.

Jimmy Southpaw checked his watch. 'You'll need to hurry it along though.' He started striding away as he casually continued, 'Apparently, there's one of those fuel trains that don't stop here coming through in thirty-three minutes.'

Chapter Twenty-Three

How Mo was managing to stand upright on the stairs the next morning she had no idea. She was wiped out. Emotionally drained. The way she felt gave a new meaning to the phrase, 'dead on your feet.' Sleep had been elusive last night. When she had managed to catch some, she'd tossed and turned in a tortuous nightmare. It was a terrifying re-run of Twinkle precariously suspended in the air by one arm, face filled with hopeless horror screaming for her life.

Help me! Help me! Help me! She'd screamed at Mo over and over again. It had wrenched Mo out of her sleep, her skin soaked in sweat, chest heaving uncontrollably as hot tears spilled down her cheeks.

The hospital must be sick to the back teeth of Mo because she'd been on the phone to them three times already this morning. The news was Twinkle was stable, hanging on in there.

'Probably gonna end up a cripple.'

Twinkle Mum's hateful and hurtful words haunted Mo. Was it true? Would Twinkle end up disabled? The hospital wouldn't give her a definitive answer because she wasn't next of kin or family. See, that's where they were wrong. She was family. The closest family Twinkle had. Family were the people who cared for you. In times of trouble provided a shoulder to lean on. Stood behind your back in case you were frightened you might fall. Family were everything. That's what she and Twinkle were to each other – everything.

How could it be right that the only family that the hospital would recognise was a Mother who'd tried to flush her unborn daughter down the lav when she found herself in the family way? How the living hell could that be family?

Mo shook off the dispiriting questions and refocused her attention on another family drama.

Delilah.

Mo's expression hardened, her hand tightening with tension on the bannister as she heard her cousin singing a hymn in the kitchen. She still couldn't believe what she'd witnessed last night during the attack on the club. Her fire and brimstone cousin, Dell, whipping out two lethal machetes from her rucksack and swinging into action like she was the East End's version of Bruce Lee and Jackie Chan rolled into one. And another thing, Mo realised that the voice singing in the kitchen sounded more South London than Jamaican.

Dell had a lot of explaining to do.

'Cousin Mo! What a beautiful morning.' Dell greeted Mo when she stepped into the kitchen. Strange thing, her accent had become pure Jamaican again. 'Doesn't it make you glad to be alive when the sun is shining, and the birds are singing?'

Mo pulled up a chair and sourly observed her cousin slicing and dicing tomatoes with a kitchen knife. It was an expert performance as the toms were turned into tiny pieces and swept into a bowl. But as Mo was coming to see, her cousin was good at all kinds of performances.

Mo observed the wicked looking scar on Dell's hand that she'd first noticed the day she'd picked her cousin up from the airport. What had her cousin's explanation been? Oh, yeah! Hard work. Hard work no doubt associated with violence. And hadn't she noticed at the airport that Dell had amazing leg muscles. The type needed to leap around while expertly wielding two monster knives.

Mo's mouth thinned into a humourless line, gesturing pointedly at the tomatoes. 'You're doing a very good job with that kitchen knife. Then again you know all about bladed cutlasses, don't you?' Mo's eyes widened with mock horror as she dramatically placed her fingers over her mouth. 'Oops! Sorry! I meant bladed cutlery.'

Dell was beginning to look uncomfortable. 'Yes, well, back home, we all learn…'

Mo slammed her palms so hard on the table a few diced toms bounced up, dancing in the air. 'Cut the crap, Dell. I'm not talking about kitchen utensils. I'm talking about those razor-sharp machetes you were swinging around last night at the club like Long John Silver.'

A flash of insolence briefly flickered in Dell's eyes as she protested in a Jamaican accent, although it was fading fast. 'You mean the cutlasses? We all have those back home. We use them to cut sugar cane.'

The nerve! The absolute bare arsed nerve!

'Really?' Mo shot back furiously. 'Expecting to cut a lot of sugar cane in the East End, are you? And where exactly is back home anyway? You're about as Jamaican as a London bus. In fact, you're less Jamaican than a London bus because a London bus might actually have a Jamaican on it.'

Dell saw the game was up. 'What does it matter where I'm from?' Her voice was pure South London with a tiny strain of Jamaican in it that you'd expect since their family was from the Caribbean.

'It matters to me.' Mo shoved to her feet. 'All that talk in Barker's office when you called the shooter, Satan's plaything.'

Dell huffed, 'OK. OK. I'm your cuz from Croydon—'

Mo butted in. 'Croydon? What's with the wide-eyed innocent country girl in the big city malarkey act for? I should've sussed you were bogus when the woman at the info desk at the airport said there were no flights from Jamaica that day. All that crap about Miami. You've really made a plonker out of me, haven't you?'

Dell reset the position of her body to that of cocky South London street girl you didn't want to mess with. 'Just be grateful you've got a guardian angel who's asked me to look after you. And you're going to need looking after. Trust me. And I know how to look after people.'

Mo stared at her shocked. 'Guardian angel?' She couldn't get her head around what she was hearing. 'What guardian angel? And why do I need looking after?' More importantly, 'Who set you up to do this?'

The other woman shook her head emphatically. 'That I can't say.' She continued in a hushed tone. 'Believe me when I tell you that this person has your best interests at heart.'

Mo's head was swimming. She couldn't understand any of this. Why would someone want to protect an eighteen-year-old girl on the make? She was a no one on the underworld radar. Unless…

'Is it Barker?' He was the only one that made sense.

Her cuz arched a brow refusing to confirm or deny.

Mo kept up the pressure. 'And why would they ask *you* to look out for me?'

Suddenly Mo could visibly see the hard girl that Dell was revealed in every nook and cranny in her face. 'Let's just say I'm handy and leave it at that.' She had that right … handy with a pair of vicious machetes. Her cousin cautioned her, 'Your Mum and Brother Bertie are none the wiser about any of this. So, let's keep this between you and me. I have something for you.'

Delilah left and went upstairs leaving Mo confused and flummoxed. Was Barker her guardian angel? But when they'd met, she hadn't known him from Adam. And how would he have known to connect to Dell? Mo's head throbbed trying to make sense of it all.

Before she could join the dots her cuz returned. In her hand Dell held a strange looking necklace that resembled a black shoelace. Attached was a small black spider with legs made of strange knots. It looked well creepy. To Mo's distaste, Delilah placed it around her neck. Mo went to yank it off, but Dell stayed her hand.

'It's a charm necklace.' Dell's whole demeanour told Mo that her cousin was being dead serious. 'It will protect you.'

Mo's lips rippled with disgust. 'But it's horrible.'

'The more freaky they look the more powerful the protection,' Dell adamantly insisted. 'It belonged to my Mother and it kept her safe. When she was attacked in her home by a man, it warded him off.'

Mo wasn't convinced and lifted a dubious brow. 'A charm-spider warded this burglar off?'

'Yeah, it did. Well that and a semi-automatic she kept on her bedside table. But it was the charm mainly. I promise you that with this charm round your neck and me by your side, you can face any danger head on.'

Mo sent her a quizzical and assessing look. 'So, you ain't one of them hell and damnation church ladies?'

As Dell straightened Mo's spider, she stayed closed mouthed for a few seconds. Then, 'I believe in God. But the world of the duppy and spirits is strong too.'

A shiver slivered down Mo's spine. Her gramps had told her all about duppies and jumbees and other types of spirits and ghosts who inhabited the Caribbean. When he spoke of them it was always in a hushed, reverential tone as if he was terrified of waking them. Mo thought it all sounded like a load of ol' cockle frankly … Still, she stroked one of the spider's legs and left the charm in place.

The front door slammed quickly followed by cries of anguished muttering and muffled sobs. Mo and Dell found Brother Bertie trembling in the passage, hunched over his stick.

Concerned, Dell asked, 'What's the matter?'

Red-rimmed, cloudy eyes stared back at them. 'It's Ruddy. She's gone. Disappeared.'

Mo resisted the urge to roll her eyes. That woman was a law unto herself. It wasn't the first time she'd done a flit without telling anyone. The last time she'd managed to wangle a spot on Sister Aggi's church's trip to Lourdes in France on a holy pilgrimage to Saint Bernadette. The story goes Ruddy had spent the trip eyeing up male pilgrims and pinching a bum or two with religious appreciation.

She hunkered down and held his hand. 'What's the problem, gramps? Has she gone and decked the wrong person this time?'

Ruddy had been a bruiser when she was young, and she hadn't seen why her getting on in years should change that. Mo always suspected that one of these days her fists would land on a person who wouldn't take her age into consideration.

Brother Bertie flashed blazing eyes at her by way of an answer. His tone was hoarse and broken. 'She's gone. I can't find her.'

Mo knew at once this was different. He knew Ruddy better than anyone. If he was worried, it meant there really was something to be worried about.

'Don't stress yourself.' Mo's main concern was calming down her grandad. 'She's always doing a Harry Houdini and turning up again like a bad penny.'

Mo observed Brother Bertie's gaze skid uncomfortably away. 'I don't know. She's always upsetting someone. You know what she's like.'

Mo scowled. That was odd. Why wouldn't gramps look her in the eye? She had the strangest feeling he was holding out on her.

So, she asked, 'It's nothing to do with me, is it?'

He had the needle. 'You?' He blustered. 'What would it have to do with you?'

Mo fingered the charm around her neck, her fingers trailing over the knots in one of the spider's legs. 'We'd better go and look for her.'

Chapter Twenty-Four

'Ruddy?' Mo yelled loud enough through the letter box of the prefab for all of Mile End to hear. 'You in there? You alright?'

No response.

The ancient prefab Ruddy lived in resembled a caravan minus the wheels. Painted a vivid sea-blue, it stood out from the dreary prefab on its left side. Ruddy's home dated back to the post-war era when prefabs offered a quick solution to homeless victims of the Blitz. Ruddy had acquired hers on a temporary basis while waiting to be rehoused in the sixties however when a place came up in a high-rise, she turned it down. She'd grown as happy as a clam with her little home on the corner of the street. As Ruddy always liked to say: 'Nothing lasts as long as a temporary fix, dahlin.'

As Mo straightened, the front door of the neighbouring prefab opened to reveal a short, bulky woman. She was dressed in what Mo could only describe as a gaudy magician's outfit. Long kaftan and pointy hat both patterned with stars and moons.

The woman frantically waved her hand in a shooing

gesture at Mo. 'Oi! Get outta here. We don't want no weirdos around these parts.'

Mo's brows shot up. Weirdos? Was this woman for real? The woman wanted to take a long, hard look at her reflection in the mirror before throwing that insult around.

Then the woman caught sight of Mo's grandad and visibly relaxed. 'Wotcha, Brother Bertie. You looking for Ruddy?'

Brother Bertie looked at the Ruddy's neighbour, hope brimming bright in his eyes. 'Eileen, thank God. Have you seen her?'

'Nah! Haven't seen hide nor hair of her for a couple of days now. Very odd indeed. Normally, when she goes out on her travels, she tips me the wink by knocking on my window. Likes me to keep an eye on the place while she's gone, know what I mean.'

Mo left them talking while she felt inside the letter box. Gotcha! What she'd found was a piece of string with a key at the end. The old girl was always losing keys down pubs and clubs. Mo knew there must be untold keys to this prefab in circulation in the East End.

She opened the front door and went inside, quickly followed by her grandad. The place was spotless as you might expect from a former professional cleaner. And it was clear it was looked after with love. There were family snaps everywhere, most of them of Ruddy and her long-departed husband, through the ages.

Mo was drawn to one of Ruddy and her grandad back in the sixties. Wow! They looked supercool. Brother Bertie in a killer showy suit and trademark pork pie hat tilted at an angle. What a handsome devil he was. And Ruddy! Wow, what a stunner! In a black and white boxed mini dress and white go-go boots. A wave of shame came over Mo as she thought back to the times she'd secretly sniggered at Ruddy's plastered on make-up and precarious beehive. Just because you got old didn't mean you had to give up all the pleasures and treasures in life. She wanted to ask her grandad about the photo … but now wasn't the time.

Brother Bertie was getting into a right state, yelling, 'Ruddy, girl? Where you hiding?' His shoulders slumped in defeat when the only answer was a damning silence.

Mo did a quick search of Ruddy's home looking for any sign, any clue of where Ruddy might be. She found nothing. No sign of forced entry. That was something. Brother Bertie sat immobile at the kitchen table staring, dazed, into space.

Mo eased down next to her grief-stricken grandfather. 'Don't worry, we'll find her. She can't have vanished.' She hesitated for a moment before asking, 'Was she in trouble with anyone? She hadn't fallen out with somebody?'

Brother Bertie's voice was shattered as his head bowed. 'She's always falling out with people. But I…' The words choked in his throat. 'I shouldn't…' He shook his head.

Suddenly Mo's mobile pinged with a text. He looked up hopefully.

'Perhaps that's her?'

Mo took out her phone. The message wasn't from a contact in her phone book. In fact, it stated: 'Unknown.'

The Docker's Return. 3 p.m. Tmr. Something to your

advantage. Tell the landlord you're here to see a friend. Come alone.

Scowling, Mo rapidly text back: *And who might you be? Friend? And what might be to my advantage?*

When she attempted to send the message, it wouldn't go.

'Is it her? Is it Ruddy?' Her grandad's desperate plea swiftly reminded Mo what she was meant to be focusing on.

She laid a comforting and reassuring arm around his shoulders and squeezed. 'I'm afraid it's not her gramps. We'll find Ruddy.'

Mo cast an eye at her phone. 'In the meantime, I've got to go and see a man about a dog.'

Suddenly Mo froze. What if this 'friend' was the guardian angel Dell was working for and being so secretive about?

Chapter Twenty-Five

Scowling with dissatisfaction, Jimmy examined his navy tie in the mirror. He was in his private toilet in the bookies. It reminded him of the sort of khazi you might have found in the sort of spit-n-sawdust boozers he'd favoured in his youth. The sort that had once been quite grand but had now gone down the crapper along with the area. Originally, the Gents had been put in to stop desperate punters, who couldn't miss a race on the TV screens but desperately needed to splash their boots, from going outside and doing it on the street. It was done out in three urinals and a cubicle with green slabs of mock marble. What Jimmy particularly liked about it was the full-length gilt mirror he stared in now that covered one wall. Long and wide enough to allow him to check out his look before he presented himself to the world.

The *Gents* sign had been replaced with a brass and bronze solid *private* one. For his use only. Any guests needing to spend a penny were pointed in the direction of the boozer across the road. Jimmy had a thing about other people's piss in his lavatory.

Just then he heard Violet walking on the stairs. A cheerful

smile slapped on his face. That's what he loved about his eldest kid, she always seemed to know when he needed her.

He called out, 'Get me one of the silk ties in my desk. The red one. I'm in the can!'

When the toilet door opened Jimmy was still examining his reflection. Blimey, she was quick! He didn't bother turning, instead held out his hand to receive the tie. All his hand got was empty air.

Jimmy sensed danger. He went into automatic defensive mode. Every muscle in his body tightened, his breath coming out shallow and harsh. A glint of something the colour of silver reflected in the mirror. Something clattered to the ceramic floor. Jimmy twisted. Froze.

The point of a vicious-looking thin sword was a hair's breadth away from his heart.

Well, well, well. If it wasn't Brother Bertie, Jimmy thought sarcastically. And cautiously. He went years back with Bertram Watson, so knew not to underestimate him. The other man held the sword with an expertise that shouted loud and clear he wouldn't hesitate to plunge it into Jimmy. Jimmy eyed the razor-sharp weapon. He hadn't seen one of those swords for years, the type of sword that was concealed inside a walking stick.

Brother Bertie prodded his chest with the tip. 'Where is she?'

Jimmy raised his hands. 'Woah! Woah! Calm down! Put the sword away! This ain't *Treasure Island* and you ain't Captain Bluebeard!'

The older man growled. 'I'll cut your lying heart clean

out of your chest if you don't tell me what you've done with her.'

Shrugging, Jimmy shook his head and dared to slowly lower his hands. 'Done with who?'

A furious Brother Bertie cut a sharp line into Jimmy's shirt, missing his flesh by a whisper.

'Don't mess me around, you little pimp. Ruddy. You know what I was Jimmy Southpaw, so don't think you'll be able to sweet talk me.'

'Ruddy?' Jimmy sighed heavily. 'I ain't seen the old girl.' His voice was soothing. 'I know who you are, but you should know who I am too. Or don't you remember?'

Brother Bertie held Jimmy's steely gaze, but his voice weakened a fraction. 'Yes, I remember.'

'How long have you been carrying that overgrown shaver around?' Jimmy asked referring to the sword that was usually concealed in Brother Bertie's walking stick. 'I seem to recall you were more of a flick knife and revolver kind of guy back in the day. You've obviously moved up in the world.'

There was a slight tremble to Bertie's hand. 'That's not a period of my life I like to dwell on too much.'

Jimmy erupted with a bark of explosive laughter. 'Have you gone soft in the head? Personally, I dwell on it all the time. Running round town, ripping the place apart, making a name for ourselves, cheeking the cops and all that sort of caper? Those were the days, my friend.'

He had a history with Jimmy Southpaw he wished he could forget. The way he'd lived when he was younger was not something he ever wanted his baby-girl granddaughter to find out about. He didn't want the same for her. He wanted her to have a life where the road she walked was straight. Not constantly having to look over her shoulder like he'd had to do for so many years.

Now it had all backfired. Because he was worried about Mo, he'd sent his best friend into the clutches of this fearsome man. If anything happened to his brave Ruddy, he'd never forgive himself.

Bertie forcefully restated his question. 'Where's Ruddy? What did you do with her?'

Jimmy shook his head with apparent sadness. 'And you know that's what makes your visit here today so disappointing. You know me better than that. You come bursting into my gaff waving a sword around like a character in a pantomime up Stratford East. You should've come knocking politely at my door asking to have a quiet word. Dear, oh dear, oh dear.'

Brother Bertie inched the tip of the sword higher until it touched the skin on Jimmy's throat. He could feel his heart doing overtime. He had to be careful. His ticker wasn't what it used to be. 'You know where she is.'

Jimmy got red in the face at not being believed. 'Give me one good reason why I would know the whereabouts of Nora Baxter? And I'll tell you something for free. Anyone who had the misfortune to nab Ruddy would soon be sending her back home, ransom or no ransom.' Scorn transformed his expression. 'She's a busybody who has too much time on her hands so sticks her beak in other people's business—'

That pressed Brother Bertie's buttons. He leant with

menace into the sword. A tiny bubble of blood appeared on Jimmy's neck 'Don't talk about her like that—'

'She always did have you wrapped around her little pinkie. Then again you and her were always as cosy as two ferrets in a sack.'

'Keep your filthy tongue to yourself. I'll admit she's got her quirks and ways, but she's got the purest heart of gold a person could ever have.'

'Heart of gold?' Jimmy roared with the laughter of a loon. 'See, that's always been the difference between me and you, Brother Bertie. You're a romantic. You want to believe that there's still good folk roaming the earth, holding hands, teaching the world to fecking sing.' His features set into a chilling mask. 'The day my sister, Sin, walked out of my life was the day I learnt the only good in this life is the type you make yourself.'

Brother Bertie's already cracked heart nearly fractured wider at the mention of Jimmy's sister. He wouldn't allow the harsh memories to take him. Break him. Focus only on Ruddy.

Both men were breathing hard. Brother Bertie spat, 'That's why I don't want you anyway near Mo.'

'Mo?' Jimmy questioned innocently. 'Who's this Mo when she's at home? Ruddy's twin sister?'

This was too much for the older man who looked ready to plunge the thin piece of steel straight through his one-time partner in crime. He never got the opportunity because he was interrupted by the deadly click of a hammer being pulled back on a shotgun.

Violet Steele stood in the doorway with a sawn-off. The knuckles on her already pale hands were nearly white where she gripped the gun too tightly. She was grim, determined, meant business.

She ordered, 'Chuck the sword on the floor. Nice and gentle-like.'

Before Brother Bertie could do as told, Jimmy intervened, telling her, 'Blimey! If it's not bad enough having one old bird waving a deadly weapon around, now I've got a young one doing it as well. You've come in here to save me have you, sweetheart? Took you long enough. If my mate here had really been up for it, I'd be cut to pieces by now.'

He waved his palm impatiently at her. 'Put that long piece of iron down and do me a favour. Get me a red tie from my office. This one' – he stroked the tie he wore – 'is a total eyesore.' He sent his daughter a quizzical look. 'By the bye, babe, are you sure that thing's loaded? Here's a tip from a guy in the know – always make sure your shooter's got plenty of lead in its pencil.'

Violet did as she was told but there was a faint air of resentment as she did so. 'I know how to load a shooter, Dad. I know lots of things you don't know I know.'

Jimmy was put out. He didn't approve of her giving him lip especially in front of company. 'Alright, girl, don't get the hump. I'm only joshing with you.'

When Violet left, Jimmy turned to Bertie. 'She's a good kid but' – he tapped the side of his head – 'not much up here, know what I mean?'

The men stared at each other, both lost in memories of a joined, criminal past they would never forget.

Jimmy sighed as he collected the sword. He shoved it inside its walking stick frame with such force a loud sawing sound ripped through the air. He handed it back to the Brother Bertie with the gritted warning, 'Next time those ol' legs of yours bring you to my door, press the doorbell like everyone else.'

Brother Bertie snatched his walking stick. Then he gobbed on the tiled floor at Jimmy's feet. 'If my Ruddy doesn't turn up soon, hale and hearty, I'll be back. And it won't be for a yarn about the old days. Trust me on that.'

Once on the street, Brother Bertie disappeared down the first alleyway he came to. He almost crumbled as he shoved his back against the wall. He could barely catch his breath. He should never have involved Ruddy in this. Sent her into Jimmy Southpaw's den. A man he knew was capable of cold-blooded murder.

Chapter Twenty-Six

Inside his Wapping riverfront duplex, Harry snorted two lines of nose candy and downed a couple of Black Beauties with a mouthful of Stella. He grabbed a bottle of Polish Vodka. Then he hit the night-time road looking for trouble. He jumped into his soft-top convertible, knocked back another Black Beauty and a burning mouthful of voddy as he motored towards a club he knew down Bethnal Green way. Harry urgently needed to let off steam. Best way to achieve that was to give his fists an outing. And the club was the perfect spot to pick a row with some twat and proceed to smash his face in.

He was spitting mad over the stunt his Dad had pulled tying him to the railway track. And to that big-gobbed bitch Robbie had married. Harry clenched up. He was barely holding it together. What was eating away at him was not what his Dad had done at the Docklands Light Railway station. It was what Jimmy Southpaw had said at Robbie's funeral for all to hear:

'Robbie, you were the best son a geezer could ever have. There won't be another one like ya.'

It had left Harry stunned. Swallowing back the tears that had thickened in his throat. The pain couldn't have been any worse than his Dad slashing him with a thousand cuts.

What about me?

I'm your son.

I'm still here.

Alive and kicking and breathing.

All that and more he'd wanted to rage at his Dad. Get right up in his face, so his old man had to look directly at him to acknowledge he still had a son.

What made it ten times worse was Jimmy Southpaw had declared it in front of all the mourners. Proclaimed it like he was reading it from the scriptures. All those people would now think that he, Harry Steele was second best.

Second rate.

Not fit enough to be The Southpaw Prince-in-Waiting while his old man still sat on the throne.

But hadn't that always been the story?

Robbie the firstborn.

Robbie the favoured son.

And what about me? What about me? Harry thought with a belly full of bitterness. Second fiddle, that's what he'd become. An accessory Robbie had around him like the chunky rings he'd worn on his fingers.

Harry knocked back more voddy to get rid of the rank taste in his mouth. When he hit Bethnal Green instead of proceeding towards the club, he found himself driving somewhere he had not been since he was a nipper.

He stopped the car besides the railings of a place he

would never forget. A place where he'd been forced to understand exactly where he stood in the pecking order in his family.

As he drank deeply Harry looked out onto the green called Weaver's Field. Some said it was a park, but it was more like a huge area of grass where, the story went, it got its name because it honoured the textiles trade of weavers from the East End's long ago past. It was off Valance Road near Bethnal Green overland train station.

Harry's tanked out mind zoomed back to his school days. It had been the day of the Summer Sports Day at his and Robbie's primary school. The school put on a smashing, picnic-style fun day event for all the family on Weaver's Field.

The sun had well and truly popped its hat on. Hot and glorious. Harry had been charged with excitement. Couldn't wait to show off how fast he could sprint in the one hundred metres race. Winning that race was a symbol of how he was going to grow up to be a force to be reckoned with like his legendary Dad.

Everyone knew his father. From the bolshie lady who ran the laundrette with an iron fist to the governors of his school. Other geezers tipped their hats to him. The ice cream van man always gave them their 99s for free. Take a penny off Mister Southpaw's kids? Don't talk effing silly buggers. His Dad had a rep and that's what mattered in East London. That's why all the other kids treated him and his older brother like royalty.

Each year the parents would turn up to cheer their kids

on. That year had been no different, except his Mum had still been alive then – bless her departed soul. Although her given name was Vera everyone called her Mini on account of her being so small. A perfect, porcelain doll. Dead ringer for a model many whispered enviously behind their hands. Slap always expertly applied, hair turned out to perfection and clothes that were especially made for her measurements by a tailor in his basement up Brick Lane way. Jimmy had worshipped the ground his wife walked on. Mini never raised her voice. 'A proper lady' was one of the epitaphs engraved forever on her tombstone.

He and Robbie had each won the heats of their race so they'd ended up in the final together. When the whistle blew, he had raced his eight-year-old heart out, waiting to hear his parents cheering him all the way. But all he heard was:

'Come on, Robbie, shift yourself,' from his Dad.

'Get those knees up, Robbie,' from his Mum.

The race couldn't have lasted thirty seconds, tops, nevertheless it had been one of the longest stretches of time in his life. He'd waited and waited and waited for his parents to shout his name. To spur him on his way. Instead they'd only screamed his brother's.

Robb-eee.

Robb-eee.

Robb-eee.

That's all that had buzzed in his ear. It should have knocked him back. No way. It had provoked the opposite. Made him kick up his heels and belt closer and closer and closer to the finish line. Fucking yeah! He'd won to the ecstatic cheers and whoops of his class and teacher. He'd shown them. Harry Steele was going to grow up to be as strong and as tough as his legendary Father.

Robbie had come in second. There were no hard feelings on his side. That's why so many people had loved Robbie, he was so laid back. In fact, he had taken Harry's hand and raised it with his own. Jimmy Southpaw's boys conquering the world together.

They had sprinted over to his parents, who had a huge spread of sarnies, bickies and fizzy drinks.

His Dad beamed as he congratulated and slapped him on the back. 'My boy done good.' Then he'd squinted at him, some of the light leaving his face. 'What's that on your chops?' Jimmy Southpaw had looked over at his wife. 'Mini, give my champ here a brush up.'

She smiled at her husband and it widened when it touched Harry. 'I've got some more tissues in the car.'

Harry had practically skipped, hand-in-hand with his Mum to the car. Once there, she made him sit in the passenger seat. Turned his face to her. And belted him a stinging slap across the face.

Harry had never been so shocked in his life. The pain hurt like he was fighting for breath under water.

Tears pricked his eyes. 'Mum, I—'

His Mum's face was mottled with anger. So angry. Her eyes, which were usually so soft and kind, were as tough as stone. Harry was scared. He didn't know what he'd done.

Her biting words cut over him as she stabbed a warning

finger in his face. 'Hear me, Harry Steele and hear me good. You don't ever, *ever*, show your Dad up like that again. You hear?'

'But I don't understand.' How could he have shown his Dad up? 'I won the race.'

Mini Steele cracked her youngest son another one on the other cheek. 'And there's the problem. Robbie's your Father's heir. The next in line to run your Dad's firm when your Dad decides to retire. If you win a race over Robbie all those people are going to think your Dad's raising a weakling. That Robbie won't be fit to run the company. Next time you let him win. You hear me?'

Oh, he'd heard her, so much so that it had stayed with him for the rest of his life. The emotion from that day choked Harry up as he looked over the field of grass that had taught him so much about life. The tears were in his eyes the same way they had been when he realised not everyone started the race in the same place.

He took another swig of his voddy. He loved his brother Robbie. But he would always hate him too.

Harry got back in his whip and changed his travel plans. Instead of the club he was on his way to somewhere else. He ditched Robbie from his thoughts, replacing him with thoughts of his fecking widow. Kristal. He had already set in motion a plan to take her out of the game. For good.

The problem with Harry Steele was that he didn't always keep his eye on the ball. He was so busy plotting and planning against his sister-in-law that he never clocked that he was being followed. The person wearing shades in the other car followed Harry after he left Weaver's Field and watched him like a hawk as he finally parked up. Observed him stroll down the street and go into a certain establishment.

Kristal Steele slowly pulled off her lilac-tinted Jackie O sunglasses. Her mouth spread into a nasty, knowing smile.

Now why would Harry Steele be visiting a Turkish Bath so late at night?

Chapter Twenty-Seven

'You keep palming off that third-grade shite on me instead of the real deal, I'm gonna come over there and shove your bollocks so far up you they'll be whizzing around your body like a pinball machine. Got it?'

Mo hesitated outside the private snug-room inside The Docker's Return because whoever was the mysterious 'friend' she was meeting was giving someone a right, royal rollicking.

Since getting the text Mo had dismissed this being a potential meeting with her so-called guardian angel. It was more likely to have something to do with the feud between Barker and Southpaw. The situation between them was barbwire tight and deadly, so this could be a trap. The last thing Mo wanted was to be a casualty in a war she hadn't created. Then again, she was a member of Barker's crew and had proved her loyalty in the battle to defeat Southpaw's firm.

The man on the other side of the door abruptly stopped talking. Mo figured he'd been giving it some on the phone. That gave Mo her first clue about him. The geezer was used to giving orders. The one-sided convo she'd just heard was delivered by a guy who dished out the crap but didn't take it. A man who was willing to threaten a good kicking if his orders weren't obeyed. Mo nervously bit her lip. Maybe, just maybe, this wasn't someone she should be meeting. He'd sounded like a proper nutter on the ole dog just now. What if…?

Mo pushed her doubts aside and got her guts – and smarts – back on track.

Here goes!

Mo pushed the swing door. She recognised him immediately. This was no guardian angel.

Harry Steele.

'Told you we'd meet again.' Harry spread his arms wide from his seated position. 'I come in peace.' He topped it off with a cocky, lopsided grin. Smoke from a ciggy between his fingers wriggled in the air.

Mo held her shock down. Made sure it didn't show on her face. But she was knocked for six, no doubt about it. What the triple bloody hell could Jimmy Southpaw's son want with her? Especially after his family had taken a kicking they'd never forget at Barker's club? She recalled how she'd found him as snug as a bug in his wheels outside, having a barney with his dead brother's widow and then throwing Mo off her game with some nifty sugar-coated words. What had he said again…? Oh yeah!

'You're good. I like you. I think you're going to go a long way in this business.'

'What do you want with me?' Mo asked him straight,

standing her ground by the door. Her body was on full alert. If he tried any funny business, she'd be on him like a piranha on flesh.

The cocksure sod touched the ciggy to his lips and inhaled. He took his time, getting the measure of her the same way she was taking stock of him. Flash wanker! She summed him up. His threads weren't off the peg but designer, right down to his Egyptian cotton socks. He loved his bling – belcher chain, two bulky gold rings on one hand, slim silver one on his pinkie. Probably wore one round his cock Mo concluded sourly. And the way he sat – legs and arms wide – this was a geezer who adored being noticed. It was clear as day that Harry Steele was a legend – in his own mind.

Which begged the question why he was holed up in this back room without an adoring audience?

Smoke wafting from his mouth Harry used his foot to push out the chair opposite him, an invitation for her to park herself. 'I've got a tasty business proposition to put your way, so why don't you take a pew.'

Mo took a chance and did as he asked. He poured them both a brandy from the bottle on the table. She held up her hand when it looked like he was ladling on the sauce too thick. Mo suspected she needed to keep her wits about her around Jimmy Southpaw's boy.

Mo wet her lips with the brandy and then asked, never taking her hard-edged gaze off Harry's face. 'So, what's this golden opportunity you want to send my way, *friend*?'

Harry relaxed back, drumming his fingertips on the table.

He was needled. 'You know what? Most people would jump, give their eye-teeth to work for me. The chance to do business at the behest of Harry Steele is a dream come true for many.'

He flashed his pearly whites in a way that said she should be honoured to be breathing the same air as him. Harry Steele clearly loved the sound of his own voice.

Mo scoffed, 'I've had a lot of dreams in my life and funny enough none of them have featured you.'

That smacked some of the smugness out of him. He stubbed out his smoke. Leaned forward. 'Like I said at that night at Barker's, you're good. Too good to be at the beck and call of a geriatric numpty like Barker.'

Mo didn't react outwardly to his slagging her boss off. Instead she calmly took another sip of the brandy. The booze burnt her chest. Mo placed the glass very quietly down. 'You offering me employment, Mister Steele?'

'Harry, please.' He enthusiastically insisted. Harry knocked back the last of his drink. He caught her cool gaze and held it. 'Word is that you've only recently been added to Barker's books. So I says to myself, "I wonder if that young lady is still testing the waters with her new boss, and not quite made up her mind whether she's found herself the right family".'

Harry relaxed back, never breaking eye contact. 'You impressed me. I liked the way you handled yourself.' He shrugged with one shoulder. 'If you've decided you're happy as a lamb where you are, no probs.' His tone deepened. 'However, if you're looking to expand your operation, I'm your man.'

Mo tilted her head, confusion marking her face. 'Expand? How?'

Harry pulled out another smoke and lit up. 'A spot of freelance. I've got a job that needs doing. The person doing the doing has to be someone no one – not even God hisself – would connect to me in a million years. The last person anyone sticking their beak in will suspect is some pint-size chick who gave the Steele family a good hiding.'

'Hiding' seemed to stick in his throat. Fair dues, Mo could understand that. The pain and humiliation of getting a sound beating … Ouch! That kind of pain took time to scab over and heal.

Mo's mind ticked away, mulling over what he'd laid out on the table. He poured another generous measure of booze into his glass. When he tried to do the same to hers, she placed her palm over it. More alcohol would only make her brain fog. Muck up her thinking.

Finally, she asked the million quid question. 'And what is this job?'

His cheeks splashed with red heat. Whatever the job was, it was personal. Whoever he was looking to sort out had obviously trod on his corns one time too many.

'A spot of tidying up,' he finally answered. 'Time to chuck out the rubbish.'

Mo audibly sucked in her breath. She knew exactly what he was talking about. Waste disposal is what he was discussing. He wanted someone dead. And her to do the doing. Taking out someone on Harry Steele's say-so? Nah! She wasn't even tempted. Come on, how's it going to look if she's working for Barker with her right hand and doing hush-hush work for a member of the Steele family with her left? Disloyalty, that's what. Serving two masters was not a good look.

Decision made, Mo drained her glass and stood. 'Been good meeting you, *friend*.'

Harry was out of his chair, face mottled with displeasure. He was puffing air like the Big Bad Wolf. His fingers flexed uncontrollably by his side.

'You're gonna regret this.' He vowed retribution. 'Think I've forgotten what you did to my boys that night? Have I fuck.'

Whatever! Mo thought as she turned her back. It didn't take him long to show his true colours. He'd be the worst kind of person to work for. Nicey-nicey one minute and then blowing up in your face the next. Nah! She didn't need that type of aggro.

He hissed, shouting the odds. 'You'll regret turning your back on Harry Steele. You'll…'

Mo closed the door. The noise of his raging words now muffled gobbledygook following her until she reached the main door. The first thing Mo did outside was to draw in an almighty punch of air. Well, that was a turn up for the books! She hadn't seen that one coming.

Mo pulled out her mobile to contact Barker. The bossman needed to be informed pronto that Jimmy Southpaw's son had approached her. She'd probably earn Brownie points with Barker for telling Harry to get on his bike.

'What happened?' a voice rasped in her ear.

The phone nearly jumped out Mo's hand. She twisted to find her cousin. A very different looking Dell. The two chunky plaits were gone replaced with individual twists and she was rocking some proper fashion puss street wear. Mid-rise blue jeans, large looped earrings, and designer trainers. And – Mo could hardly believe she was seeing this – her cuz wore a high cut blouse that showcased Dell's belly, including belly button. Dell had turned into the embodiment of the women Bible bashing Delilah had cried out were, 'Daughters of Satan.'

Mo kissed her teeth in disbelief. 'What the heck are you doing here?'

'I'm your shadow. Wherever you go, I go too.' The rucksack with the machetes sat comfortably on Delilah's back, as per usual.

Mo pushed her fingers through her curls, aggravated beyond belief. 'Why won't you tell me who you're working for?'

By way of an answer, her cuz smiled brightly and mockingly started singing, 'What A Friend We Have in Jesus.' Mo almost screamed in exasperation.

As they walked off, Dell stopped with her hymn-singing nonsense and asked, 'Who did you meet?'

Mo resigned herself to having Delilah as her shadow. Plus, having a bodyguard could come in very handy. 'Harry Steele—'

'What?' Delilah stumbled back in shock, which surprised Mo. The look on her cousin's face was like she'd seen a ghost or one of her duppies.

'I'll tell you all about it behind closed doors.' Mo promised.

As they crossed the road Mo remembered her mobile was in her hand for a reason. But the mobile started to ring before she could contact Barker.

Caller unknown.

Mo ground her teeth. Better not be Harry Steele again…

It wasn't. It was a nurse on the hospital ward where Twinkle was.

Chapter Twenty-Eight

Mo flew into the hospital room. Twinkle was sitting up in bed, eyes closed, head resting heavily against a plump pair of pillows. The shade of her skin still looked like death warmed up. Mo didn't care about any of that. Twinkle was awake. Twinkle was alive. ALIVE. A lump of pure joy lodged in her throat. Then she noticed her best friend's leg, bandaged and dressed.

Mo tried to stop her mind flashing back … But couldn't.

Twinkle dangling by one arm. Twinkle falling. Falling. Falling. Smash. She hit the ground. Red, thick blood creeping, spreading…

Mo snapped out of the sickening memory. What she couldn't shake off was the guilt. All the guilt she felt about what had happened came flooding back.

Twinkle sensed her presence, her weary eyes opening. A mammoth grin burst over her face when she saw Mo. She held her hand out. Mo was in her embrace in no time. They held onto each other so tight it was a wonder bones didn't break. Locked together they sobbed their hearts out. Couldn't seem to stop. Mo realised how close she'd come to losing her best friend.

'East End Girls Forever,' Twinkle whispered.

'East End Girls Forever,' Mo uttered breathlessly back.

Mo pulled away, tears still streaming down her cheeks. Her hands ran convulsively up and down Twinkle's arms as if she needed reassurance that her friend was really alive. They smiled, almost shyly at each other.

'Hark, get you,' Mo joked to relieve the tension. 'With your own hospital room like bloody Lady Muck of the manor.' She winked. 'Betcha got a butler who brings you G&Ts at noon and a maid to straighten your sheets.'

Twinkle didn't play along. Instead her hand suddenly clutched Mo's so tight. Her voice was thick with anguish but with a thread of steel. 'I know you blame yourself. It's written all across your face. But you didn't' – her hand squeezed – 'make me come to the club.'

Mo's gaze swiped away with wretched grief. 'But if I wasn't working there—'

Twinkle slapped her palms impatiently on Mo's shoulders and twisted them with surprising strength to force Mo to face her again. 'I ain't having it, you hear? I went to Barker's club on my own two feet, no one carried me there.' The forcefulness in her tone gentled. 'I wanted to see where you worked. You in your new job. I'm that proud of you. That proud of what you've made of yourself. Proud to call you my mate.'

Twinkle croaked the final word, lips wobbling. She teared up again. They wrapped their arms about each other again, not so tight this time, and simply stayed like that for a time as if the world outside didn't exist.

Mo couldn't put into words what it felt like to feel her best friend's heart beating against hers. How it felt to feel Twinkle's skin warm and alive. The feel of her breath fanning Mo's skin. Mo had been so afraid, petrified to her very soul, that the next time she saw Twinkle, her friend would be a blue-lipped, deathly cold corpse on a mortuary slab.

'What's the doc say about your leg?' Mo asked awhile later, sitting on the edge of the bed. She held her breath knowing the answer wasn't going to be one she wanted to hear.

Twinkle tried to put a brave on, but her voice was filled with bleakness. 'They said it could've been so much worse. I could've ended up dead.' Mo winced. 'I've damaged my hip. I'll probably have to have a hip replacement.'

Twinkle inhaled a steady breath, her cheeks losing a touch of colour. 'Me being young and that, they think my body should cope with it really well.' She appeared to perk up with a stunning smile. 'I'll be doing cartwheels before you know it.'

Twinkle's smile was over bright. Mo knew it was to cover-up the fact that she'd had a knock back no young woman should have. Oh Twinkle! Mo wanted to take her in her arms again … But what was that going to do, eh? Only make Twinkle feel even more crap about her situation than she already did.

Somehow, she had to lift her bestie's spirits. 'Your Mum shown her face again?' *Including that vile creature, Eric Brown*? If Twinkle's Mother had had the brass to bring that demonic monster anywhere near her best friend Mo was going to swing for her.

Twinkle momentarily shut her eyes in exasperation. 'She's been doing my head in. Ringing up, giving the nurses a right hard time.'

Mo cosied up close. 'You should've seen her when she arrived while you were out cold. Carrying on like she was the Mum of the year.'

Mo sprang to her feet and did a bang on imitation of Sheena Brodie's dramatic arrival that day. Twinkle hooted and creased up so hard she was in danger of falling out of bed, bad leg and all. That's more like it. Twinkle should be laughing herself silly, forgetting her troubles. For a time at least.

Mo didn't want to leave, but knew she needed to see Barker about Harry Steele. In the end it was Twinkle's exhaustion that made the decision for her. When her bestie drifted off to sleep, head slumped to the side, Mo gently kissed her. With the gentlest caress she pushed Twinkle's red hair off her forehead.

Then, head high, Mo strolled calmly through the ward. When she reached the lift, she punched the wall with such force she grazed the skin on her knuckles. Sometimes she hated this world. Fucking hated it. Twinkle wasn't even twenty yet. Not even twenty! Mo wanted to SCREAM!!! It wasn't fair! How can it be right that a woman that young with her whole future ahead of her should have to face such a tragedy?

Mo knew in her heart that Twinkle was never going to walk properly again.

Mo looked on in startled bewilderment when she entered Club Class. Not only had everything been put ship-shape after the raid but the place had been transformed into somewhere that resembled Darby and Joan meets *Come Dancing*. The dance floor was filled with seniors, who were dancing in couples, rocking to Bill Hayley's 'Rock Around the Clock.' And boy, could they move! Hips twisting and turning, legs a-shaking and a-grooving. These older folk were taking the dance floor by storm.

Mo couldn't help but smile. It was cracking to see the grey-haired brigade having fun. It seemed to Mo that she lived in a world where the prevailing belief was when you reached a certain age you should have the decency to stay put in an armchair, sit in your own piss and then do everyone a favour by popping your clogs. Older people should be looked after and respected not shunned and shunted to the side.

Mo sidestepped the dancers by moving along the edge of the room towards the stairs to the lower floor where Barker was in his office. She was one step away from the door when she let out a yelp as an arm encircled her waist and neatly tugged her onto the dance floor. She was in the arms of a wizened-faced character, with a few tuffs of hair and a sparkling twinkle in his rheumy eye. His partner left a space for him to uncurl Mo between them. Then they started dancing and Mo guessed they wanted her to join in.

Ah! What the heck!

Mo started shaking her stuff with them. Doing the works: back foot curls, funny-feet tapping moves, twisting those hips limbo-like down to the floor. She threw her head back because she was having Fun! Fun! Fun! Mo couldn't honestly remember the last time she let her hair down.

Brother Bertie loved to drop foot. He had some moves on him. When she was a kid, especially on a Sunday morning, he'd pop on some reggae classics and they'd dance away. She'd never forget the time they were slow dancing along to Susan Cadogan's 'Hurts So Good' and seeing tears glisten in his eyes. She wondered if he was missing Jamaica. It couldn't have been easy to pack up his belongings and travel across the globe to start a new life.

As much as she was having a grand ol' time, business beckoned. It always did. She blew a kiss to her dance partners, used some nifty footwork to spin away and headed down to Barker's office.

Inside, Barker was doing paperwork at the large desk while Josh sat all comfy-like in an armchair, one ankle crossed over the other. He chucked daggers her way, she smirked right back. He was still hating on her for avoiding all his subsequent advances. They hadn't discussed anything, but it was clear she was giving him the big brush off.

Mo turned her attention away from the monkey to the organ grinder. 'What's with the old timers disco upstairs?'

Barker looked up and settled back in his chair. 'A couple of hours, once a month, I give the club over to the wrinklies to shake a leg. Gets them out of the house, know what I mean.'

Mo considered this new side of her boss. 'That's very generous of you.'

'Nah, it ain't. It's what they're owed. That generation saw us all right. Made sacrifices for us. The least we can do is provide them with a space to enjoy themselves.'

Amen to that, Mo thought. Then she recognised the impatient gleam in his eye, so best step to it. 'I had a meeting earlier you won't believe.'

She told him.

Barker stilled for a second and then straightened. 'Jimmy Southpaw's git?'

The strangest thing was his expression was a dead ringer for Delilah's when Mo had informed her about the same thing. Sure, his face was stamped with disbelief, which she'd expect, but there seemed to be something else lurking beneath. Mo mentally shook her head. She must be seeing things that aren't there.

Barker motioned for Mo to park herself and tell him the whole of it. At the end Barker did something she wasn't expecting. He banged the table with his fist and leapt to his feet. His face was like thunder. He was not pleased. No pleased at all. Mo fought to maintain her cool as he leant menacingly over the table.

Fuming, face getting redder by the second, he let rip. 'You should've told that weasel you were up for the job.'

Mo couldn't hide her shock. 'Why? I don't get it.'

Josh jumped in, seizing his chance to attack her. Make it looked like she wasn't up for the job. 'Told you, Uncle, she ain't worth the time of day. As thick as a docker's sandwich that one.'

Barker breathed heavily through his nose as he straightened and re-took his chair. 'Josh, why don't you tell her why she should've taken up young Steele's offer?'

Relishing his moment in the limelight, Barker's nephew

took his time unfolding his long limbs to stand. He moved towards the desk and parked himself at the corner near Mo. She wasn't sure if it was a sneer or smirk, he directed her way, whatever it was was meant to put her squarely in her box.

He gave her the lowdown. 'Sometimes life is all about getting certain pieces into the right place. And one of the best moves you can ever make is to have a friendly face in your enemy's camp.'

Suddenly Mo got it. Knew where this was headed. Her eyes narrowed on his incredibly beautiful face. 'I should have accepted this job offer, cosied up to Harry Steele and kept my ear to the door for any information that might be of service to Mister Barker.'

A bark of big laughter threw her boss's head back. '"Be of service". Got it right in one. Love your turn of phrase, darlin'.' The muscles in his neck clicked as he centred his head. His gaze was as hot as coals as he stared Mo dead in the eye. 'Ring him back. Tell him you'll take the job with both hands.'

Josh caught up with Mo in the corridor outside his uncle's office, spun her around and kissed her deeply. Mo endured it and could only be thankful he wasn't using his tongue. Then she raised her knee and let him have it in the family jewels. Josh cupped his delicate parts, groaning, back slamming into the wall.

'What did you do that for?' he got out between painful gasps.

Mo stared furiously at him. 'First off, I never gave you permission to put your lips on mine.' She wiped the back of her hand over her mouth. 'Second, you seem to be under the misconception that me and you are sweethearts coz we've done the dirty one time.'

His brows knitted together in dumbfounded confusion. 'But you let me make love to you.' His mouth twisted. 'Unless you're some slag and like putting it about.'

Mo restrained from rolling her eyes heavenward. She thrust her fists on her hips. 'Where do you think you're living? In the 1950s? This is the new millennium, babe. Maybe you haven't heard, but us girls like to sow our wild oats too.'

There was a bitter tightening of his mouth, although beneath it he appeared crestfallen. 'You saying we're through? That's why you've been giving me the brush off?'

Mo leant towards him and lightly kissed his mouth. 'What I'm saying is you wanna be keeping it in your pants until you've completed a course called Ten Steps To Finding The G Spot.'

And with that little nugget of knowledge she left him, her mind consumed only with thoughts of Harry Steele.

Chapter Twenty-Nine

A council rubbish bin of all things. That's what Harry Steele had directed Mo to find. It was a couple of days later in the afternoon and she stood with her cousin, Dell, on a street in the suburbs where East London fades away to become Essex. You knew that because of the wide gaps between the houses and the sleek German-brand motors on the driveways.

They were both decked out in black clothes, hoodies hiding their faces.

Harry Steele had text her two things:

The name of a street.

A map of the street.

On the map an arrow pointed to where the bin was located. X marked the spot.

Mo threw her gaze around with hyper alert suspicion. It was a touch quiet for her liking. 'I don't like this. It's all a bit too James Bond on a treasure hunt for my liking.'

Dell nodded in agreement, her trademark rucksack shifting on her back. 'Feels like shifty eyes are checking out our every move from behind net curtains.'

'They probably are. It's that sort of area. You get what

you pay for.' Mo inwardly sighed. 'The sooner we crack on, the sooner we can bounce out of here.'

The shakiness in her voice clearly showed how nervous Mo was. She might've signed up to do this on Barker's say-so in order for him to have another way to discover what Jimmy Southpaw was up to, but truth was she had a bad feeling about it. Uppermost, she didn't like being at the beck and call of flash Harry Steele.

Mo did one final check up and down the street before proceeding, with Dell, towards the freestanding bin that had 'litter' in peeling gold paint on the front. Mo wrinkled her nose as she looked inside. Urrrgh!! Disgusting! She was going to have to put her hand in there.

The people round here must love their KFC because there were enough of its takeaway boxes to feed an army. Beneath them was a half-eaten banana. Under that … Mo's hand froze. A plastic shopping bag from an upmarket clothes store. Her eyes rolled. What a dimwit Harry was. Any bin diver would have it away in an instant to stick their beak inside.

On a neighbouring street, out of view of any houses and their accompanying CCTV cameras, she and Dell looked inside the bag. There were two items inside:

A black box about the size of a brick.

Something that resembled a small TV remote with a single button on it.

Mo gingerly examined the box while Dell shook her head, saying, 'That's not a tracking device.'

Mo kept her intrigued eyes on the box while she asked, 'How do you know?'

'Too big. They're tiny these days. Some are the size of a watch battery.'

Mo now jerked her gaze curiously at her cousin. 'How do you know?'

Dell shrugged, seeming slightly irritated that Mo was persisting with the same question. 'I know stuff. I watch TV. They have them in all the action thrillers. That ain't a tracking device.'

Mo compressed her lips. It was written all over Dell's face that she wasn't telling the whole story. Mo was beginning to suspect there was heaps still she didn't know about her cousin, including the so-called guardian angel who had made her Mo's shadow.

No point wasting my breath asking her more, Mo decided. Deffo not the time or the place.

Mo was jittery because this wasn't her manor. She was off her own streets with two suspect devices doing a job for a seriously suspect geezer. Her phone pinged with the next set of instructions:

The name of a nearby street.

The registration of a BMW convertible.

The instructions were for her to locate the BMW on the neighbouring street and to attach the black box to the underside of the car.

Mo went still. The blood rose to her face, turning her brown skin much darker. It was dawning on her what this job was.

On the same street as the BMW Jimmy Southpaw inspected the facilities of the largest function room at one of his commercial properties that marketed itself as a banqueting hall. Proper proud of the place he was because it was the kind of dinner-dance joint a celeb or professional footie player might hire to kick up their heels with friends and family. The chandeliers weren't glass imitations but the real deal. The trimmings were teak and mahogany not plywood. The dance floor was properly wood sprung rather than the cheap substitutes found in a spit and sawdust fleapit that's about to be turned into a bingo hall.

Jimmy Southpaw wrapped his knuckles on one of the tables in the dining area and was reassured by the noise it made. Proper timber. He squeezed the plush on the chair, which yielded to his touch like a woman's Bristol's.

His searching gaze did a three-sixty. 'Nice. Very nice indeed.'

His three guests, Harry, Kristal and Damien stood mystified watching as he inspected the premises. What the hell was the ol' fella up to this time? Finally, he gestured at a round table for them all to park themselves.

Jimmy rested his elbows on the table with his hands fastened. 'Nice, eh?' he said again referring to the premises.

Kristal chirped, 'Yeah, lovely.' She might sound all sunshine and smiles but those glinting eyes of hers betrayed her bafflement.

Harry wasn't the type to lavish praise on a property. *Did it bring in money* was all that concerned him. So he relayed nothing, but he did seem to have an obsession with his phone.

Jimmy thought the time was right for him to tell them why he'd called for a family sit-down.

'You know me. I'm not one for second chances. A fuck

up's a fuck up, even when it's your own family fucking up. I don't do sloppy seconds when it comes to women and I don't do sloppy seconds when it comes to jobs. That's why I've decided to sort bollocks Barker out my own way.'

Harry leapt up, shooting his mouth off, just like Jimmy knew he would. His son's hands fisted. 'I can do it, Dad. Just give me another pop at the bastard and I'll take him down quicker than a wrestler at Wrestle Mania.'

Not to be outdone, Kristal was fast on his heels with, 'Me and Damien have already been hatching plans on that front.' She took hold of his son's hand. 'Ain't that right, sweetie?'

Damien vaguely moved his head, which his grandad took to be a nod. Jimmy inwardly cringed. He couldn't help it. He still couldn't get his nut around how his Robbie had produced a weird lump like that.

Jimmy wasn't about to repeat himself. The silence did all the talking for him about his response to their offers. He settled back in his chair as he surveyed the faces of his family.

'I didn't just bring you here to give you the lowdown on Barker. I wanted to let you know that this is where I'll be holding my retirement bash. This Saturday.'

Harry and Kristal watched him both on the edge of their seat. They knew what he was going to say. What they'd been waiting for.

'I'll be announcing who will be filling Robbie's shoes. Who will be my successor.'

'It's a bomb,' Mo stammered in terrifying understanding. Her hand tightened on the bag as she paced like a caged animal. 'That's what it is. Shit, Dell, that fucker wants us to blow up people. Place it under the car and…'

She didn't have to finish. Mo bristled with anger, but it was with herself. Of course it was a bomb. How could she have been so stupid? Why else would the instructions tell her to wait until two people were in the car and then press the button on the remote?

Boom! Blown to kingdom come.

Mo shook her head in a frantic motion of denial. 'I'm not blowing up anyone.'

Dell wasn't fazed, appearing as if this was all in a day's work. She took the black box and remote from Mo and stashed them back in the carrier bag. 'Stay here. I've got a plan.'

Mo felt a weight lift from her shoulders as her cousin disappeared around the corner. Whatever plan Dell had up her sleeve, Mo prayed it panned out.

Thought you wanted to make it in bizz? A vicious inner voice taunted. *You're gonna have to get your fingernails well and truly dirty to become a Face. Muck right up to your elbows. This ain't flippin' Playschool.*

Mo wanted to slam her palms over her ears to shut the knowing voice out. Naïve. Stupid. Fool. She called herself all the names under the sun. Did she really think she could join the criminal underworld and not be presented with having to take a life? Mo prayed hard that Dell was getting shot of the bag and its deadly contents. However, when she clocked Dell's stony expression and that her cousin still carried the bag, which appeared heavier now she knew her prayers hadn't been answered.

Expressionless, Dell held the bag out to her. 'Just do it.'

Mo was horrified. Her feet nearly tripped her up as she staggered back. 'Why's it looks heavier? What did you do?'

Dell remained steadfast. 'Just do it. Or you'll go back to being Little Mo forever.'

'Titch.'

'Short-arse.'

'Pint-sized dwarfy.'

That was the life of Little Mo. Bullies beating on her. People taking liberties. Did she really want to go back to that?

With feet like lead and robotic legs, Mo took the bag and walked towards the BMW.

'Damien! Get a fucking move on. We've got work to do.'

Kristal was in a hurry as they headed across the foyer of the building. And in a fury. She would have to move up her plan to take Harry down. Time had suddenly become very pressing. Jimmy and Harry were long gone.

'Nag, nag, nag…' Her son had the brass to chant under his breath.

In a rage as red as the colour of her Jimmy Choo's Kristal grabbed her son by the scruff of the neck like a kitten that had made the hideous mistake of doing its business on her kitchen floor.

She shook him violently. 'Now you listen to me. Our big break has come early and I'm not going to let your grandad, your Uncle Harry or anyone else, including you buster, get in my way.'

She dragged him out onto the street, down to where her BMW was parked.

From a distance, Mo's breath knifed inside her throat as two figures appeared on the street, heading for the car. One was a youth who was struggling with and yelling at a woman. Even when Mo realised who they were, she didn't believe it. It was the same woman who had fought like a demon during the night of the raid on Club Class.

Kristal Steele. And no one had to tell Mo that the lad with her was her son, Jimmy Southpaw's grandson, Damien.

Now Mo understand with horrifying clarity what Harry Steele's job was. He wanted her to kill his sister-in-law and nephew. Mo looked down at the remote and rubbed her thumb along the switch. When Mo looked up again Kristal was in the driver's seat while Damien stood by the open passenger door. He was giving his Mum plenty of verbal.

Then he climbed into the car.

Mo looked down at the remote again, then at a steely-eyed Delilah.

It was now or never.

Her finger touched the button. One press, that's all it would take…

A raised voice made her head shoot up.

'Fuck off, you bitch. You ain't my boss.'

That was Damien shouting the odds as he jumped out of the car and slammed the door.

He marched back down the street, pursued by his fizzing Mother who screeched, 'If you're old enough to speak to your ol' Mum like that, you're old enough to get her fist in your moosh.'

Kristal and Damien disappeared down the street taking their screaming match with them.

Dell took the remote from Mo's stiff, cold hands. 'We can't stay here any longer; it's too dangerous. Tell this Harry-boy that he made the wrong choice of venue. He should have wired the bomb to the ignition of the car before his two targets set off this morning. That's what a pro would have done.'

Ten minutes later, Damien sat like a sulky teen in the passenger seat of the BMW while his Mum started the engine.

Kristal was still making her feelings known. 'And don't give me any more of your lip or I'll drag your nuts over your face this time.' She sighed heavily, her voice catching with an emotional gentleness. 'This is all for you, you know. I ain't doing it for the benefit of my health.'

As Kristal pulled her car out, she asked him, 'Have you got a pair of swimming trunks?'

'Have I got a what?'

'Are you fucking mutton and Jeff as well as stupid?'

Damien's nostrils flared, the skin on his face suddenly flaming. 'Course I ain't deaf.' He seemed overly angry at her insult considering it was nothing compared to what she usually threw his way.

His expression suddenly brightened. 'I've got loads of swimming trunks. The ladies love 'em.'

'You're going to need to slip into a pair tomorrow morning.'

Damien sneered. 'Nah! Screw that.'

Kristal slammed on the brakes, bringing the car to a screeching halt.

She grabbed her son by the ear. Pulled him close. 'Get it done.' Then she added, 'You're looking a tad unhealthy. What you need is a proper going over in a spa. So you're all set to go to one tomorrow morning.'

Kristal let go off his ear and smiled with smirking delight. 'It's a nice spa. A Turkish Bath. Your Uncle Harry will be there...'

Chapter Thirty

'Two pairs!' Jacko, the young heavy, hooted in triumph, fist pumping the air.

His luck was finally changing. He was sat at a table in a cottage somewhere on the Kent coast. He now barely noticed how drafty the cottage was with the gale blowing in off the English Channel.

With glee he stared at his opponent. 'Come on, love. Get your skirt off.'

Nora Baxter, aka Ruddy Nora, squinted. 'I don't think so, laddy. Cop a load of that.'

She laid her cards on the table with delight as she chuckled away. The hand was a straight flush. She'd won another round. Fifth one in a row.

Ruddy had lost track of how long she'd been stashed away in this cottage. Her mind cast back to the day at Jimmy Southpaw's HQ at the bookies. He'd caught her red-handed. No matter how many fibs she'd spun to lie her way out of it he hadn't fallen for one of them. She'd figured she was in for a good thrashing if not something worse. You didn't put your mitts in Jimmy Southpaw's business and expect to come out of it with five fingers still attached to your hand. Especially considering what she'd found out. What she hadn't counted on was Jimmy getting one of his goons to transport her to a cottage on the coast.

Jacko had kept her under lock and key in the back room for days. Gradually she'd worn him down, so he'd at least permitted her in the sitting-room to watch some telly. It had been Ruddy's idea to break the boredom of her captivity by tempting Jacko to a game of cards. She'd told him there was a pack of playing cards in a drawer in the room he'd stashed her in.

To start off with his jaw had gone south when she suggested they play one of her favourite games.

'I ain't playing strip poker with an old crone like you. What kind of pervert do you take me for? I mean, no disrespect love, but you're knocking on a bit. I don't get my jollies off clocking saggy old dears in the buff. That's a bit too niche for me.'

Ruddy had her answer ready. 'Got a small todger, have you? That's the usual reason men back out of strip poker. I might have guessed. The bigger the mouth the smaller the weenie.'

He was outraged. 'I've never had any complaints.'

Ruddy sniggered. 'Yeah, that's probably because there's never been any women in your life to complain about it.'

'Cute.' Jacko thought on it. Then warned his prisoner, 'I'll soon have you stripped off. They don't call me Cool Hand Jacko in the casinos for nothing.'

That was thirty minutes previously. Now he sat at the

table in the freezing cold with only a West Ham T-shirt, a pair of boxers and one sock to cover his modesty. Playing poker with Ruddy gave a new meaning to losing the shirt off your back.

Ruddy meanwhile was down for one button on her blouse. 'Come on, sonny, get your sock off and it's your turn to deal.'

Mumbling and muttering under his breath, Jacko angrily pulled off his remaining sock. He shuffled the deck and threw Ruddy's cards belligerently across the table. He'd made the fatal mistake no one should ever make at the card table. He'd lost his temper. Ruddy had him right where she wanted him.

He got even more nettled when she turned down the chance to change some cards. 'Nah! You're alright, pet. I reckon I'm doing cushty, thank you very much.'

His face turned from anger to despair when he clocked his card. He looked at her with something approaching hate. 'Right, that's it. Show's over. Time for you to get back to your room.'

Grinning for all she was worth Ruddy snatched the cards out of his hands and spread them gleefully on the table. 'Oh dear. You've got nothing at all while I was only bluffing with a pale pair. I don't think cards is really your thing, is it?' Eyes glittering with glee she mocked, 'Come on, son, get your top off. You don't want to turn into a bad loser.'

Jacko pulled his West Ham T-shirt off.

Ruddy inspected his torso with an arched critical brow. 'You could do with working out a bit more. Maybe if you did your boxers wouldn't look like a pair of fart crackers. You know, way too tight up your bum.'

He bared his teeth forgetting all about how this woman reminded him of his Nan. 'I'll work you out if you don't pack it in.'

Ruddy clucked her tongue. 'Nice way to talk to an old lady, that is. Come on, let's have another round. Have your shorts off. Then you can get me a glass of water from the kitchen for my pills and we can call it a night.'

Ruddy's bag with her meds were tucked up against the leg of her chair.

'Tell you what, I'll save you the trouble.' He rose to his full impressive height of six-four. With a flourish, he jerked down his boxers. He stood with his hands on his hips and shook his naked body with a flourish. 'There – satisfied?'

'That's cheating.' Ruddy took not a bit of notice of his John Thomas. 'You should have played the last hand.'

'I ain't going to give you the satisfaction, love, especially as that's the only satisfaction an old dear like you can expect at your time of life.'

In a huff, he stormed off towards the kitchen in a right strop to get Ruddy her glass of water.

As soon as Ruddy heard him turn the tap on, she swung into action. It was now or never to execute her plan of escape. In five minutes, she would be locked up in the back room again with no way out. She always kept two packs of playing cards permanently in her bag. Both marked, of course. The dopey, golem had believed that she'd found a pack in the drawer in the room. It never crossed his incy wincy teeny-weeny mind she'd planted them there.

Ruddy checked his jacket, one of the spoils he'd handed over in their game of strip poker. Desperately she searched and came up trumps with his car keys. She pocketed them. Dived back into his jacket and searched. And searched. Flipping Nora. She couldn't find the front door key.

The water stopped running in the kitchen. Crikey!

Ruddy left his jacket and focused on her bag. She took out something and held it in her lap where Jacko wouldn't see it. The kitchen door swung open as he moved towards her holding the glass of water for her meds. As he leant forward to place the glass on the table Ruddy took her chance.

With the yell of a warrior, she twirled the carrier bag partly filled with coppers and hit him a solid one in the temple. He went down like a tree. His moaning attested to him not being out cold, which meant Ruddy didn't have any time to lose. She was back in his pockets with the knowhow of a pickpocket but couldn't find the door keys. Jacko groaned and rolled on his side. Ruddy left his jacket and went to Plan B. She picked up a chair and crashed it against the window. The glass smashed outwards but then the smaller pieces blew back in with the raging gale blowing off the sea. Ruddy climbed onto the sill and jumped out, her thin body blowing in the wind. She hurried over gravel to where her jailer's Land Rover stood.

Ruddy could just hear Jacko screaming at her over the storm. He was furiously peering through the broken window. She fumbled with the keys. There was a time when pinching a car was just a matter of smashing a quarter light and wiring it up. But these days, it was a lot more difficult even if you had the keys.

Ruddy climbed inside and pressed a button by accident. The windscreen wipers went loopy. Ruddy started the ignition. In the rear-view mirror, she caught sight of Jacko, stark-bollock naked, jogging in his bare feet on the gravel. His hands were cupped over his family jewels. He closed in but he was too late. Ruddy was driving away.

She drove down the drive that led to the open road but stopped after a hundred yards. When Jacko saw that she'd come to a halt, he got his hopes up and yelping with pain with each step, he set off in pursuit, thinking she might have stalled.

When he was close enough she wound down the window, leant out and shouted in defeat, 'Alright, laddie, I give up, you win. I can't drive this thing.'

In the red rear lights, his features curled with triumph and retribution. He strode with menace towards the rear of the motor. When he was a few yards behind Ruddy grinned with pure delight. She had another ace up her sleeve. She slammed her foot on the accelerator and spun the rear wheels. Jacko was pelted with sharp-edged gravel all over his naked body. He yelped and growled in pain.

Ruddy wanted to do a jig of pure happiness. 'You need to get up very early in the morning to get one over on Ruddy Nora! So long sucker!'

And with that she disappeared into the night. Her mind now on getting to Brother Bertie to tell him what she'd found out. Her face grew grim. She was going to have to be very careful though because Jimmy Southpaw would be on the prowl to hunt her down.

Chapter Thirty-One

Sister Aggi thrust her large wooden cross threateningly into the dark at the ghostly apparition she could just about make out in the corner. The chill from her bare feet spread through her body as she stood in the cold, dark corridor in her ankle-length nightie and heavy dressing gown.

Of course she knew what she was looking at was no ghost, but whoever it was might as well have been because they were doing a bang-up job of scaring the sweet bejeezus outta her. God knew what time of the night it was, but when she'd heard a noise in the corridor, she hadn't hesitated in getting out of bed. Such occasions demanded that Sister Aggi take her special cross with her. It doubled up as helping to ward off evil and if evil didn't get the message to hop off it became a weapon to bash the idiot over the head with.

'Be gone!' she exclaimed, pushing her cross forward. 'Be gone, Satan's hood rat! The Lord does not take kindly to anyone robbing a bunch of harmless nuns—'

Her words caught in her throat. She inhaled a sharp intake of breath when she saw who emerged from the shadows. Not a junkie, as she'd believed, robbing the convent to get something to barter for their next fix. No, it was Little Maureen Watson.

Good grief, the girl looked terrible. The biblical embodiment of 'wretched' if Sister Aggi had ever seen it. And she'd seen many many wretched souls in her life. Hadn't she been a wretch herself when she turned up on the steps of the convent all those years ago?

Sister Aggi pushed her past back where it belonged – in the past.

The cross dropped limply to her side as she asked Mo, 'How about a nice steaming cuppa, my girl?'

Over the years Sister Aggi had learnt that the daftest thing to say to someone with the haunted expression Maureen wore was, 'Is there something wrong?' How stupid can you get? It's as clear as the nose on a body's face there's something terribly wrong. Best thing to do was to get them all nice-n-comfy and then gently draw the problem out, one step at a time.

Mo moved completely out of the shadows and didn't answer. Instead she walked past her former sewing teacher into her bedroom and sat on the edge of the nun's single bed. Sister Aggi pursed her lips. So, it was going to be one of those, was it? No comforting tea, but a tell-it-as-it-is session.

Sister Aggi had barely sat down next to Mo when her unannounced visitor opened up: 'Have you ever hurt anyone?'

Aggi's heart pinched tight at the anguish she heard in the question. 'Is that what's happened? You hurt someone, Maureen?'

Mo's little hands twisted in her lap. 'I nearly did.' The words wrenched out of her. 'All I had to do was press something. I didn't even have to touch them. So easy. And I couldn't do it.' Finally, her gaze caught the nun's. 'Some badass I'm turning out to be.'

The nun felt a sudden fury that was so hot. If she got her hands on that Barker…

'Did that sinful man you're working for put you up to hurt someone?'

Sister Aggi sucked in her breath when Mo snapped her gaze away. It wasn't quick enough for the nun not to see that whatever had gone on it hadn't been Barker pulling the strings. Thoroughly puzzled, her brows creased together. Who else would ask Mo to hurt someone? Unless … Unless … The thought running around inside Sister Aggi's head was almost too unbelievable to entertain. No way. Mo wouldn't do something that dangerous? Would she?

The nun asked her straight. 'You playing for one side while batting for the other team, Maureen?'

Mo bristled with anger. 'You must be off your rocker. I'd never do anything like that. I'm loyal to the core—'

'Loyal enough to hurt someone who's never done a thing to you in your life?'

Mo flew off the handle. 'I never done it. I couldn't.' She swallowed hard, the emotion a ball of fire in her throat. 'It was a young man and this woman. Strangers.' She lifted stark eyes. 'I've been telling myself for years whatever I have to do to make it, I'm going to do. No problem.'

Sister Aggi's temper rose. Whoever had put this darling

of a girl in this terrible position should be shot. *Sweet Jesus, forgive me!*

'Hurting someone always leaves its scars. And sometimes those scars never go away.'

Suddenly Mo's head fell into her hands. Dejected, soul-destroying words bled out of her. 'I don't want to be a killer. Have blood on my hands.'

Sister Aggi pulled her into her arms. Tremors shook Mo's body. Mo was so young, so very young. The way Mo strutted around, playing the Big I Am, it was so easy to forget how young she was. Eighteen-years-old was that crossover age. Stepping into adulthood but, at the same time, still letting go of being a child. What bastard would do this to such a young girl? Her arms tightened about Mo. Sister had seen this so many times. How the seasoned Faces of East London's underworld took advantage of eager beaver kids, full of false swagger and bravado desperate to do anything that would see their name in lights.

Even murder.

'I knew this girl once.' Sister Aggi spoke quietly. 'Had the world at her feet. She could've done anything – anything – that she wanted. But she falls in love with this handsome young man. The problem was they were involved with the wrong people. They had all their dreams ahead of them. What they forgot about was the innocent always get hurt. Always.'

Mo stilled, beguiled by the power of the story that Sister Aggi told. So she asked, 'What happened to them?'

The nun drew in a deep punch of air. 'I can't tell you

where she or he is now because that would breach their confidence in me.' Her tone hardened. 'But I'll tell you this, the woman, she blamed herself for the innocent member of her family who got hurt. It was her who brought trouble to her family door. That's what's going to happen to you if you keep mixing with the type of people who bring the evilness of death and destruction to decent folks.'

Mo gently pulled free and flicked her fingers through her curls. 'I suppose you know I never knew my Father.'

'I heard that.' Sister Aggi's voice became fierce. 'Anyone who judged you for it should be consigned to hell's burning bonfire for all eternity.'

And she meant it, with her whole heart. Anyone who made a child feel less than nothing because she only had one parent or no Mum and Dad at all didn't have any business living in this new century. Who the heck were they to cast the first stone anyways? Throw it and Sister Aggi wouldn't hesitate to pick it up and pelt it right back in their judgemental face.

Mo went on. 'It ain't that, Sister. I don't give a flying monkeys what other people think. It's what *I* think that matters.' She turned to face the other woman more fully, her voice urgent. 'I dream that one day he'll come back into my life and when he does, I'm going to be somebody. Someone with plenty of dosh. When I tell people to do something they jump and do it in a heartbeat.'

An aching, heavy sadness descended over Sister Aggi. What a rotten world we live in when a child feels they have to impress the Father who abandoned them. It should be the other way round. The fella should be on his knees begging for everlasting forgiveness.

'Surely you can do that with a lovely job in an office.' Sister Aggi reasoned. 'Plenty of jobs going down the city, which is only a hop, skip and jump away.' She deliberately caught Mo's gaze and held it. 'And they won't ask you to kill someone.'

Mo suddenly jumped to her feet and began pacing. 'Do you see me at a desk? Filing papers? I'm a woman of action. I need to be moving—'

'Get a job as a PE teacher then.' Sister Aggi cut in with conviction. 'Drive a bus. Plenty of jobs where you have to shift and shake yourself.'

The nun eased to her feet. Moved towards Mo and took her hands. 'I never forget the way you'd stand up for yourself against those bullies. Day in, day out. And do you know why that is?' Sister Aggi didn't wait for her reply. 'Because you're a defender, Maureen. You have your fists ready, like a boxer, not to hurt the innocent but to defend the underdog.'

She pulled Mo into her embrace again. 'You're a good person, Maureen Watson. And don't you ever forget it.'

Sister Aggi fell to her knees beside the bed once Mo had disappeared into the night. She clasped her hands together and prayed.

'Holy Father, please shine your golden light of goodness on young Maureen Watson. She is lost. In the darkness where evil lurks and waits to snatch her up and use her to carry out its wicked deeds. Shine your heavenly light upon her to guide her to the mouth of the road that will be the start of her journey to a decent and rewarding life.'

Sister Aggi wasn't the only one on her knees. Mo was too, inside her grandad's allotment shed. Her breath caught when she picked up the gun she'd stolen from Jimmy Southpaw. The moonlight slipped through the slats in the shed, shining on the golden handle of the gun. Now she knew how to use it Mo hid it securely beneath her jacket.

Chapter Thirty-Two

That's strange! Mo thought as she eyed the partially opened main door of the club the next day. Barker was shit-hot on security. The security in the club was usually tighter than a hangman's noose. Doubly so with the feud between Barker and Jimmy Southpaw hotting up. Then again, there might be a delivery going on. Mo frowned as she glanced out on to the street. No sign of any vehicle offloading goods.

She was here to meet Barker to give him the lowdown on what had happened with the job for Harry Steele. Mo suspected that her boss would go ballistic when she told him she couldn't go through with killing someone.

Killing someone. Taking a life. Just thinking about it made Mo want to chuck up. Talking to Sister Aggi last night had eased her conscience somewhat. However, it still left her with the question of whether the criminal path she'd chosen was right for her. In the meantime, she had Jimmy Southpaw's gun. Some sixth sense had driven her to go to her gramp's allotment last night to retrieve it. Something kept telling her she needed protection. Maybe Harry Steele was going to come gunning for her since she'd not carried through with his plan?

Now she was going to have face Barker. And prayed he understood why she hadn't blow Kristal and Damien Steele to pieces. If she'd gone ahead with it that would have properly triggered one of the bloodiest gangland wars in the East End's history.

Cautiously, Mo pushed the door and stepped inside. Then listened. Silence. The only sound was the laboured noise of the short spurts of her breathing. Usually the place was a hive of activity getting the club ship-shape and its groove heels on for the punters. Something wasn't right here. Mo could taste it in the air.

Mo eased out Jimmy Southpaw's flash shooter. Mo gripped it the way that Josh had taught her. She moved, one careful easy step after another. Not a soul in sight at reception. *What the heck's going on?* Without exception, there was always someone front of house. First impressions are everything in this business, Barker had told her.

Mo went on high alert. Her heartbeat tripled as she considered what could be going on here:

Entrance door open.

Empty reception.

These were the trademarks of an attack having been carried out on the club. Had Jimmy Southpaw's crew launched another raid, this time a total surprise to Barker and emerged victorious? Were they still here? Or long gone leaving behind a room littered with dead bodies and splashed with blood?

Another damning explanation suddenly slammed into her. What if word had reached Southpaw what she'd nearly done on the orders of his son? Been on the verge of killing his grandson and daughter-in-law?

Mo desperately shook her head, trying to clear the fog getting thicker and thicker within it. Mo inhaled deeply. On the out breath booted in the door of the main club room. The gun did a sweep of the room.

No one there. No Jimmy Southpaw. No dead bodies. Nothing.

Mo stood there for a time in the pulsating silence. *Maybe I missed the memo about today being a team away day.* Mo mentally chuckled away at her little private joke. Some of the tension left her. Mo put the shooter away and made her way to the bar. There she treated herself to two shots from an eye-wateringly priced bottle of Cognac. The heat of the alcohol warmed up her insides. A blessed sigh escaped her. She needed that.

Well, best not beat about the bush if she was meeting the boss. And if Barker wasn't in his basement office, Mo cheekily thought she'd try her luck at sitting in the Big Man's chair, popping her feet up on his desk. Get a taste of what it felt like to be a Premier League Boss.

Mid-way down the lower ground floor corridor a creepy sensation slithered over Mo. As if someone had their filthy eyes on her. Was following her. The baby hair on the back of her neck stood wildly to attention. Heart pounding, a terrible tension coiling and twisting in her tummy, Mo spun on her heels.

Something dark moved. A shadow. Instinctively, Mo's hand flew up to defend herself. But she was too late. A hand as large as a bear's paw grabbed her by the throat. Lifted her up. Slammed her into the wall.

Shockwaves of electric pain travelled throughout the whole of Mo's body. A sickness swirled in her gut. A head splitting buzzing shrieked in her ears. A cloak of darkness started smothering her.

Don't faint. Don't faint.

Don't. Fucking. Faint.

Mo shook off the dazed sensation as the paws holding her tightened. Her vision came back, and she couldn't help the heaving gasp that left her when she identified her attacker. The personification of pure evil.

Eric Brown.

The nonce who couldn't keep his raping paws off young girls. The dirt bag Twinkle's Mum had let have his evil way with her. Mo knew she was in real danger.

He pushed his hideous face with its pockmarked craters right into her own. Foul breath stained her skin.

'Been watching you, lovely. Told you I hadn't finished with you. Bidding my time, that's what I've been doing. Waiting for the right moment for me and you to have some one-on-one action.'

That's what this sick bastard did. Hunted. Tracked. Lurked in the shadows. Pounced on girls when they least expected it.

Despite his meaty fingers circling her throat, battling to inhale air, Mo screamed.

He cracked up laughing because her scream was more like a pitiful high-pitched wheeze. His laughter was one of the sickest sounds that Mo had ever heard. Gruff, rattling with phlegm, sliced with manic, heavy breathing.

'There's no one here, lovely. Not a fucking soul to hear me play with you.'

He was right. He had chosen his time well. Mo kicked into gear and fought furiously, kicking and pounding, but it seemed to have no effect on him.

He leered, displaying his revolting nicotine-stained teeth. 'Gonna have fun with you. Gonna fuck you into this side of next week, including that ripe rump of yours.'

He licked his furry tongue along the curve of Mo's neck. She shuddered violently at the reptilian contact and the disgusting sticky wet he left on her skin. He rubbed his raging hard on against her.

Ominously, he vowed, 'They won't find you when I've finished with you. That's the mistake I made with the last one. Leaving her alive to tell her tale.'

Mo head butted him on the bridge of his nose. An audible crack sounded as it broke. He roared as blood spurted in her face and down his. But the bastard wouldn't let go. He strengthened his hold, shaking her like a rag doll. He carried her as if she were a sack of rubbish towards Barker's office.

No! No! No! Once inside Barker's office it would be easier for this monster to corner her so harder for her to escape. With all her might, Mo clawed the wall, using her feet, her hands, trying anything she could to stop him getting her inside that room. Mo hit, punched, scratched for her very life.

He wouldn't let go.

A dreadful fear descended over Mo. She would never see her precious Gramps again. Never cross swords with her Mum again. Never see Twinkle. Sister Aggi. The river. London. He was going to brutalise her. Murder her. Dispose of her body so no one found her.

No fucking way. That wasn't happening to her. Big Mo? No chance! This rotten scumbag was about to discover he'd put his filthy claws on the wrong little girl. Mo calmed her breathing. And waited. Waited for the right moment to take this monster down.

And she got it as soon as he dragged her into Barker's office. He made the mistake of dumping her on the ground. Mo was on her feet in such a swift flash he never saw her coming. She rushed around him. Used her schoolgirl gymnastics skills to run part way up the wall behind him, which gave her the momentum she needed to leap on him and bringing him down. He crashed onto his front, Mo still clinging to his back. She tangled her fingers into his greasy hair, yanked his head back and smashed it against the floor. Again. And again.

As he groaned and moaned Mo jumped off him. Without hesitation she took out Jimmy Southpaw's gun. This bag of shite had been terrorising girls and getting away with it. That couldn't be allowed to happen again.

Mo became Lady Justice.

Bang! Bang! Bang!

'Good.' A firm voice applauded her action.

Shocked, unsteady on her feet, Mo swung the gun in a

shaky arc towards the doorway. Josh and Dell stood there solemn faced looking at the crime scene before them.

'Good,' Dell repeated. 'He deserved to die.'

Josh added, 'Good riddance to putrid rubbish.'

Mo gazed back down at the dead body. *I've killed someone*, the voice in her head screamed with disbelief. But inside, Mo felt numb. All she felt was she'd done the world a massive favour.

Chapter Thirty-Three

The windows on Kristal's BMW were so heavily tinted she had to lower the driver's window to peer out to get a proper butchers at the building down the road. She pulled a pair of binoculars from her Gucci black leather, crystal fringe handbag to get a better look.

She checked the place over and knowingly sneered to her son beside her. 'Turkish Baths? I ain't seen no Turks going in so far. The punters all look like they've had a thorough scrub up at home, if you ask me.'

Damien fidgeted in the passenger seat. He had no idea what his Mum was rabbiting on about. He still didn't have a clue why she wanted him to go into a Turkish Bath to see Uncle H. He could see and speak to his uncle anytime he wanted.

'I'm bored,' he droned, backing up his words with a wide and noisy yawn that earned him a smart whack on the arm from his Mum.

'This might come as a surprise to you, son, but we're not just in business with a view to keeping you amused.' Suddenly her voice changed to one of almost panic. 'Get down! Get down!'

Kristal did it for him, her hand forcefully cupping Damien's head and pushing him low in his seat while using her other hand to shield her face. A few seconds later a man walked past the car carrying a holdall, looking furtive as if he was about to commit a crime.

Harry.

Kristal purred with pleasure. It was all coming together. She let her son up and righted herself.

Her eyes were lit up like a child who'd just been given the Xmas prezzie they'd always wanted. 'Well, well, well. Looks like *our* Harry is going for a steam, so to speak. How careless of him.' She glanced sharply at Damien. 'Let's give him ten minutes and then you can pop in and say hi.'

Damien scowled deeply. 'What's a steam? Sounds painful enough to have my bollocks off.'

Kristal ignored him. He would do as told. She checked over her shoulder at the sports bag on the back seat. She mulled things over for a while. It was high risk sending Damien into the Baths as the boy had problems following instructions. They sometimes got all jumbled up in his head.

Sod's Law, though, he was the only candidate available. She wouldn't trust her plans to anyone else. The wider the circle of people who knew your business the more likely it was that someone would blab. After that it didn't take long for the person you were trying to trip up to find out about your plans. Game over.

Kristal did a double take when she saw what her kid had in his hand. A mobile phone. Gimme strength! Damien was never going to make it into the Baths at this rate because she would've murdered him.

Kristal snatched the offending device. Switched it off. She pinned her son with a withering glance. 'I told you no fecking phones. You know the law can trace you everywhere if you've got one of these.'

Damien shrugged a voiceless 'who give a toss' gesture. 'It's only a burner. And anyway, I don't care, the law can chase me if they like. I ain't scared of them.'

And he weren't. He was going to be as fearless as his old man. A wave of yearning trembled through Damien. He missed his Dad so much. He'd never voice this aloud. Never cried at his funeral. Why had it been his Dad who was taken and not his Mum? Don't get him wrong, he loved his Mother, although God knows she could do his head right in sometimes, but he missed that bond with his Dad so much.

Inside Damien was this hollow space that his Mum couldn't fill. He should be able to go to Grandad Southpaw, but he suspected the legendary man didn't like him. Damien knew he had a funny look about him, the way he positioned his head to the side most times. He did that for a reason. One he'd been too ashamed to tell his Dad about. He wasn't going to be weak; he was going to be as tough as shit like his ol' fella.

Kristal checked her watch. 'Follow your Uncle Harry in. You know what to do?'

'Yeah.'

'Are you sure?'

Damien got the nark. 'Oh, shut up, Mum, you're getting on my tits.'

Kristal had to restrain from bitching back, *'At least you*

know you've got a pair with all that flab.'

What she told him instead was a reminder. 'Remember – don't take it too far.'

Kristal couldn't disguise the note of fear in her voice as she warned him. She wasn't blind to the fact that her boy had a tendency to use his fists and feet when others would opt for the use of words.

Damien got out with the sports bag and swaggered down the street. Instead of the confidence she should be feeling at finally trapping Harry like a beetle under a glass, Kristal's gut was having a meltdown. She almost called the whole thing off. But this was her only chance to get Harry bang to rights.

So, she watched her son go inside the Turkish Baths, her fingers anxiously tightening around the steering wheel.

The first thing Damien noticed in the reception area was a sign that read: 'Strictly no photography.' The second thing: the young woman at the reception desk seemed to be the only bird about in the gaffe. Plenty of geezers coming and going, but not a sign of any ladies.

'Can I help you, sir?' she asked him.

His brain went blank. He couldn't recall what his Mum said he should do. He blurted out the first thing that came to his mind, confessing, 'Dunno. Can you?'

She smiled gently back. 'If you tell me which of our *services* you would like, I'll see if I can.'

His Mother had suggested with a whisper in the car that Turkish Baths might be for Turks who wanted a bath. Damien was now unclear exactly what it was that blokes –

Turkish fellas – came in a place like this for and he wasn't sure it was anything he'd be into.

'What have you got?' he asked, noting a couple of blokes striding across the reception. Neither one of which, he would swear, looked Turkish in the least.

The receptionist got his attention again when she passed him a leaflet detailing activities and facilities. Swimming, cold room, steam room, massages and body washes. Damien looked at the list with suspicion before finally settling on the 'executive service'. Not that it mattered, he was under orders from his Mum to get in and out of the place as fast as possible, an instruction he was starting to warm to. His curiosity got the better of him, as he flat out questioned, 'Don't you have any skirt in this place?'

The surprised huff of air she sucked in was noisy. 'I beg your pardon, sir?'

Damien gave the place the once over again with a very sceptical eye. 'Only it seems a bit boysie, know what I mean?'

She knew what he meant, and her pursed lips was all she needed to do for him to get it she didn't approve of his comment. 'Monday, Wednesday and Friday are gentleman only. Tuesday, Thursday and Saturday are for ladies. It's mixed on Sunday.'

Damien knew how to amuse the ladies. 'Perhaps I'll make my second visit on Sunday and try my luck?'

His winked. She stiffened. And slapped a form beneath his nose.

'If you can complete this.' She snidely added, 'Or perhaps you think a Turkish Bath isn't for you?'

Po-faced troll! The form was an arm's length list of diseases and conditions that might prevent him from accessing the service. And he couldn't have that. Mission complete was the only result his Mum would accept. He ticked 'no' to every question and passed it back to misery guts. He paid the membership fee – cash of course. No credit cards trail to trace their tracks his Mum had warned him.

Damien was in!

In the changing room he slipped on an orange pair of trunks. Then he should've been off to find his uncle H, but he was lured for a splash in the pool and then tried the hot sauna. He noticed the place was well plush with exotic blue tiles everywhere and marble, the sort his grandad had kitted out his personal gym in. And it was very blokey. What kind of red-blooded bloke would pop into a place like this on a Tuesday, Thursday or Saturday when he might catch a bit of eye candy on a Sunday instead? It made no sense.

Damien put the hunt for his Uncle H on hold and enjoyed the empty sauna. The hot coals blew steam around the wooden walls and benches and he sweated like a racehorse after a steeplechase. He dubbed his brow with a lemon-fresh scented towel as he whispered, 'What this place could do with is a Swedish bird to give me a good pummelling and rub down.'

The door opened and a second person came in. But the hope blew away with the steam when he realised it was some old git with a heavy tan and a belly to match. The guy took a seat on the bench opposite.

He sent Damien a sweaty smile. 'I say, they certainly

know how to work up a sweat in here, don't they?'

Damien deliberately stayed schtum. He had a thing about talking to naked men with only a short towel wrapped around their waist to cover their excuse-me. It was one of his house rules. He didn't even like standing next to another geezer at a urinal.

Damien smiled and nodded at the bloke and decided the time was right to locate his uncle. Plus, he understood why the guy was smiling at him. Not his thing!

Three things bounced in his head:

He needed to find his Uncle Harry.

Do what his Mum had instructed and then get out of here fast.

Finally have a word with his Mum and put her straight on sending him to a knocking shop for blokes. Of course, she'd do her nut. She'd clipped him royally round the ear once for using a very offensive word for gay guys. And sternly put him straight, 'Don't let me *ever* catch you using language like that again. You hear me. Only ignorant cretins use shit words like that, got it? Besides, there's no need to be jealous just because they've got better bodies and get more sex than you do.'

He looked high and low for Uncle Harry, poking his head around doors and peering through windows. Damien began to fear his quarry had bolted when, through glass frosted with condensation, he found his prey. It was the cold room that resembled something out of the North Pole and felt like a butcher's cold freezer.

His uncle was parked on a bench, shivering away, in close

conversation with a handsome young man who was snuggled up close to him.

Damien couldn't believe his eyes. His uncle Harry! Of all people! Jimmy Southpaw's son! In a cold room with a handsome young man!

He threw open the door. He stood in front of the couple on the bench.

Stunned, Harry scrambled to his feet in disbelief. 'Damien? I mean what the actual?'

Damien delivered a full-on bunch of fives to his uncle's face. That's what his Mum had told him to do. Dish out a beating. But, don't take it too far.

He bent his uncle's arm for maximum effect before hitting him on the other side of his face. Harry fell moaning to the floor. That would be a couple of fractures, nothing too serious but enough to put his uncle in hospital for a few days. Damien turned his attention to the other bloke, who appeared to be frozen in shock at the suddenness of Damien's unleashed violence.

His Mum had been clear. Any fella with his uncle was to get a portion too.

But when Damien took a swing, he was about to discover the other man was no push over. He ducked and dodged Damien's fist. On the up, the man levelled a stinger right jab to Damien's mouth. Damien momentarily skidded back. Gingerly, he inspected his mouth with his fingers. In the cold room steam started to come out of Damien's ears. No one, fucking no one, took the rise out of him.

He growled at the man currently giving him a pasting,

'You wanna make something of it, do ya, cowboy? I'll make something of it for you.'

Kristal's nerve dug in so badly while she waited, she pulled out her hip flask, that had 'Holy Water' engraved on it. And knocked back her brand of holy water, Baileys mixed with Tequila. Where was the little bastard? How long did it take to put that other little bastard, her brother-in-law, in hospital?

Finally, her son appeared, sauntering slowly, as cool as you like, from the Turkish Baths back to the car.

When he got in the passenger seat beside her, she barked, 'Well?'

'Well what?'

A strange, strangled sound emitted from the back of Kristal's throat. Whether that was through despair or she was about to nut him for his cheek wasn't clear. But her hands were curled as if she was about to grab the front of her boy's shirt.

'Did you find him? Did you do enough damage to put him out of action and in ozzie?'

Damien appeared unfazed, shrugging. 'Yeah.'

Kristal peered at him hard. Something wasn't right here, taking note of the bruise at the corner of his mouth. 'Are you sure?'

Her son got the nark. 'I know how to do a bloke over, Mum. I might not be any good at exams, but I know how to inflict grief.'

Kristal sighed with relief, easing back into her seat. 'Good. Was there any other bloke with him?'

Damien nodded. 'You never said that place was for geezers, know what I mean.'

Kristal smugly smiled. ''Course I knew that. I just wanted to catch your uncle at it. Nothing wrong with being gay. However, I'm not sure your grandfather will see it that way.'

Kristal felt a twinge of guilt and rotten about having to 'out' Harry. It wasn't her preferred option. However, when she was securing her son's future her motto was: 'By any means necessary.'

The guy with Harry, did you knock him about?'

When Damien sharply nodded, Kristal was delighted. High-fived her kid. 'But you didn't take it too far? I mean the guy's still in one piece?'

Damien averted his gaze, staring straight ahead through the windscreen. 'He wasn't looking too clever when I left. But that's to be expected' He had a final think before admitting, 'But I'm sure he'll be on his feet in no time helping little ol' grannies across the road.'

Chapter Thirty-Four

Damien's head throbbed with confusion as he walked beside his Mother in the hospital ward the following day. They were making their way to the room where his Uncle Harry was laid up in the private wing.

'I still don't get why you wanted Uncle Harry thumped. Is it because he's…' he chose his words carefully because he didn't want to piss off his Mum. She wouldn't stand for any iffy words about fellas who fancied fellas. So, he finished with a tentative, 'gay?'

Kristal was like the kitty that had got the cream with a side helping of catnip. She was triumphantly on top of the world. She looked a knockout in her eyes. Strutting beside her son in a tube-top that showed off her belly button, a pair of denims accessorised with a thick black belt that had 'Kristal' monogramed on the front sparkling with diamante. Her hair was super-sexy Mariah Carey to the max. She cradled a huge bunch of flowers in her arms.

She was so euphoric that even having to explain her cunning plan to her son for the umpteenth time couldn't break her sunny disposition.

'How thick are you?' she told him, merrily flicking her hair back. 'I mean, seriously? Can't you see? I've got Harry by the short and curlies. If he doesn't make way for us so you can take up the reins as the new boss, I'll grass him up to the old man.'

Kristal abruptly stopped and shifted in front of her son. 'I'll tell your Grandad Jimmy that Harry got caught with his towel down in a gay hang out and that's how he ended up in hospital. I know we're all super broadminded these days and a guy's personal sexual desires are his own business.'

Kristal paused. She'd thought long and hard about doing this. On a personal level she didn't give tuppence who Harry was shagging. He was her enemy, plain and simple. And because of that she would use any weapon she could against him to advance her son.

She started walking and talking again. 'Your Grandad Jimmy's old school. He ain't going to want his son bringing the boyfriend along to family functions, now is he? He'd be a laughing stock. Jimmy likes his men to have a bird in the nest.'

Damien remained baffled. 'But Uncle Harry knows it was me doing the damage. If he spills to Grandad Jimmy, grandad will suss it's you who is behind the whole set up. And then I'll have fractured bones and you'll be lucky to get a gig as grandad's char lady.'

They stopped outside Harry's room. Kristal narrowed her eyes dangerously. 'Your unc isn't going to say dick to the old man, you dipstick. Harry will be finished if he fesses up to his ol' man where he was when he got duffed over. He knows it and I know it.'

She set her features into what she deemed to be a sympathetic pose. 'Now then – do I look worried and concerned?'

'Eh?'

Huffing, she rolled her eyes. 'Oooh! Never mind.'

Balancing the bouquet with one hand, she used the other to throw open the door to Harry's hospital room and strode in like she owned the place. She almost stumbled back when she caught sight of a grim-faced Jimmy seated at his son's bedside. She hadn't factored on him being there. Surely Harry hadn't fessed up? She didn't have a plan B for that. But that couldn't be. He knew his old man better than anyone except his dead brother.

'Harry, baby.' Kristal cooed, jumping into her act as she hurried over. Perching on the side of his bed she hugged him, as a Mother does, to her breast. Her voice was all aquiver. 'You alright, babes? What happened?'

He looked into her face a slight whisper of a smile on his own. Then he glanced the length of the bed to Damien.

Harry's voice was hushed and crumpled. 'Yeah! I'm sweet as, dahlin. A few bruises, a couple of deep cuts.' Kristal winced dramatically as he laid his injuries bare. 'The quacks want to keep me in overnight for observation, I said screw that, boys; I'm made of stern stuff. Steele stuff.'

His Father butted in. 'Too right you're coming out today. It's my retirement do. You've got to be there.'

His retirement do. Kristal had to rein in her glee. Just thinking about tonight was almost making her wet her undies with excitement.

Her voice was tartier than one of those live models working out of Soho. 'Did you hear that, Harry? You're *coming out* today!'

Kristal squeezed his hand significantly on the 'coming out' but was slightly disturbed when he squeezed her own back. Something wasn't right here.

But she pressed on. 'That's the great thing about going private; they pull out all the stops for you, don't they? It's not like you have to lay on a trolley for hours in a corridor trying to catch the eye of a nurse who's off on another tea break.'

Kristal smoothed his hair. She nearly jumped out of her skin when he took her hand and bestowed an old-fashioned kiss to the back of it. 'Thanks, sis. I know we've had our problems in the past but it's good to know your family's there for you at a time like this.'

Something was definitely up. Harry should have been bricking it at this precise moment not carrying on like her knight in fucking shining armour.

Kristal's good humour was fading like a teenager's crush. Her voice was uncertain. 'So tell me, what happened?'

It was Harry's turn to look like the kitty that had got the cream with a side helping of catnip.

'I'm just telling Dad here I had a snout who works in admin for the coppers. I met him regularly at a Turkish Baths, which has got a rep for being a gay hangout. It was the perfect cover for a meet. Cops and robbers ain't going to be seen dead in a joint like that, now are they?'

His Dad backed him up. 'You got it on the nail there, son.'

Kristal felt sicker and sicker as her brother-in-law continued. 'My guy would check the police computer in return for a round of drinks. He was a gold mine for our family firm. Anyways, two-twos, we're sorting out business in the cold room when this guy bursts in wearing bright orange swimming trucks.' Harry levelled a long, beady eye at Damien. 'You know the sort. What I call a *special-needs heavy.*' Harry shook his head. 'The plonker only goes and has a pop at me. Then lays into the cop. Reckon, it must've been one of Barker's boys.'

Harry and Kristal stared openly and knowingly at each other. Neither was now under any illusion that they were playing a game.

Kristal's voice was reedy and weak. 'Had?'

Harry's brows crunched together. 'Sorry?'

Kristal's words were now as slow as a funeral cortege. 'You said you *had* a snout. Has he given you the boot?'

Harry bristled with anger now. 'I suppose you could say he's quit. Thing is, Barker's fuckwit went in so hard on the guy, he killed him.'

The breath caught harsh and hurting in Kristal's throat. *The guy was dead. Dead. Dead. Her son had killed him.*

Harry resumed. 'Of course, the law are trying to cover-up what actually happened but they're already hard on the killer's trail. In here earlier, they were, trying to get a description out of me. 'Course, I told them I had concussion and the details were a bit hazy.'

He caught his nephew in the crosshairs of his intense stare. 'The funny thing is though, I'm sure I knew the guy from somewhere. But you know how the mind plays tricks on you when you're battered. Maybe it'll come back to me.'

Harry leant back into his fluffy pillows. 'You know what the Bill are like when one of their own gets stiffed even if he was really playing for our side. I don't reckon the guy who topped him will make it to the Bailey for a trial when he's caught. Probably shoot him while he was trying to escape, you get me? Dead men tell no tales.'

Kristal was barely hanging on. Her plan had turned into a nightmare of biblical proportion. She looked over at her son who had the decency to avoid her gaze. When she got him home…

Jimmy Southpaw stood up. 'I've got to go and make some phone calls.' He looked pointedly at his son. 'Get dressed, Harry, you're leaving.'

When his Dad was gone, Harry didn't waste any time levelling his triumphant gaze on a frozen Kristal. 'You've really done it in your trousers this time, ain't you girl? What was it? Heard some spiteful rumours about my private life and decided to cash in?' He was spitting fire and didn't give a fuck about who got burnt. 'Sent Mister Mastermind here' – he stabbed a finger Damien's way – 'to put me in the frame with my Dad? Oh dear.'

Harry swung his furious gaze between Mother and son. He became calmer and more logical. 'You back up my leadership bid with Dad and I reckon my concussion won't clear up and the events in the Turkish Baths will remain a confused jumble. But if you don't, or if you cut up rough at any stage in the future, I'll have no choice but to advise my

Dad of what my dumb nephew here was really doing in the cold room.'

The door swung open and Jimmy Southpaw strode back in. 'Why are you still in bed? Get moving.'

Harry swung his legs round and put them in his slippers. 'Don't worry, Dad, I'm ready to roll. In fact, I've never felt better. And Kristal here is offering to make up my face, so it looks less swollen for your party. Isn't that right, babe?'

With a supreme effort, Kristal managed to choke out, 'You betcha!'

Harry told his Father, 'Tell you what Dad, you go ahead and I'll catch up with you later at your retirement do.' Then he switched his smug gaze to his sister-in-law. 'Kristal will get me back home, won't you, sister dearest? After she's done my face, o' course.'

Jimmy's phone rang as soon as he got in his motor. He took the call and the message he was given left him grim-faced and seething.

'I give you a simple job to do, probably the simplest job I've ever given anyone, and you fuck. It. Up.'

It was obvious to Jimmy that the chancer down on the coast, to whom he'd given the task of keeping Ruddy under lock and key, had invented the story of how she'd escaped. The twit was obviously terrified of retribution from Jimmy.

The version of what happened was a bit vague, but it seemed his guy, Jacko, had ordered a pizza in. But when it turned up, a gun was hidden in the box which Ruddy had got her hands on and used to make her get away. Obviously, his guy told him, he'd shot it out with her as she fled but she was too quick for him. He reckoned she must have had outside help and a car waiting down the track. She was a slippery one was that Ruddy.

Jimmy had never heard such a pile of steaming horseshit in his life. A shooter hidden in a pizza box? A shoot-out? A woman in her sixties was quicker than Jacko? Jimmy knew Ruddy from the old days. The one thing his guy had got spot on – she was a slippery customer. She'd probably outsmarted the pillock.

'So you gave chase in the 4x4? Is that right.' Jimmy challenged.

'Well, boss, that was the plan but the ol' dear had shot the tyres out. She'd thought of everything.'

Jimmy's voice was as quiet as it usually was when he had the real nark. 'We're talking about an old crone who'll need a stick soon enough to walk around with, not the cockney Jesse James. She ain't Mile End's Bonnie and Clyde. She's the kind of old girl who knows her way around a bingo card not how to bang it out with a heavy like you.'

Jimmy drew breath. He could feel his blood pressure zooming towards code red.

'I'm upset that you let her get away and I'm even more upset that you're trying to sell me a dodgy watch of a story to cover it up. And believe you me, when I catch-up with Ruddy effing Nora the first thing I'm going to want to know is how she had it away on her toes while under your eagle eye. Now then, you best track her down. And fast. Otherwise, the next visit you pay to the coast will be tied in a mail sack weighed down with lead. And they'll have a delivery note attached that will read – *"The middle of the English Channel."* Do I make myself clear?'

Jimmy furiously cut the call. If Ruddy got to Brother Bertie all Jimmy's plans would be shot. Jacko had best find her.

Jimmy checked his rear-view before driving off. His eyes a stormy shade of grey that saw right through people. Eyes that were the same striking shade as Mo Watson's.

Chapter Thirty-Five

There were other blokes and a few ladies weeding and planting on the allotment but for Brother Bertie the place was lonely and desolate. There was no Ruddy and he might never see her again. Jimmy Southpaw was lying through his crooked back teeth. Any other old dear would be OK with Jimmy. One promise from the old biddy that she'd keep her trap shut would be enough to persuade the gang boss to let her go.

But Ruddy wasn't your typical garden variety of old woman. She was a fighter. She'd kick, punch, cheek and bait. She'd swear revenge and push over those that got in her path. Whatever the outcome, she'd be got rid of afterwards. It wasn't worth the trouble to let her go. No, it was over for Ruddy. Jimmy Southpaw had gotten rid of her.

And it was all Brother Bertie's fault. That's what he kept beating himself up about over and over again. He should have never sent her into the lion's den. This wasn't going to end the same way as the story of Daniel and the Lion. Southpaw chewed people up and never spat them out. They disappeared. Why didn't he just go to see Jimmy Southpaw himself? Ask the man point blank what he was up to regarding Mo? Brother Bertie sighed heavily. He knew exactly why. They had a history. A bad history. One neither man was willing to forgive or forget.

Brother Bertie watered his vegetables while his eyes watered themselves. As a thin spray spread out over the green leaves, the steady flow of water began to splutter and choke as the pressure died. He looked along his hose to see what could have cut it off but the line was clear. Baffled, he headed towards his shed with the hose in his hand to see what the deal was with the tap. When he checked it, he discovered that the water was turned off. What was going on? Bertie looked around but could see no sign of any kids who might be playing the fool. But someone had turned the tap off.

'Psst! Psst! It's me. Are they around?'

His head jerked up to find the upper part of a woman's head peaking over the open window of his shed like a jack-in-the-box. What looked like a woollen hat with a knob on it was pulled down over her forehead so only her eyes were visible.

Ruddy.

Brother Bertie was so shocked to see his friend all he could splutter was, 'What's that on your head?'

'It's a tea cosy, what does it look like? I nicked it from an Oxfam, it's part of my disguise.'

The old man fell silent with disbelief, holding the limp hose in his hand. Then he started to smile. Long and happy. Ruddy was back. She was back.

Ruddy shrilly asked, 'Are they around?'

Bertie sparked back into life. 'Is who around?'

'Jimmy Southpaw's goons, stupid. They'll be looking for me in all my regular haunts and they'll know this is one of them.'

'How long have you been in there?'

Ruddy started to lose her rag. 'Since last night. Southpaw had me locked up in a hidey-hole down on the coast, but I jumped the wall. I burnt out the motor I escaped in case it's got a trace on it and walked the ten miles in the middle of the night to come here.'

Ruddy started shaking, the enormity of the situation and what she'd been through hitting her. The hose dropped from Brother Bertie's hand as he rushed forward and took her in his arms. And rocked her. They'd been in some tight spots in their time.

He cried, 'I shouldn't have made you go—'

'You didn't make me do anything, you old doughnut. I did it myself. He has got to be stopped.' Ruddy pulled away from him. 'Check outside to see if there are there any geezers in dark glasses with bulges in their jackets hanging around, keeping a beady eye open?'

Brother Bertie was still dumbstruck, but he looked around. When he established there was no one around Ruddy yanked him back into the shed and slammed the door. She got him sat down.

Taking his hand, she gravely told him, 'We've got no time to lose. I've got some urgent information you need to hear.'

Much later, a despondent Brother Bertie sat on the balcony of the maisonette that overlooked the river. He gulped deeply from his 'Lord Have Mercy Rum Punch' praying that the weed marinating in the liquor would numb his brain. Take away the crippling pain that consumed him. He felt like crying after what Ruddy had told him. All these years he'd protected his granddaughter as best he could. And now…

'Daddy? What are you doing out here?' Precious peered quizzically at him from the French doors.

He was pleased to see that his daughter was nicely turned out tonight. Back to the beautiful lady she always was. He'd never been one of those Fathers who'd tried to lock their daughters away. That way only led to disaster. As soon as the sheltered girl walked into the world, she went batshit crazy. Drinking, screwing, drugging. Usually ended up in the clutches of some evil man who fucked her up as a full-time job. His daughter was truly precious to him but he understood that she was her own person. So, he'd only ever given her one, solid Jamaican piece of advice before she'd stepped out into the adult world:

'Wise monkey know what tree to climb.'

Know who your friends are. And who aren't your friends. That included the men you chose to open your heart to.

Precious had forgotten everything he'd advised her.

Precious immediately spotted the sorrow covering his face. She stepped onto the balcony. 'What's wrong?' Her lips crimped together. 'If that girl of mine has—'

He cut her dead. 'Mo's found out who her Father is.'

His daughter's skin turned an appalling dead-brown shade as the blood drained away. 'What?'

It hurt Brother Bertie so much to see his daughter in so much pain. But he wasn't a man to back away from the truth. 'If she doesn't know already, she will soon.'

Precious collapsed in the other chair. 'How? Who told her?'

He looked out at the river, the waves turbulent tonight, as he sipped from his glass. He told his daughter, 'Mo's a woman now. Maybe it was time for her to find out.'

Precious' head fell into her hands as she sobbed her heart out.

Mo ignored the call from her Mum for the umpteenth time, just as she had her grandad earlier on. Mo was lost in her thoughts as she paced by the river near her home. Mo didn't need any interruptions while she was thinking. Things were troubling her. She couldn't put her finger on it, but there was something whacko going on.

That unsettling sensation had been there ever since Jimmy Southpaw's abortive raid on Club Class. One question bugged Mo. How had Barker known that the raid was coming? The exact time and day? Her boss claimed to have a grass prettily set up in his enemy's camp, which is how the whispers about the attack reached him. Okay, Mo internally reasoned, say Barker was being straight up? Then why was she plagued by lots of other it-don't-make-no-sense questions?

Why was the package she delivered for Barker empty?

Come to that, how did those sleazeballs who waited to mug her off know she had a package in the first place?

Who had appointed Dell as her shadow?

How did…?

Mo was so lost in deep thought that she forgot one of the cardinal rules of being in the bizz. Always remain alert. Eyes, ears, front, back and sides. She never heard the footsteps behind rapidly gaining on her. What finally snapped her back into the dangers of the real world was the breathing. Rasping and heavy. Mo spun on her heels. Staggered back at the scary as shit sight of the man almost looming over her. He was the size of a mountain, the shadows playing harshly over his face so that it was impossible for Mo to make out his features.

Huge hands lunged for her. Mo jumped back, swerved, expertly turned and ran for her life. She almost took out Jimmy Southpaw's gun that was concealed beneath her jacket. But bullets are loud. They could draw attention including some do-gooder calling the cops. Besides, she had a big advantage over whoever was on her tail. The Island was her manor. She knew where all the nooks and crannies were to hide. All she had to do was get away from him first.

They played a game of chase as Mo ran and ran. Damn! She couldn't dislodge him. The only way she could do it was to delve into her bag of dirty tricks. Her racing mind flashed with a plan.

Mo abruptly stopped. Her pursuer was taken by surprise and, not expecting her to stop, he nearly collided with her.

His hand whipped out and grabbed her. 'Gotcha!' he proclaimed,

The heat of his hot flesh seeping through her skin, Mo's remarkable steel-grey eyes shot deeply into his as she let rip,

'Think you've got the wrong way round mate. It's me who's got you.'

His eyebrows furrowed together in confusion, not able to figure out her meaning. What a dopey dolt! He probably expected her to faint on him or some other style of female melodrama. Mo swiftly turned the tables with a one-two move she'd honed years ago. Her foot slammed down on his with the crushing strength she'd learnt as a gymnast at school. Howling, he let go of her. Her foot came up and kicked with the power of a mule into his dick.

Mo didn't hang about to watch him sink to his knees with a groan of pain so deep it sounded as if his intestines were being ripped out. Usually she'd be whooping out loud at outwitting an opponent. She wasn't laughing now though as she bolted. Her face was filled with stone cold dread. The attack was yet another question that had no answer. What was going on? Mo was terrified and all she wanted to do was get inside the four walls of her home and secure the door tight. For the first time in years, she experienced the yearning sensation of herself as a young girl wanting the security and shelter of her grandad's arms. To protect her from the bogeymen and duppies who roamed this world.

Mo left the river and leapt up the old river stairs to road level. She dodged through the swings in the deserted children's playground. Twisted and turned through the cars parked in front of her block. Reached the stairwell…

Mo was lifted up at both ends. Carried away. Her mouth was taped. Something placed over her head. No one searched her or found her gun as her world went dark.

Chapter Thirty-Six

There wasn't a seat to be had at Jimmy's retirement party. For that matter, not a spot at the bar either. The bash was in full swing, bursting to the rafters. All Jimmy's men were there, turned out in their best spit and polish. This was a family affair, which meant wives and girlfriends only. The guys knew better than to bring a piece of side totty along to an event like this. The man himself did the rounds, slapping backs, making idle chit-chat, guffawing to a joke regardless of whether it tickled his funny bone or not, tucked a sixpence into a pocket or two to celebrate the arrival of a new baby. Jimmy was the perfect host.

He'd splashed the cash, turning the function room into a stunning feast for the eye. Lit up by the huge chandelier and flamingo shaped wall lamps the place sparkled; as polished as the sleek wooden floors. The drink flowed and the food was top nosh courtesy of a chef who owned his own restaurant Up West. A string orchestra serenaded the crowd with popular music from the '60s.

A hard lump lodged in Jimmy's throat as he surveyed the merry making scene. He would be giving it up. All of this.

He'd built this up from nothing. The boy who'd grown up in a mildewed-ridden one-room with his Mum, Dad and sister, who society expected to amount to sweet FA had created all of this. These people depended on him, looked up to him. And, in many cases, would give their right arm for him. But, he reminded himself, never ever forget these people aren't your family. Being his people wasn't the same as being his family. Family were those with the same thick blood causing through their veins as his own. The same people who could hug you one minute and then plunge a knife into your back the next.

Which reminded him neither his son nor his daughter-in-law plus that accessory of her's Jimmy called a grandson had shown their faces yet. Typical!

Jimmy headed to the top table, where he took the chair of honour. A waiter quickly offered him some fizz. He impatiently waved it away. The only fizz Jimmy was interested in was the sound of the fireworks that would be going off with a bang later. He downed a glass of whisky and smiled for his own secret pleasure.

Harry Steele strode into his legendary Father's retirement knees-up feeling like a king. He was also off his face after snorting a few lines of Special K. He was suited and booted in a classic slim-line charcoal suit with polished to the hilt black Italian brogues to finish off the look. Deffo not his style, but his Dad would approve. No way did he want to make a show of his ol' man when he was presented before the gathering as the Steele heir apparent.

He'd seen off Robbie's widow and that wank nephew of his. The pair had chucked the lot at him, including the proverbial kitchen sink and had failed to take him down. The law of nature had been restored. He was his Father's son, the next in line to take over his Father's empire. Kristal must've been off her rocker to think she could outsmart him.

Bitch!

He was the man of the hour.

You're da man, Harry Steele, da man.

The Special K was giving him an all-time buzz as Harry mingled with the crowd, lapping up the respect he received, although he was getting well pissed with the condolences for Robbie. His brother was dead. He was not. Finally, Harry took the seat next to his Father at the top table.

The drugs swirling in his system made him daring enough to slap his Dad's back, grinning like an idiot. 'How's tricks, pops?'

He got a curled lip for his troubles. '"Pops?" Where the hell do you think you are? The Wild West?'

Feeling slightly foolish, Harry tried to laugh it off. 'More like the Wild East. Just passing the time with a joke or two.' He leant in close, his pupils growing large with the effects of the drug. 'So, when's the big announcement? The crowning of the prince?'

His Dad surprised him by cupping a gentle palm around his neck and hugged him close. 'Soon. Very soon.'

Harry couldn't recall the last time his Father had embraced him, pulled him close. His heart filled with elation as he clasped his Dad right back.

Finally! All his dreams were about to come true.

Kristal timed it to perfection when she finally put in an appearance. As people were taking their seats for the sit-down dinner, she stole the moment as she sashayed in. Her face might be on the brink of cracking from the fake smile fixed to it but no way was she going into that room on her knees like a beaten dog.

Kristal wore a knock-off of the famous safety pin Versace dress that Liz Hurley had taken the world by storm with back in '94. With one difference. Kristal's was blood-red. The colour matched her super super glossy lips and criss-cross lace six-inch heels. Her purple beaded, flapper's bag matched the tint and sparkle of her eye shadow.

Silence gripped the room. No one noticed Damien by her side, they only had eyes for Kristal. And she milked it for all it was worth by swaying her hips from one end of the room to the next. She waved like the Queen looking down at her subjects from the balcony at Buckingham Palace. She brightly greeted guests as she made her very slow, stylish way to the top table.

Kristal buzzed a kiss on both Jimmy's cheeks. 'What a lovely spread, Daddy.'

As she and Damien took their seat Jimmy snapped, 'You're late. I was about to send out a search party for you.'

Kristal graced him with her most brilliant smile. 'I wouldn't miss this for anything.' The corner of her lips drooped ever so slightly. 'How could I miss you announcing to all concerned that Harry will be filling Robbie's saintly shoes?'

The words cut and ripped like barbed wire in her throat. What she really wanted to do was to take the bottle of bolly on the table and smashed it over Harry's smug skull. He knew he had her on the ropes. As long as her bruv-in-law had the upper hand and continued to blackmail Damien that he'd killed that cop in the Turkish Baths she was going to have to suck it up.

Kristal hit the bottle. It was the only way she could deal with her dreams vanishing right before her eyes.

An hour later the ringing-tinging sound of Jimmy gently tapping a teaspoon against the side of his glass drew everyone's attention. An expectant hush fell over the room, everyone waiting for the Big Man to speak. The lights dimmed dramatically. Jimmy was not a believer in beating about the bush.

He addressed the gathered crowd, who hung on his every word. 'A man of sixty knows when it's time to start putting his house into order. And that's why I've asked you all here tonight. To announce who will be my successor…'

Mo looked around the room where her kidnappers had dumped her. They had removed the tape covering her mouth and the hood over her head. The place was dark. She had no idea where she was. Something caught Mo's eye. Hold up a minute! Mo crept forward. Grinned because she'd lucked-in. The plonkers had left the door open. Mo did a small fist pump. Yessss!!!!

Mo didn't even think about it, she took her chance and was gone. She found herself in a long dark corridor, a peek-a-boo of light coming from one direction. Quickly, Mo followed it. The light was getting stronger and stronger, brighter and brighter. Mo soon realised what it was. It was the light from a room seeping beneath a door.

Mo hovered and hesitated when she reached the door. What if this was where her nabbers were stationed? Going in there could mean she fell right back into their hands. Then again, that door could lead to outside and her getting away from here. Mo's heart started racing. She couldn't go back …

On tiptoes Mo inched closer. And closer. Her hand grasped the handle. And turned.

Stepped inside.

Mo nearly jumped out of her skin when a spotlight pinged over her bathing her in light. Momentarily blinded by the strong light she raised her hand using the back of it to shield her eyes. Mo knew it was game over. They had caught her again.

Then she heard the scattered gasps.

WTF!

She shook her head, blinking rapidly to see properly again. Mo's jaw dropped when she saw what was around her. She stood in a room filled with people. The people, every last one of them were staring at her. Their faces matched the expression on her own – shock and surprise. Mo couldn't understand what was going on because this looked like someone's big party bash.

'Welcome,' called a man's cool deep voice.

Disorientated, Mo twisted in the direction it had come from. It came from a large man standing at the head of a table where … Mo couldn't believe her eyes. Present at the table were the members of the Steele family – Harry, Kristal and Damien. There was another woman at the table she'd never clapped eyes before, but from the looks of her she was another one of the Steele brood.

OMG!! That meant the man who'd spoken to her was the Big Man himself, Jimmy Southpaw. What Mo couldn't get her head around was why had he welcomed her like he'd been expecting her to put in an appearance?

Mo had had enough of this carry on. She pulled out her gun and flew across the room. The crowd gasped. She leapt up and landed on the top table. The others at the table dived back. Not Jimmy Southpaw though, he stood steadfast. Mo ran down the table until she reached him. She pointed the shooter, his very own gun, in his face. The gasps turned to shrieks. Not from Jimmy, he just chuckled.

Mo looked him dead in the eyes. Eyes that were the same peculiar striking grey colour as hers.

Mo's world went into meltdown. She knew who this was. Who he *had* to be. She couldn't believe it. Couldn't believe it.

'You're my Father, aren't you?'

When he answered her, Mo's whole world fell apart.

'I'm your grandfather. Your Dad was my son, Robbie.'

Mo and the guests sucked in their breath in one collective motion.

Jimmy Southpaw addressed the room. He stepped slightly back leaving Mo the centre of attention. He lifted his chin proudly as he pointed to her. 'Meet my new heir. My granddaughter.'

Chapter Thirty-Seven

The reception room was empty except for the Steele family. And Mo Watson. After his earthshattering grand announcement, Jimmy had given the guests their marching orders. No doubt about it, what had gone down here tonight wouldn't just be doing the rounds of the gossip vine in East London it would be travelling across the crime vine of the whole city. Probably across the country.

Mo was sitting in a chair, listless, in a state of profound ear-buzzing shock.

Robbie Steele is my Dad.

Robbie Steele is my Dad.

Robbie Steele is my Dad.

Mo thought she was inside a dream. Or a nightmare? She wasn't sure which one yet.

Jimmy Southpaw had just made it known she was his heir. While Mo was grappling with all this new info the other members of the Steele family were not backward about coming forward to make their feelings known.

A furious, lip-curling Kristal was pacing, every now and again chucking dirty looks Mo's way. 'If my Robbie had another kid, I'd know about it. I'd bloody know about it.' She shouted at Mo, 'How old are you?'

Mo told her. 'Eighteen.'

Kristal threw her hands dramatically in the air. 'My Damien's seventeen…' She mumbled fast to herself. Then, 'Fuck me! That means he was shagging some other bird while he was married to me.' Although she knew full well that Robbie hadn't been able to keep it in his pants.

Mo winced. Precious Watson having it away with a married man? Never! Her Mum was a modern lady, for sure, but she also had a moral code which drew the line at seeing married men.

Harry Steele looked like a volcano ready to blow. He argued with his Dad. 'You can't put her before me as your heir. I don't care if she's Robbie's kid or Santa Claus's, she's a friggin outsider. Plus, look at the size of her. You could tread on her if you weren't looking straight.'

'I'm Violet.' The woman who Mo hadn't seen before tonight introduced herself. She smiled ever so sweetly. 'It's good meeting you. Any child of Robbie's is welcome in our house any time.'

Damien was the only one who sat there not saying boo to a goose. In fact, he'd taken out one of his digi devices and was playing a game.

Jimmy had had enough. He struck his fist against the table. Bang! 'I've made my decision and that's the end of the matter.'

End of the matter? Not by a long shot buster, Mo snarled in her head. There were too many unanswered questions here.

She sharply addressed Jimmy. 'Did you deliberately bring me here?'

He parked himself opposite her before answering. 'My men's instructions were to bring you here by any means necessary—'

Mo jumped in. 'You deliberately made them leave the door open so I would try to escape. But all the time you were luring me to this room. Get me in the spotlight and viola! Present me to the world as your next in line.'

Kristal screamed, 'That position was earmarked for my Damien.' Not that her Damien was paying any mind.

'Shut. It.' Jimmy briskly ordered. 'This is my empire. I created it with these' – he displayed his work-hardened hands – 'so stop bleating about what is and isn't yours. Got it?'

Harry hadn't finished by half. 'Dad, you can't give it to her. How do you know she's any good? She ain't been tested in our world. She'll probably fall arse over face the first time you send her for a spin.'

In shock, Mo sucked in a heavy, revealing breath because it was all starting to become clear. She'd been the victim of a wagonload of dirty tricks. She'd been well and truly played.

Dazed, the words fell limply from her lips. 'Barker offering me the job was a set up. He never was your rival, was he? He's always been your man. You needed to get me in a position where you could test run me. Put me in different situations to see how I would react.' Mo looked him directly in the eye. 'There's no gang war, is there? It was all made up? In reality it's been a contest to see which one of us is worthy to sit in Robbie's seat?'

The others looked dumbstruck. Seeing the truth on Jimmy's face Kristal collapsed in a chair, grabbed a bottle of fizz and knocked it back. Harry looked like an animal caught in the headlights, shaking his head over and over. Damien was the only one where it was hard to read what he was thinking. Then his lips flickered with a tiny smile and he went back to his digi game.

A new voice explained, 'The job, the empty package you had to deliver, the raid on the club, they were all tests. All of which you passed with flying colours, doll.'

It was Barker, standing there as bold as brass just near the door. Josh stood to the side of him. He was fighting to restrain his anger.

Mo levelled an accusing finger, not at Barker, but at his nephew. 'Did you know about this? Is that why…?'

'Never!' Josh cried. '*That*', they both knew what he meant, their one and only time hitting the sack, 'was a genuine thing. I really liked you. Still do. I never knew about none of this.'

Mo turned back to her newly discovered grandfather and asked, 'But how were you sure I'd work for Barker…?' No way! He couldn't have. 'You set it up, didn't you? Me and my crew jacking your Bentley?'

Jimmy shrugged. 'You were an easy mark. A well-known teenage scally wanting to up her stakes in life. Set someone to whisper in her ear that there will be an unattended Bentley with God knows what inside it.' Jimmy's tone changed. 'That's something you're going to have to be careful of in future. People whispering in your ear. Not everyone has your best interests at heart.'

Mo's brown skin flushed with mortification. 'As God's my witness, I never knew that you were burying your son, my Dad,' Mo stumbled over the last two words, 'that day. I'd have never done it…'

'Despicable.' Kristal whiplashed over Mo's apology. 'Robbing and cheating while my husband was being put in the ground.'

Mo quickly took out the gold-handled gun. Jimmy's shooter. She placed it on the table between them. 'I apologise for nabbing this as well.'

Jimmy picked up the gun. His expression looked far away as he touched the handle. 'I found this in a shop in Istanbul. The colour of the handle made it look special. So, I bought it. I knew exactly who I was going to give it to.'

He put the gun back on the table and slid it back across to her. 'I left it in the glove compartment knowing you wouldn't be able to resist taking it. I got it for Robbie. He loved it. Now you'll be walking in his shoes, it's yours.'

'And the bomb thingie?' Mo carried on, trying to get every piece of the puzzle firmly in its place. 'Was that a set up too? Pretending to plant a bomb under Kristal and Damien's motor—'

Mother and son were both out of their chairs in record time. Kristal blasted at Jimmy, 'You did what?'

Damien's fisted hands shook, the strange way he angled his head looking even more pronounced.

Jimmy and Barker's gazes fell on a squirming Harry. Jimmy twisted his mouth with disgust. 'No, that wasn't me. Someone was using their initiative to get some of the opposition, permanently, out of the game.'

Kristal hurled the bottle of bolly at Harry as he ducked, the bottle missing him by inches. The bottle crashed into the wall.

Jimmy pointed a warning finger at his grandson, who was on the verge of charging his uncle. 'Easy, lad. Best take a seat and cool off.'

Harry dared to raise his head as his nephew reluctantly followed his grandad's order. Kristal glowered her hatred at him.

Mo said, 'If you didn't set it up, and it was Harry, that meant it was a real bomb. My cousin Delilah was with me. She went off to do something with it….'

Delilah! Guardian angel! Mo leant forward. 'It was you she contacted, wasn't it when she walked off with the bomb device?'

'He's your guardian angel,' a voice uttered and then her cousin sauntered into the room, her rucksack as usual on her back. 'Mister Southpaw contacted me to make sure no evil came to you.' Her glance fell pointedly on Harry. 'Including blowing people up on behalf of people who should know better.'

Jimmy suddenly had had enough. 'Everyone, take a walk. I want to talk with my granddaughter. Alone.'

They all did as he asked, some reluctantly so, others, like Damien couldn't get out of there fast enough. Only Dell didn't follow his orders straight off. Calmly she walked over to her cousin and squeezed her shoulder reassuringly. 'I won't be going far. You need me, just shout.'

Granddaughter and Grandfather stared at each other with the same colour eyes. Mo was the first to shyly avert her gaze. She couldn't get over the fact that this East End legend was her blood. Her grandfather. That she was Robbie Steele's girl.

Jimmy linked his fingers together as they rested on the table and told her, 'My wife was small like you. That's where you get your height from, my Mini. God rest and keep her. Mini weren't her real name, but coz she was like a little doll folks called her that.' He shook his head. 'She was a toughie. She had to be where we grew up. She had the biggest heart I'd ever seen. Family was everything to her. She lost hers when she was little, you see. Ended up in one of them Barnardo Homes. The first time I saw her I knew she was destined to be mine.'

That's when Jimmy smiled. Really smiled. The creases and lines deepening around his eyes and mouth. The light glowing in his eyes. And that's when the final piece slotted into place because Mo knew that smile.

She gazed at him in wonder. 'You're the Big Man. The one who helped me all those years ago when those bullies were having another go at me.' Mo couldn't believe it. She'd modelled herself on this man. The way she stood, the way she thought. And all this time he was her own blood. Her Father's Father.

'That's why you wore the shades that day, so I wouldn't clock the colour of your eyes.'

Jimmy's smile broadened. 'I'd had my eye on you for ages. From a distance, of course. But that day I couldn't resist. I had to talk to you, see what my Robbie's girl was really made of.'

'And were you impressed?'

His smile faded away. 'You betcha! You were like a little bulldog. You wouldn't grass on the bullies, didn't need back-up, weren't going to lay down and take shit from no one.'

Mo dipped her head as another thought came to her. Concerned, Jimmy questioned, 'What's on your mind? What's suddenly troubling you?'

Mo's finger swept through her hair. 'There was this geezer. He followed me to Club Class. Real evil scumbag—'

Mo didn't get any further because Jimmy laid his large palm over the back of her hand. 'I know all about it. You made the right decision.'

Her head flicked up, gaze burning. 'So, him coming for me wasn't one of your tests?'

Jimmy's head slammed back in incredulity. 'Get outta here! I'd never let foul scum like that breath the same air as you much less let them anywhere near you.'

Jimmy carried on. 'There's a lot to talk about. You're part of this family now. The Steele family.'

Then he popped the question Mo knew had been coming.

'Are you ready to be Jimmy Southpaw's heir?'

Chapter Thirty-Eight

'Why didn't you tell me that Robbie Steele was my Dad?' Mo asked her Mum point blank.

She stood in the doorway of the sitting-room staring hard at her Mother. Precious looked like hell. Eyes bloodshot and red from crying, the heavy bags beneath them making it appear that she hadn't slept in a week. She cradled a half-gone bottle of cheap supermarket brandy.

Mo hadn't come home straight after leaving Jimmy Southpaw. When she hit The Island she'd gone for a walk along the banks of the river trying to clear her head. Jimmy Southpaw her grandad? His son, the same one who'd burnt to death in a fire in a police station was her Dad? Robbie Steele? Jimmy had been testing her skills to see if she had it to be his heir?

Mo had walked and walked in a shocked stupor. Her world had been flipped upside down, sideways and upside down once again. Then it had hit her in the gut, as she gazed out at the sleeping river, that she had another family. The blood of the Steele's thickened in her veins.

Her Mum's hushed voice brought Mo back to the present. 'Robbie's your Daddy, there's no doubt about that.'

Seeing the gobsmacked expression on her daughter's face made Precious want to cry a river all over again. And curl up and die. That Mo should find out the truth from that fucker Jimmy Southpaw made her want to go gunning for him.

Precious wiped the back of her hand across her damp eyes. 'I don't want you to have nuthin' to do with that Southpaw—'

'Too late.' Mo stepped fully inside the room, closing the distance between her and the only parent she'd ever known. 'He wants me to join the family. He—'

Her Mum was on her feet with such frightening speed, Mo stumbled back. 'Over my fucking dead body. You ain't going anywhere near them nutters.'

Mo had never seen her Mum in such a state. Rage vibrated like a surge of electricity as Precious' trembling hands curled and uncurled by her side. And that's when Mo really got a good look at her Mother. Her Mum's appearance had nosedived again, back to where it had been a month back. Hair a state, no make-up, the bottle once again her closest friend. Mo's mind did a quick calculation...

Understanding hit. 'It was Robbie Steel's death that sent you on the skids, wasn't it? He perished in the fire right about the same time you hit the bottle and stopped caring whether it was night or day.'

Of course, it all made sense. It was the day after the fire at the police station. Mo could've kicked herself for not joining the dots. Then again, how the heck was she meant to know there were any dots to connect between Robbie Steele and her Mum?

A horrible, chocking sound crawled from the back of her Mum's throat as she swayed like a branch about to snap in the wind. Her gaze was glassy, as if she wasn't really there. 'I couldn't believe it when I heard he was dead. I was stood at the bus stop and these Herberts are gassing about the police station fire. Someone dying.' She sucked in such a fierce pull of air Precious was in danger of falling backwards. 'Me and Robbie were over years back, but to hear he'd passed over was a shocker.'

Abruptly, Precious found her legs and staggered towards the brandy. Tipped it to her mouth, drinking greedily.

Mo was puzzled by her Mum's behaviour. 'I don't get it, Mum. You don't want me to have sod all to do with Robbie's people, you said you and him were washed up long time and yet you're putting on a production like he was the great love of your life.'

Precious shot daggers her way. 'You watch your mouth, young lady! Accusing me of putting on a show! I ain't putting on no show.'

'So what?' Mo's eyes bulged. 'Robbie was your one and only?'

Precious waved the bottle around to underscore what she was saying. 'I ain't saying that. For fucking one thing, I never knew he already had a Mrs Steele warming his slippers indoors.'

Mo was relieved to hear that. At least her Mum hadn't made a play for a married man. There was plenty bad in the world and her Mum turning out to have had relations with a married man didn't really even rank. Still, it left a very bitter taste in Mo's mouth.

Precious slumped in a dejected heap on the settee, the bottle of booze slipping from her slack fingers rolled onto the carpet. 'To make you understand me and Robbie you'd need a gazillion years to hear all of it.' Without warning, her high-pitched laughter should have brightened up the room. Instead it sounded freakish. 'No one could make me laugh like Robbie could. He comes waltzing up to me one night, flash git, while I'm having a ladies' night out with my mates down Club Class.'

Ah! Now Mo got it why her Mum maybe didn't want her to work at the club. Maybe Precious thought there were those who'd remember her and Robbie being an item. Then put two and two together that Mo was the outcome and start whispering sweet nothings about the past in Mo's ear.

Mo stepped closer. 'I don't get it, Mum? If you and Robbie were the perfect hook up, why didn't I ever know him? Why wasn't he in my life? I wouldn't have minded sharing him with his missus and son.'

To have had a tiny slice of her Dad, even if it meant sharing him with others, would've been better than having no Dad at all in her life.

Precious never answered, instead she pointed at a love-heart shaped photo sitting on the cabinet filled with her Mum's best drinking glasses. What a gorgeous photo it was. A beaming dewy-eyed Precious held her precious baby in her arms on the day of Mo's birth.

Her Mum instructed, 'Turn it over.'

And that's what Mo did with expectant curiosity. Inserted into the back of the frame was another photo. Mo couldn't hold back her gasp. It was another baby photo. Baby Mo being held tenderly in someone else's arms on the day of her birth. Robbie Steele. Her Dad.

Mo's breath caught. She was seeing her Father's face for the first time ever. She couldn't even put into words what she was feeling.

Robbie gazed up at the camera lens with such pride. Mo couldn't get enough of looking at him. The guy looked hot and obviously liked to play hot too. He had a face that could tempt even Sister Aggi to sin. What caught and held Mo's attention were his eyes. Her eyes. Glossy-grey. Jimmy Southpaw's eyes.

'Did he love me?' Mo achingly whispered, running a fingertip over her Dad's face.

Her Mum's laboured breathing filled the air, striking tension back into the room. 'I've said all I'm going to say. Maureen, you're to stay away from Jimmy Southpaw and the rest of the clowns in that family. You hear me?'

That got Mo's feathers up. Who did her Mum think she was throwing out orders after the damning secret she'd kept hidden away from Mo all these years? Eh? The only person willing to cough up the truth was Jimmy Southpaw. Sure, he'd taken her through her paces before spilling the beans, but he'd told her, which is a damn sight more than her Mother ever did. And why had he told her?

'Know what he said to me?' Mo slammed back. 'That he wants me because I'm his flesh and blood—'

'So, where the backside fuck has he been all these years?' Precious screamed.

Mo stretched her neck and scoffed, 'It ain't easy to see why that was. He wouldn't have been welcomed around here.' She puffed out her chest. 'Now Robbie's gone he wants me to take over his place. To become his heir.'

'Noooooo!!!' Precious cried. The sound was like the dying cry of a person falling from the top of a building.

Mo had it up to here with this dramarama. She stalked towards the doorway.

Her Mother's claw-like fingers dug into her jacket yanking her back around. Precious' face was like thunder as she stabbed a warning finger at her girl. 'I'm telling you not to get involved with that man. Spit in the eye of his offer. Don't—'

Mo roughly shook herself free. 'You don't have the right. Know why? Because Jimmy Southpaw is as much my flesh and blood as Brother Bertie is. He. Is. My. Family.'

And with that Mo shoved past her Mum and rushed up the stairs to her room.

All the way, Precious wailed, until her voice was hoarse, 'He's a bad man. A monster…'

Brother Bertie sighed as he took a deep lug of his 'Lord Have Mercy Rum Punch'. He'd been listening to every word that passed between his daughter and granddaughter. He'd made the conscious decision not to intervene. The main reason being it was finally time for the two women he loved most in this life, along with Ruddy, to confront the truth. After Ruddy had briefed him about finding the copies of emails Jimmy Southpaw had sent Barker and legal documents that were just waiting for Maureen Watson to sign, Brother Bertie knew there was no way to hold back the truth about his beloved baby-gal's parentage. He was frightened for his gorgeous granddaughter. God! He hoped it wasn't history happening all over again.

'Nothing good is going to come from this,' he whispered, 'Nothing good at all.'

Chapter Thirty-Nine

Jimmy Southpaw woke up because he sensed danger. Someone was in his bedroom. The temperature felt a lot cooler which left him thinking whoever had been fool enough to have the brass to break into his home had climbed in through the window.

He lived in a seven-bed, six-reception house that rose tall in five acres of land in Kent. Palatial some called it others fuck off. No expense had been spared inside or out. Especially on knowing who was coming and going from the house. Security was a premium. The place was rigged out in a state-of-the-art security system including an armed twenty-four-seven patrol. Which begged the question, how had someone bypassed it all and got in? And not just his frigging house, but his room for Chrissakes! Heads were going to roll once Jimmy dealt with the intruder. By God, if it turned out to be that scheming bob tail, Kristal or his thick as a plank son, Harry he was going to knacker them to within an inch of their lives.

After today's revelations and finally playing his trump card he'd downed a malt when he got indoors and then hit the sack. He'd been a wreck. Crippling tired, feeling every last one of his sixty years.

Jimmy remained lying down as he mockingly asked the intruder, 'What's a geezer got to do to get any rest around here?'

He waited for the answer. When it didn't come, he added, 'They do say that an Englishman's home is his castle.'

'Can I spend the night in this Englishman's castle?' The request was hesitant and so very quiet.

Jimmy knew that voice. He swung his legs over the side of the bed, popped the side lamp on and shifted himself into his dressing gown. Then he looked over at the person standing in front of the window in his immense bedroom.

Mo.

His granddaughter was decked all in black, had a rucksack over her shoulder and, he didn't know her properly yet, but he could swear her red-rimmed eyes showed she'd been crying. Give the girl her due, she was putting on a brave face.

First things first though. 'How did you get in?'

Mo tilted her head cockily to the side. 'You've got a weakness around the back. The part that leads to the quickest route to your neighbour.' Her brow arched suggestively. 'Now if I didn't know any better, I'd say that was a deliberate occurrence on account of you not wanting anyone to know you go for a gander every now and again next door.'

It had been eons since Jimmy had blushed, but he did so now. He had a clandestine arrangement with his stunning neighbour when her hubby was away on business. A couple of decades younger than him, he suspected she got off on him as her bit of rough. Mo might've caught him out that didn't mean he was admitting to sneaking over to his neighbour for a shag.

Jimmy smiled with pride. This girl was good. Smart as a fox looking to sneak inside someone's garden to dig a hole. She had a bone fide brain inside that loaf of hers, unlike others. One that bloody worked exactly as it should. Jimmy couldn't help feeling proud of his choice. Robbie's daughter. Perfect.

He suspected that Mother of hers had nearly had a coronary when she found out he was in her life. Not only in her life but offering her Robbie's golden seat. *And Brother Bertie*? he thought sourly. Had the old codger had a hizzy tantrum or played a cool hand? Either way it didn't matter. The girl was his now. A member of the Steele family. His heir. If anyone *dared* try to take her away from him, including her other family, Jimmy wouldn't hesitate. He'd cut them to pieces.

He stood up. 'I've got the perfect room all ready for you.'

No one had to tell Mo who the boy in the large gilt-framed photo was on the wall of the bedroom Jimmy escorted her to. He was a younger version of the man who was holding her as a baby in the hidden picture her Mum had kept. Robbie Steele.

Robbie was seven years old looking up at the camera lens as if he owned it. He was casually togged out in black jeans, navy T-shirt and trainers with an added touch of style from the shades perched on his little nose. And what a killer smile complete with cute dimples. *He'd grown into a devastatingly handsome man*, Mo thought. No wonder her Mum fell for his charms. And fell to pieces when he died.

Jimmy started speaking, 'It's a bit of a tradition in the family that I take our older generation off for a day trip to the seaside. I've been doing it for years, since the boys and Violet were small. That was the year we all went off to Margate. Proper poser, Robbie was. And the best son a man could ever have.'

Mo asked him something he wasn't expecting. Her gaze remaining fixed on the photo of her Dad. 'I don't know what to call you.'

Jimmy sent her one of his rare big smiles. 'Jimmy. Mister Southpaw. Southpaw.' His voice caught slightly. 'Grandad, if I'm lucky.'

Mo's teeth worried the inside of her cheek not sure what to say about that. Truth was she was having a major league conflict. Brother Bertie was her grandad. The person who'd lifted her with one hundred per cent love and gentle care to his breast when she was a babe-in-arms. He'd been a Dad and grandfather all rolled into one. No one could ever ask for a more precious grandparent than Brother Bertie. It felt wrong to name-check someone else as her grandad. So very wrong.

Some of her turmoil must've shown in the sudden stiffness of her shoulders because Jimmy insisted, 'I'm not trying to replace Brother Bertie in your life—'

Startled, Mo spun to face him. 'What? You know my other grandad?' Never in a zillion years did she think that someone like Jimmy Southpaw would know her Mum's Father.

The Big Man shrugged, his smile dying. 'You know what the East End's like. You know someone who knows someone who knows someone.'

Codswallop! That was Mo's response to what he told her. She didn't believe it for a minute. Jimmy Southpaw knew Brother Bertie. But how? Her beloved grandfather had never been involved in London's underworld. The common link between both men was her. Maybe they'd met when she'd been born?

Mo pushed the unanswered questions aside. 'I'm going to call you Grandad Jimmy, if that's okey dokey with you?'

Her Grandad Jimmy looked well chuffed. 'Total honour, sweetheart.'

Mo's brows knitted together, her brain ticking away. 'So, Barker never burnt down the police station and killed … my Dad?'

Her grandad stared at her as if she were mad. ''Course Barker never. Think he'd still be breathing if he had? That was all part of the fake story we told so Barker could offer you a job, y'know that.'

Mo stayed silence. Then, 'But if Barker didn't do it, who did?'

'Did what?'

'Murdered my Father.'

A brightness seeped into Jimmy's eyes. 'No one did. It

was bad electrics is what done it. And bad luck.' Sorrow was plain in his voice. 'I'll leave you now, girl. Get a good night's rest.'

Before he closed the door, he added, 'Welcome to the family.'

Chapter Forty

The following week, Precious flung on her coat with single-minded determination and was almost at the door when her Father appeared at the top of the stairs.

Brother Bertie's heart beat badly, too much for his poor ticker, when he caught the haunted expression on her face. Since Mo had hit the door, Precious was barely sleeping. Every night, she sat out on the balcony, staring at the river with sightless eyes, drowning her sorrows in a bottle of fruity Taboo and cherry Lambrini.

He quietly asked, although he suspected he already knew the answer, 'Where you going, daughter?' He made his way slowly down the stairs, his faithful, unique walking stick supporting him.

Precious was barely keeping it together, body trembling from not only lack of sleep and booze, but heartache. 'I'm going to find my daughter and bring her home.'

Precious had given Mo a week to recognise her mistake and then come back. They would say no more about it and get on with their lives. Precious was even prepared to tell her more about Robbie. Not the whole of it, of course, but enough for Mo to understand there was never any future in their relationship.

Brother Bertie shook his head, a wave of tiredness suddenly threatening to drag him under. 'You don't know where she is?'

His daughter went postal. 'That fucking man has got her in his clutches.' She croaked, 'He's going to ruin my girl's life. Turn her into something she wasn't meant to be.'

Precious whipped out a long kitchen knife from the sleeve of her coat and brandished it in her Dad's face. 'When I get my hands on Jimmy Southpaw I'm going to chop off his knackers. Then his hands. You know why? So, he can't nab any other respectable women's children.'

Brother Bertie was shocked at the state his daughter was getting in. Her eyes were wild, as if she didn't even know where she was anymore. She was truly losing the plot, snarling, teeth grinding. No! She wasn't losing the plot, Brother Bertie realised. Precious was the picture of a Mother who would do anything to defend her child. Anything.

A whisper of a sigh left him, travelling across the passage to stand before his daughter. There were times in life when you have to decide whether to speak a little white lie or tell the honest to God truth. The beauty of a little fib is it can sometimes bring the sunshine out, y'know, make the badness go away. And if there was ever a time that his daughter needed an injection of goodness it was now.

Brother Bertie surprised himself by going for the other option. The one that can cut and wound. The truth. Precious knew the truth about Mo as well as he did. He reminded her of that truth now, whether she wanted to hear it or not.

'Mo was already walking on the wrong side of the street,' he told her strongly. 'She was bound to meet the sorta trouble one day that she wouldn't have been able to handle. Maybe this way is best. He can protect her—'

'I'm her protector not scum-scrote Southpaw.' Brother Bertie's head swerved back as the knife swished in circle in the air. 'I've been protecting her since she came out of my womb after carrying her for nine months. And she wasn't an easy baby to carry, making me eat apricots with hot pepper sauce on them. I'm her Mother,' wrenched out of Precious in a loud wail.

He took her in his arms and held her sobbing heaving body close. The knife fell and clattered to the lino floor. 'Let her go. When she's ready, she'll come back.'

Brother Bertie also prayed hard that Jimmy Southpaw would keep the promise he'd made all those years ago. That he would never breathe a word to anyone of what had happened between their families so long ago.

Mo caught the bunch of keys that Grandad Jimmy threw her way. They were in the main room inside Club Class. The staff beavered away, as per usual, getting the place tip-top for another night. There was no sign of Barker or his nephew.

Mo scowled, brows slashing together, as she stared hard at the keys. Very heavy keys. Then she looked up at the giant of a man standing before her, confusion mounting.

'What are these for?' She asked, jangling them.

Voice low, a glint in his world-weary eyes he answered, 'They're the keys to the kingdom.'

Her bafflement grew further. 'What kingdom's that then?'

Jimmy opened his arms wide, indicating the room. 'Club Class—'

'You what?' Mo gushed. 'The Club? Mine?' Mo could barely find her breath. 'But it belongs to Barker.'

Jimmy escorted her over to the bar and ordered a whisky for him and a snazzy tropical cocktail for her.

While their drinks were being prepared, he told her, obviously as pleased as punch that she was gobsmacked by his surprise. 'The place has always been mine. Barker's been running it for me for years.' He pitched his voice to a 'just between me and you' tone. 'Sometimes in the bizz you've got to perform magic tricks. Make people think they're seeing one thing when all the while it's an illusion. The truth is something else entirely.'

Mo greedily stored that nugget away. She still couldn't get over how, the first time they'd met all those years ago, she'd dreamed about learning more from him. And now it was happening. Really, really happening.

Later that day Jimmy and Barker clinked glasses of whisky, congratulating themselves as they sat inside Jimmy's office in the betting shop.

'Thanks, me ol' mate,' Jimmy said to Barker. 'You did a bang-up job of keeping our girl on her toes.'

Barker nodded his agreement as he tucked into his drink.

Brows snapping together, scowling, he asked his old friend, 'Did you tell her that you were the one to set her up with Eric Brown?'

Jimmy's wet lips smacked together in disgust thinking about that filth who thought he could roam around the East End, putting his dirty paws on innocent girls. When no one would speak against him after what he did to the fourteen year old girl, because of his underworld connections, the girl's distraught family had come to see Jimmy and begged him to take action on their behalf. They'd tried to pay him. With pleasure he'd told them this was on the house. Then Jimmy had got to thinking, what about killing two birds with one stone?

So, he'd discreetly tipped Eric Brown the wink where Mo would be to set things up. And his girl had taken care of the rest.

He confided in Barker, 'That was her final test. Whether she can kill. I can't be handing over my empire to someone who can't pull the trigger when need be. Now she's done it once, she won't hesitate to do it again.'

He'd lied straight to his granddaughter's face about knowing anything about Eric Brown finding her. About it not being one of his tests. Jimmy Southpaw was a man who'd come up the hard way where sometimes to get what you wanted you had to use a bag full of dirty tricks.

Mo made her way to a place where once a police station had stood. Now it was empty, desolate, cleared of any evidence of a fire. Mo was convinced she could still smell the fire that had been here in the air. The burning ash and cloying smoke and gushing flames.

'Who killed you in that fire, Dad?' she whispered to Robbie in the place where he had breathed his last.

Mo's gut was telling her that Grandad Jimmy was wrong. Her gut was usually right. The fire at the police station had been no accident. If it had been, why wasn't Robbie logged into the police station's computer as being in a cell?

Mo vowed, 'As I live and breathe, if it takes me a lifetime, I promise to hunt down whoever murdered you, Dad.'

Coming Soon

Mo Watson Crime Series Book 2

FIGHT DIRTY

Her enemies are closer than she thinks

Notorious East End gangster, Jimmy Southpaw, has made his long lost granddaughter, Maureen 'Big Mo' Watson, the new head of his criminal empire. But not everyone's happy about it, including Mo's tough as nails new stepmother, Kristal Steele.

When a mysterious new gangster goes to war with her, Mo begins to doubt her ability to fill Jimmy's shoes. Feeling her enemies circling, Mo contacts South London Boss, Nico Sinclair to help find out who's trying to take her criminal crown.

Who is this gangster taking Mo on? Who's backing him up? Will Jimmy think he's made a mistake choosing Mo as his heir?

Thank you!

Thank you for reading *Dirty Tricks.* We hope you enjoyed it! We LOVED writing it!
Checkout Amazon for all our books
The Big Mo Crime Series is also available on Kindle Unlimited.

Reviews: We write for you!
We adore hearing what you think about our books. Reviews help other readers find books. So do please leave a review.

For news and loads more, head off to our website and sign up.
https://dredamitchell.com

We adore hearing from readers, so please do get in touch.
Website: https://dredamitchell.com
Facebook: Dreda Facebook
Twitter: Dreda Twitter

All About Dreda

Her Majesty The Queen awarded me an MBE in her New Year's Honours List, 2020!

I scooped the CWA's John Creasey Dagger Award for best first time crime novel in 2004, the first time a Black British author has received this honour.

After writing five books I partnered with Tony Mason to continue my writing career.

We write across the crime fiction genre – psychological suspense, gritty-gangland and fast-paced action books.

Spare Room, our first psychological thriller was a No.1 UK and US Kindle bestseller. My parents are from the beautiful Caribbean island of Grenada. I am a passionate campaigner and speaker on social issues and the arts.

I have appeared on television, including Celebrity Pointless, Celebrity Eggheads, BBC 1 Breakfast, Sunday Morning Live, Newsnight, The Review Show and Front Row Late on BBC 2. I have been a guest on BBC Radio 3 and 4 and presented Radio 4's flagship books programme, Open Book and written in a number of leading newspapers including The Guardian. I also reviewed the newspapers every Friday night on BBC Radio 5 Live's Stephen Nolan Show. I was named one of Britain's 50 Remarkable Women by Lady Geek in association with Nokia. I am a Royal Literary Fund Trustee and an Ambassador for The Reading Agency.

Some of our books are currently in development as TV and film adaptations.

My name, Dreda, is Irish and pronounced with a long vowel ee sound in the middle!

Printed in Great Britain
by Amazon

63632603R00200